A TABLE ON KILIMANJARO

By Janice Coy

"How to get the best of it all? One must conquer, achieve, get to the top; one must know the end to be convinced that one can win the end - to know there's no dream that mustn't be dared...Is this the summit, crowning the day? How cool and quiet! We're not exultant; but delighted, joyful; soberly astonished...Have we vanquished an enemy? None but ourselves. Have we gained success? That word means nothing here."

George Mallory,"*Climbing Everest: The Complete Writings of George Mallory*"

Chapter 1

Everyone has a mountain.

Some, like Kilimanjaro, are more visible than others.

Our Chagga ancestors had a mountain of fear. They told stories about a Shining Mountain with treasure guarded by evil spirits and demons. One day, they said, a brave king dared to climb the mountain. But he did not triumph. He never returned.

Those who did come back had damaged arms and legs.

David Mbowe liked to think about his father's words when he led a group of hikers up Mt. Kilimanjaro. He didn't want to be like the brave and foolish king. A proper respect for the mountain was prudent, and a good reminder at the start of another trip to the 5,895- meter Uhuru Peak. God willing, he would lead at least seven more this year. He had his own mountains to consider.

Although David did his best – tips were greater when the foreigners reached the summit– not everyone enjoyed success. The mountain had no favorites.

David surveyed the crowd of hikers – most white Europeans or Americans with a few Canadians and Australians - waiting at the Machame Gate ranger station this bright summer morning. Many could have posed for an advertisement of hiking gear with their shiny trekking poles and clean gators hanging around their calves. Further up the hill and across a stretch of asphalt by the Land Rovers, knots of African men jockeyed for jobs as porters. Most wore an odd assortment of mismatched clothes, baggy sweaters or jackets, stained pants. The two groups were separate now, but they would brush up against each other daily on the Mt. Kilimanjaro ascent.

Tens of thousands tried to climb Mt. Kilimanjaro year round: foreigners and porters. Many would turn back, too sick from the altitude or the cold to keep going. Ten to fifteen would die each year. For the porters, the numbers were higher and harder to get right. Some said twenty died on the mountain just south of the equator every year. Others put the number as high as fifty. Three porters were assigned to each hiker, and many of the porters made the ascent thirty to forty times a year. The porters were more numerous and, those hired by less honest tour companies were often dressed poorly in thin jackets and shoes. David would never forget the September storm that stole the lives of five porters from three separate groups. Grace had bought him a warm waterproof jacket and gloves afterwards.

"You are robbing from our children's education," David said. "What about their future?"

Grace folded her arms. Waited for him to try on the jacket.

"And how will they be educated if you die?" she said. "Your English is good. Work harder for tips."

David doubted the mostly white tourists – at least two hundred - lining up at the ranger station were thinking about porters dying. They laughed and told jokes. He watched as they wrote their name, passport number and age in the ranger's open logbook. They would register at each camp, and sign in the exit book when they finished– an official record they had survived.

Yesterday it rained, the water pouring in buckets from the heavens as if God were weeping for those who had been carried down the mountain on stretchers or covered in black plastic bags. But today, He must be feeling better. The sun was out and many of the tourists took off their fleece jackets. Some unzipped the bottoms of their hiking pants and made them into shorts. Porters tied their jackets around their waist. Still, the trail through the rain forest would be slick with mud and wet leaves. Many would slip and fall.

The most serious dangers of climbing the African mountain- high altitude sickness and insufficient water consumption- were listed in yellow block letters on two large wooden signs. No one stood on the thin grass below the signs. No one studied the warning. The Tanzanian National Park Service had done its duty, and David knew it would be up to him and the other guides to care for the hikers.

A black and white monkey scurried along a tree branch towards the open- air structure where some of the hikers had already gotten into their snacks. A young woman from his group had placed a granola bar on the low wooden wall, but now her back was turned and it seemed she had forgotten about it. The green foil wrapper glinted. The monkey dropped into the shadows below the solid barrier, out of David's sight. But he was patient, and it wasn't long before David saw the monkey's leathery fingers snatch the treat. The monkey re-appeared scampering back up the tree, clutching its stolen treasure. The older man with her glanced over in time to see the bar disappear and he pointed.

The young brunette shouted in dismay. Then, she dug into her daypack and pulled out a camera. She leaned over the railing, searching for the monkey. Her neat braid swung. David could see her shoulder bones under her thin nylon shirt. Would she be one of the successful ones to summit? He learned long ago it was impossible to foretell a person's success by their body shape or age.

For example, that plump man leaving the bathroom, the door banging shut behind him as he adjusted his pants. He could have the necessary will power. Or that woman with the gray hair and thick legs, checking her pockets for tissue while she stood behind two others for her last chance at a flush toilet. The lines of her chin suggested a strong will. But would it be enough?

The ranger gestured to David. It was time to gather his group, sign the register and begin the ascent. As David called them over, he silently promised his father, his ancestors and Grace he would do his best. His children needed an education. His small house needed some repairs. But he knew that in the end, the mountain would determine the success of this trip.

Three days earlier

Chapter 2

Leda Saunton stole a glance at her smart phone. Her London flight left at 11 p.m., three hours from now. Her pop was driving so they were early – as usual. He eased his Prius into the lane closest to the departures curb on the second level at the Portland International Airport. Twilight shadows pocked the busy terminal, the angle of the sun low through the glass roof covering the traffic lanes. Although the curbside drop off for international flights came first, the sign for Leda's airline was at least a hundred yards ahead in bumper- to-bumper traffic. Leda settled against the leather seat for what was sure to be a slow ride.

"Don't get out yet," her father said. "I'll take you to your airline."

"No worries," Leda said. She slid her cell phone into her purse and folded her hands on her lap so her father could see she wasn't reaching for the door. He could be overbearing at times, but she loved her pop and knew how to handle him.

The car in front of them braked, and then parked with its flashers on. A woman emerged from the passenger side and wrestled a scuffed black suitcase from the trunk. Her wrist twisted when the suitcase hit the asphalt at an awkward angle.

"She could fit a child in there," her father said. He shook his head. As far as Leda could tell, the fact that the car was holding them up didn't bother her father.

"A child of eight at least," Leda said. The two shared a smile.

The woman managed to get her suitcase settled on its wheels and bumped it up and over the curb but not before a traffic officer in a fluorescent vest blew his whistle and gestured for the car to move.

"Your duffel all ready?" her father said.

"In the trunk with my backpack."

"Got your passport and tickets?"

Her father continued through a list of other items the guides had told them to bring for the climb up Mt. Kilimanjaro. Leda answered in the affirmative although she wondered what her father would do if she said she had forgotten something important – like her hiking boots. Although if she had, he could bring them when they met at the Everlastings Hotel.

"I wish you were coming with me now," Leda said.

"What?" Her father's forehead wrinkled in a way that was all too familiar to Leda.

"Already thinking of those equations?" Leda said.

"This last minute project's proving to be more difficult than I thought." Her father moved the car forward a few inches. Leda couldn't remember how many times last minute projects at Green Solutions had cut into their time together. It had gotten worse when he was promoted to chief physicist while Leda was still in high school.

"Sorry I'm missing London," he said, "but we'll have plenty of time to talk about the exhibits at the British Museum on the trail. You know I won't miss the climb."

For once, Leda had hoped she could spend time with her father somewhere other than on a mountain trail, but she knew she could count on him showing up for the climb. He always did. She resisted an urge to touch the locket with her mother's picture hidden under her t-shirt. It pressed against her skin like a guilty conscience. This was the first time she wore the locket in her father's presence. He didn't know she had it. She wondered if he realized the simple gold heart was missing from the secret place in the back of his closet and had been for a long time. If he did notice it was gone, Leda didn't think he would mention it to her. He hadn't talked about her mother for years, and Leda learned long ago to avoid the subject.

The locket made her feel closer to her dead mother, and as much as Leda wanted to spend time with her father in London, she also felt relieved she wouldn't have to make excuses for disappearing for a few hours while she was there. She would tell him where she'd been in the end anyway; it just made it easier if he didn't know at first. He'd be happy she wasn't alone in London, that she visited distant cousins. Wouldn't he?

"I don't know why you brought a purse," her father said. "and those shoes. Wouldn't it be easier to wear your hiking boots?"

Leda wiggled her toes in the fashionable black flats. She wished she could be wearing heels, but she would be doing a lot of walking and didn't want to risk twisting her ankle on some cobblestone street and missing out on the climb.

"I refuse to walk around London in my boots," Leda said. "And I'm not lugging my backpack either. They'll be safe at the hotel."

"I suppose."

"You made the reservation." Leda patted his arm to take the sting out of her words. He harrumphed like she had insulted him, but Leda saw his slight smile, the brief deepening of the lines radiating from the corner of his eye. He kept his focus on the car in front, his eyes flickering every so often to the rearview mirror. It had just been the two of them for as long as Leda could remember. It hadn't taken her long to figure him out. She knew how to make him proud, how to get his attention for a little while with top grades and the academic awards that still lined her bedroom walls and were the first things she saw every morning when she woke up. She had lived away at college and graduate school, but she had been back for a year living in her old room while she completed her clinical training as a speech therapist. She enjoyed looking at the awards that now included her degrees. Every morning that she could, she punched up her pillows to raise her head to see the awards better. Her morning ritual always ended at her dresser top littered with photos of her with her father on various mountains. One small photo of her mother when she was a student at the university stuck out like the wrong accessory in an otherwise complete outfit.

Leda would lie in her bed looking at her awards and the pictures, thinking all's right with the world except I have no mother. When she could no longer resist the smell of the coffee wafting from the kitchen, she got up and shuffled down the hall in her slippers. Leda lived at the opposite end of the rambling one story house from her father: the kitchen divided their personal spaces. Her father ground fresh coffee from ecologically sustainable farms every morning before he left for work. Leda didn't need to be at the elementary school until later. She would probably take a job in Portland when her training was done and continue to live at home to save money and pay off student loans. Besides, she was used to her pop. Why spend time adjusting to the habits of a stranger? She had already done that in college. Leda knew her father wouldn't eat her dark chocolate ice cream bars or scrabble around in her closet wanting to borrow her favorite pair of shoes.

The line of cars moved forward at a glacial speed. Now, a Lexus stopped in front of them, and a man in a suit stepped out. His shirt was open at the neck, and Leda imagined his tie was tucked neatly in the efficient carry on he swung out of the back seat.

"There's someone who knows how to pack," her father said.

"What if a freak snow storm blows through?" Leda said. "He doesn't have a coat."

"It's summer."

"You're bringing a coat," Leda said. She liked to tease her father, loosen him up a little, he could be so serious, and he usually rose to the bait.

"We're climbing the highest freestanding mountain in the world," he said. "It makes its own weather. I hope you packed a coat."

"We went over all my stuff last night Pop," Leda said.

Checking each other's hiking gear was more tradition than necessity now, but she wouldn't want it any other way. When it came to climbing, she was guaranteed his full attention. Sometimes she wondered what it would have been like if she had a brother or a sister. Would she have worked so hard for her father's approval if someone else was around to give her attention or would she have worked harder because she would have to compete with someone else for it? Mostly, she wondered what it would have been like if she had a mother. She didn't think she would have this hole in her that her pop, no matter how much she loved him, could fill. Her father didn't remarry after her mother died when Leda was barely out of diapers. Leda imagined it was because he loved her mother so desperately he couldn't bring himself to love again.

Leda thought she saw something flicker in her father's eyes – pain maybe – when she asked about her mother, so about the time she was ten, she stopped asking. But she never stopped wondering, and now her heart raced and her palms felt a little sweaty thinking about what she planned to do in London.

The locket seemed to grow in size so that it loomed on her chest in an obvious way. She didn't dare touch it or even glance at it. What if pop noticed? Her father stomped on the brake and swore at the driver in front of him.

"This is why we need to get here early," he said, "because of idiots like him. Did you see him swerve out of nowhere?"

A young woman jumped out of the old-model BMW parked nose in at a sharp angle in front of the Prius. Her straight blond hair lay on her shoulders in a manner Leda envied. A dark-haired young man emerged from the driver's side, leaving his door ajar. He pulled a compact suitcase out of the trunk and carried it to the woman. A jaunty pink bow was tied to the handle. The man set the suitcase down, and then he lifted the woman like she was the lightest thing in the world, swinging her around so that her bare legs and her feet with the strappy red sandals flew out behind her. She threw back her head, gales of laughter spilling from her tanned throat. The two kissed in a way that reminded Leda of the movies she liked.

"Where's the traffic officer?" her father said. He honked the horn, and the couple pulled apart, staring at the Prius. Leda bent her head and rummaged in her purse, her wild dark curls hiding her red cheeks.

"Here we are!" Her father's voice sounded triumphant as he rolled to a gentle stop in front of the door for her airline. He pressed a button, and the automatic locks on the doors sprang open with a clunk. "Back's open."

Leda knew that was her cue to exit the car and grab her things in a hurry. Still, she lingered on the seat.

'Better get going!'

"Pop." Leda touched the shoulder of his favorite sport coat. Her father disliked overdone displays of emotion, she knew that, and yet for some reason her eyes felt warm and prickly almost like tears. He smelled like mint soap and dry erase marker. She cleared her throat. "Love you." She pressed a quick kiss on his cheek, and then grabbed her purse.

"I'll be there," her father said. "You can count on me."

Leda nodded. Of course he would be at the base of the mountain. He had never let her down on a climb before. She slammed the car door, pulled her duffel and backpack from the trunk. She stood on the curb, her hand lifted in farewell. The Prius eased its way into the furthest lane its distinctive back lights flickering red, merged with the jostling traffic and disappeared from sight.

Chapter 3

Leda hoped her dark jeans were dressy enough for tea with distant English cousins. Her father had raised an eyebrow at the summer dress on her bed with her hiking pants, waterproof jacket and wool socks.

"You're not bringing that?" he said.

"Of course not." Leda snatched the dress and hung it back in her closet. She planned to slip it into her duffel later, but forgot.

Luckily, she already packed a cute top she meant to consider as an alternative to the dress. The top had some serious wrinkles, but most seemed to have fallen out while she wasted time in the British Museum this morning checking out the illuminated manuscripts encased in temperature controlled glass cases. Normally, Leda would have been excited to spend time studying Assyrian art, or the ancient stone busts of the various Egyptian rulers. She would have hovered over the prints of the Lady of Shallot and wondered at the Rosetta Stone, but she couldn't stop thinking of all the questions she planned to ask the distant cousins about her mother – questions her father would never answer - and she merely skimmed along the displays, mingling with the moving crowds of visitors until it was time to leave.

She also felt jet lagged; the back of her eyes ached and her legs felt somewhat wooden. When she checked into the hotel early this morning, her room wasn't ready. Still, she saw other tourists sleeping in the deep cushions of the lobby couch and arm chairs. Leda was too excited to sleep. Changing in the lobby bathroom, she did her best to freshen up after the long flight. She brushed her teeth, applied a new coat of mascara and more deodorant.

Leda left the museum with time to spare, but jumped on the wrong subway, heading to St. John's Wood in the opposite direction from the cousins' house. She figured out her mistake before too many stops.

Now, she hurried down the street where the cousins lived. Her armpits felt damp. Her hair drooped on her shoulders like a limp towel. She wished for her summer dress. Who knew it could be so warm in London in the summer: the sun a dull misty yellow. Leda could hear church bells clanging the hour in the distance.

She had been expecting columns and cornices, at least some gargoyles on the houses – she was in London after all - and she was disappointed in the neighborhood of attached brick houses with steep roofs, one after the other looking pretty much the same like row upon row of American twin homes. Low brick walls and neatly tended bushes fronted most of the houses. Many had small black iron gates. The other side of the street appeared to be apartments. A tiny pocket of a park enclosed by a wrought iron fence matched some of her imagination. And, Leda felt somewhat satisfied when several pigeons landed on the carved metal. Pulling a scrap of paper from her pocket, she slowed her steps to search for the matching address. She hesitated on the sidewalk until she found the brass numbers of her cousins' house. Two emerald green window boxes with wilted flowers matched the house's front door. Leda's back was damp with perspiration (the word sounded more English and proper than sweat). She unstuck her blouse, and headed up the walkway. Now that she was closer, she could see the few flowers in the boxes were too perfect to be real. They and the window boxes were edged with brown dust: the silk petals limp in the heat.

Leda paused for a minute at the door before ringing the bell. Her mother's locket hung outside her top, and she worried it back and forth along the chain, thinking of the little she knew about these cousins. She had exchanged a few emails with them after finding them through a genealogy website she was using for a free trial period. They were a distant relation to her mother at best – a brother and sister who lived together in their old age. Visiting them in person seemed like an amazing idea when she was typing on her laptop in her Portland bedroom. She had spent years searching the Internet off and on for her mother's relatives with no luck. But now she stood at the cousins' door, her stomach fluttered. What if her father didn't talk about her mother for a good reason? What if he hid this locket because it reminded him of bad things instead of good things? Leda bit her lip.

"You lost?" An old woman with a cane called to Leda from the sidewalk. A crocheted shawl was draped over her shoulders.

"No," Leda said. "I'm fine."

"Can't hear you." The woman raised her voice. For the first time, Leda realized the church bells had stopped. The woman's voice sounded loud in the silence. Even the pigeons startled from their perch, their flapping wings a noisy flutter.

She might as well ring the doorbell now. The cousins must have heard the woman shouting to her. Leda waved her hand at the woman, and pressed the bell. A long angry buzz sounded inside. She didn't look, but she could feel the woman waiting behind her. The door swung open.

Leda needn't have worried about the shouting woman alerting the cousins to her presence at their door. A bent man who looked more ancient than the woman outside greeted her with a tremulous voice.

"Come in, come in," he said. "Don't be shy." He waved her forward with a liver-spotted hand. He turned and shuffled down the dim hallway towards the back of the house. Leda shut the door behind her, following the man. The hall smelled like cigar smoke and boiled beef. The man's loafers slapped on the hall runner, his heels sliding out as he moved. Reaching an open door where light spilled out onto the carpet, the man stopped and gestured for Leda to enter before him. He spoke when Leda passed.

"Don't let my looks fool you," he said, his voice cracking in what Leda guessed was a laugh. "I'm only 79."

"Don't mind Russell," a woman in the room said. She approached Leda, her hands as fluttery as the pigeons. "I'm Eleanor, and you must be Leda, welcome." Eleanor clasped Leda's hands. Eleanor had long fingers with big knuckles. Her pale skin was as soft as feathers. The older woman smelled like roses on a hot day; her affection for the flower extended to the room's décor, a plump sofa covered in cabbage-sized roses was pushed against one wall, rose-colored curtains framed the large window and a glass vase of drooping roses and brown water sat in the middle of a carved rosewood side table. The cigar smell lingered under the roses. "Tea's ready," Eleanor said, letting go of Leda's hands and settling behind a china teapot covered in tiny roses.

Russell settled into the rooms only other chair – a worn, brown plaid that showed bits of wood and stuffing along its arms.

"He won't let me get rid of it," Eleanor said. She patted the sofa cushion next to her. "Plenty of room for you here." Despite her big knuckles, Eleanor looked like a tiny bird; the soles of her shoes barely touched the carpet.

Leda perched on the sofa's edge. The cousins were older than Leda had imagined. Both had snow-white hair, although Russell's was considerably thinner than Eleanor's, Leda could see the shiny skin on top of his head spotted with freckles. Eleanor's hands trembled as she poured the tea. Tiny scones, biscuits and cookies were arranged on a plate with a pair of silver tongs.

"Help yourself," Eleanor said.

Leda selected a scone and a cookie, feeling awkward as she maneuvered each onto her plate with the tongs. The three chatted about Leda's long flight, Eleanor expressing concern about how tired she must be, Russell wanting to know if she had anything good to drink on the flight. Leda began to feel warmer than she had outside, sipping hot tea in the room with the window closed. She could feel beads of sweat on her neck, her hair stuck to her skin and she wished she had piled her hair on top of her head before she left the hotel. Her palms were getting slick like they always did when she was nervous. She set her cup down before it slipped from her fingers.

"How exactly are we related?" Leda said. She wiped her hands on a paper napkin.

"Your great- great-grandfather was our great-grandmother's brother," Eleanor said. "So that makes us." She paused, and turned to Russell. "What does that make us?" she said. A million tiny lines etched the skin around her watery blue eyes.

"Fools." Russell bit into a cookie. Crumbs spilled on his shirt. "Everyone in England's related, and we're all descended from royalty." His voice cracked again, the breath of his laughter blew cookie crumbs onto the rug.

"Don't mind Russell," Eleanor said. She turned towards Leda. "You young people always want to get straight to the point," she said, "especially being an American."

Leda started to protest, but Eleanor waved her to silence. "Let's look at some pictures, and then you'll see the connection even if we can't figure out if we're sixth cousins or seventh cousins once removed or some such nonsense."

"I'd love to look at pictures," Leda said. Her heart raced. She worried the locket on its chain. Would it be too much to hope there would be a picture of her mother? She possessed two pictures of her mother: the tiny one in the locket and the photo of her mother on her dresser. In that picture, her mother leaned against brick steps at the university, her ankles casually crossed. Her blond hair framed her face like a cloud. Sometimes, Leda studied the picture with a magnifying glass she kept in a dresser drawer; her mother's face was so small.

"Russell, please get the album," Eleanor said.

"What album?"

"The one I set out this morning."

Russell rose from his chair with a grumble "don't know why you didn't just bring it in here earlier" and shuffled out of the room.

"He's a dear, don't let him bother you." Eleanor lifted a scone onto her own plate, using the tongs as if they were part of her hand. "He's my older brother you know."

Leda smiled and nodded, pretending to listen as Eleanor chattered about various relatives, her words spooling around Leda like piles of loose thread none having even the slightest connection to the photo album. Russell seemed to be gone from the room forever. Leda wondered if he wandered out of the house in disgust at Eleanor's request and left for a walk with the shouting woman outside. Her heart slowed to a normal beat. Her hand dropped from the necklace to her lap. She strained for the sound of Russell's return.

He reappeared with a brown leather album. He presented it to Eleanor like he was handing her the crown jewels, giving Leda an elaborate wink in the process. He backed into his chair and sat down. "Hope that's the one," he said.

Eleanor flipped the pages with an agonizing slowness, talking in excruciating detail about each photo, the people and the occasion. Leda held her breath before each page turn, wondering if this could be the page with a picture of her mother. She began to lose hope as the stack of pages examined grew, and the stack of those yet unseen diminished.

"Aha!" Eleanor's voice sounded triumphant as she turned a page. "Here she is!" she said. She slapped a photo with her long fingers. "Your mother. A natural blonde. Who could forget that hair?"

A thrill of excitement coursed through Leda and she felt reinvigorated as if someone had seen her lethargy in the stuffy room and dumped a glass of ice water down her slumping back. She leaned closer so that her arm brushed Eleanor's, straining to see the face of the woman under Eleanor's tapping fingers. The smell of cigar was stronger. Leda got a few glimpses of the woman – who looked older than Leda had imagined.

In between finger taps, Eleanor spent some time reminiscing about dear cousin Natalie. "We didn't see her much. She didn't get out too often after she returned from the states."

Leda had been soaking in the details of the woman's face – her mother – and she almost missed the import of Eleanor's words.

"You must be thinking of someone else," Leda said. "My mother never returned to England. She died in Oregon when I was two."

Eleanor looked confused, her forehead creased. "Oh dear," she said. "I thought we were talking about Natalie Whitby."

"My mother's name was Natalie Whitby before she married my father," Leda said. She wiped her hands on the balled up napkin. This must happen all the time. There must be thousands of Natalie Whitbys, hundreds at least. She thought she had found a promising lead, but these people weren't her relatives after all. She had wasted their time and hers. Leda set the napkin on her plate, next to a half-eaten scone. "I think I've made a mistake," she said. "I'm sorry to have bothered you. My father is a widower and has been for twenty- two years. I hardly remember my mother."

Russell laughed his dry cackling laugh.

"Oh dear," Eleanor said. "This is a disappointment." She set the album on the low table in front of them with the page open to the picture of Natalie Whitby. Leda's eyes slid to the photo. She couldn't help it. Whether it was a stubborn vestige of hope that kept them there, she couldn't say. She had been so sure, traveled all this way, and sought out this little house instead of sightseeing during her London layover. In the photograph – a close up - the woman's blond hair framed her face like a cloud. How many times had Leda complained about her own uncontrollable mass of curls? The bright blue eyes and odd triangle of a nose could have been Leda's. Leda reached behind her neck and unclasped the locket. Maybe if she compared the two pictures. But the locket photo was too small.

"Your mother's?" Eleanor said. "May I?"

Leda handed the locket to Eleanor. The older woman squinted at the small photo.

"Perhaps a magnifying glass would help?" Leda said.

"Russell!" Eleanor spoke like a command, her tone suggesting the snapping of her fingers. Russell levered himself out of his chair. He opened a drawer in the rosewood table that Eleanor could easily have reached. Eleanor held out her soft hand. Russell lowered the magnifier with its ornate handle onto her open palm with a bow.

"Your majesty." He winked at Leda again before settling back in his chair.

Eleanor lifted the glass to her eye and examined the picture in the locket. "I knew it!" she said. She directed a triumphant smile at Russell seeming to forget Leda's interest in the photos.

"Can I see?" Leda felt as if all her longing for a mother filled those three words to nearly bursting.

"Of course." Eleanor handed the magnifying glass and the locket to Leda. The room fell silent as Leda studied the two photos. The air grew thicker and heavier by the minute until a dry hacking cough shook Russell. Eleanor had to get up and thump him on his back, helping him retrieve his monogrammed handkerchief from his sweater pocket, refilling his cup of tea.

"You shouldn't be smoking," Eleanor said. "You know what the doctor said."

"He issued the same warning to you," Russell said.

Eleanor fluttered her hands.

"Are you sure Natalie Whitby, this Natalie Whitby returned to England?" Leda said when Eleanor settled on the couch again.

"So you think it's the same person too?" Eleanor said. "The photograph in the locket and the one in the album?

"Maybe my mother had a twin?"

"No," Eleanor said. "Twins don't run in the family."

"They do look alike, but I don't see how this could be my mother," Leda said. "I'm sorry, but you must be wrong."

"I'm rarely wrong," Eleanor said. "Am I Russell?"

Russell, caught with his teacup at his lips, shook his head.

"Look at the album photograph dear," Eleanor said to Leda. "Natalie is older in that picture than in the one you have."

Leda couldn't deny that the woman in the album photo looked to be in her mid to late thirties. While the locket photo and the one on her dresser at home were of a young woman in her early twenties – the same age as Leda. "When was this taken?" she said, pulling the album onto her lap.

Eleanor worked the photo from its plastic sleeve. An identical photo was hidden behind it. She squinted at the back of the photo. "Says here it was taken twelve years ago."

Leda felt like someone had landed a sucker punch in her stomach. She leaned back against the couch, and closed her eyes. This couldn't be happening. The scent of dying roses and stale cigar stung her nose. She felt the heavy album slide from her legs to the sofa. She heard a stream of liquid filling a china cup, and she opened her eyes to Eleanor handing her a cup brimming with tea. Two cubes of sugar languished on the bottom. She watched them disintegrate, the fine grains of sugar dissolving into the hot liquid.

"Jet lag," Eleanor said. "You're pale as a ghost. Should have taken sugar in your first cup. Drink up."

Leda took the cup. She felt dizzy. Maybe the sugar would help. She raised the cup to her lips, her hand shaking. The mixture was too sweet for Leda's taste, and she couldn't help the grimace that flitted across her face. She brought the cup to her mouth again. Swallowing the sweet tea made her feel like gagging. Still, she drained the cup, hoping the sugar would give her a jolt and return her brain to normalcy. Although Eleanor was rarely wrong, the album photo couldn't be of her mother. It was impossible. Pop said her mother died a long time ago when Leda was still in diapers. Leda set her cup back on the low table in front of the sofa.

"Maybe there were two Natalies in the family," Leda said. "It happens in large families." She didn't know how her voice sounded to Eleanor and Russell. It sounded small to her, tinny like she was talking into a can.

"I'm not aware of two Natalies," Eleanor said, "especially two Natalies who traveled to the U.S." Her hands were fluttering again.

"You've let a stranger into our house," Russell said. "And now she's sitting here drinking our tea and eating our scones. Probably attack us next. Steal our things."

"You let her in Russell." Eleanor's voice was sharp.

Leda jumped into the conversation before the siblings got off track. "Did this Natalie," Leda pointed to the photo, "have a daughter?"

Eleanor's gaze swung back to low table. She picked up the album and examined the photo. "She did," the older woman said. "We thought you were her. The resemblance is striking, except for the hair color of course."

Had she stepped into an alternate universe? This woman was an older version of her mother. But how could that be? The Natalie Whitby in the photo looked somewhat confused, her eyebrows raised in a question. Her lips open as if she was about to say something.

"Where does the woman, this Natalie, in the photo live?" Leda said. There had to be a logical explanation. Leda could visit the woman. She could find out the woman was a stunning look-a-like of her mother's. Or she could find out the woman was her mother. But the odds were against it. Her pop wouldn't lie to her about something so important.

Eleanor shook her head. "She died in a tragic car accident," she said. "Not long after this photo was taken"

"Drunk driver," Russell said. "Head on. Saw it on the evening news."

"It was a very old tree, quite large, blown over into the road," Eleanor said. "She couldn't avoid it."

Leda sank against the sofa back while the siblings argued. Eleanor reached for the album and started to slip the photo back into its place.

"Could I have that photo?" Leda said.

Eleanor hesitated. "There is a duplicate." She pursed her lips. "What do you want with it?"

"I want to show it to my father," Leda said. "He'll tell me the truth."

Chapter 4

Leda snapped a picture, but when she ducked back under the shelter to look at it, all she could see on the viewing screen was the flash of the monkey's white tipped tail. Disappointed, she pressed the delete button. She was sorry she had left her granola bar on the railing. She didn't want to be one of those hikers who fed the wild animals and littered the park with trash. Her pop had taught her better.

He stood behind her now, unaware of the locket tucked under her shirt again and the picture of the unknown woman slipped between the pages of her trekking guide. Leda's flight from London was delayed, and she arrived late last night. She went straight to her room, collapsing on the thin mattress. She had stared at the picture during her flight until she thought her eyes might cross and still had no answers. If this was Leda's mother, her pop was a liar. He had deceived Leda for most of her life. She didn't know how that could be possible. Only her father could tell her if it was a photo of her mother. But now she was with him, Leda was nervous about asking, afraid to upset the balance they had achieved: a balance where she didn't mention her mother, a balance where the truth was that her mother died in Oregon, a balance that had always seemed secure. Leda ducked her head and slipped her camera into her daypack.

It was easy to avoid her father this morning. The shower was little more than a trickle of cool water, washing and rinsing her hair was a labor. Still, the shower would be her last for the next seven days. Leda braided her wet hair. She took her time repacking her duffel, making sure she had all the necessities for the climb. She was bent over her duffel, her long underwear in her hands when there was a light rap at her door. Her father's voice called to her through the thin panel. But, Leda sent him away, calling back that she wasn't dressed. At breakfast, the hiking group of six plus the lead guide had filled in the table already. The only chair left was one at the opposite end of the table from her pop.

The group exchanged names, but Leda only remembered one. Wyatt sat next to her at the small table, his knee brushing hers. Later, Leda waited for everyone to climb into the Land Cruisers that would take the group to the Machame Gate, and found herself on the bench seat next to Wyatt. She had been thrown against him on a sharp turn. He smelled fresh – his shower must have worked better than hers - and had a very hard shoulder. After, she braced herself against the car door.

Now, Leda ducked her head and slipped her camera into her daypack.

"We travel around the world and end up in a group with a family of Californians," her father said. "Can you believe it?

Leda straightened. Normally, she would have commented that they all looked like movie stars or surfers – and the one young woman kind of did look a movie star with her perfect tan and nice teeth and Wyatt could pass for a surfer. But, Leda said nothing. She unscrewed the lid of her water bottle and swallowed some water. Her smile was wan. She looked into the jungle with its thick green growth and hanging vines as if she were hoping to see another wild animal.

"Excited?" Her pop wasn't giving up. He could be so clueless sometimes.

He looked comfortable in his hiking clothes. Leda had seen him wear the same shirt and pants on many of their trips. And his scuffed boots appeared older than her twenty-four years, but she knew he had purchased them just six years ago. A Tilley hat covered most of his thatch of brown hair going gray. He had knotted his favorite red kerchief in a jaunty manner around his neck.

Looking at him now, it was hard to tell he flew straight from Oregon to Tanzania, shuttling from one plane to the next in a twenty-three-hour journey. He had said he would be here, and he was. All her life, Leda had known he was a man of his word. Could he carry out such a horrible lie about her mother? Maybe it had gotten easier for him over the years. Maybe he had convinced himself the lie was the truth. Leda fingered the locket under her shirt.

"Are you wearing a necklace?" her father said.

Leda dropped her hand; she hadn't realized she was touching the necklace. "For good luck," she said.

"That's new. I don't remember you with a necklace on our other hikes."

"This climb's different," Leda said. She tried to sound casual about the necklace; this was not the right time to let him know about her mother's locket, or the picture burning a hole in the pages of her trekking book. Her pop needed to be approached with care and in privacy – not in this crowd of hikers milling around at the Machame Gate. Besides, Leda hadn't spoken her mother's name to him in thirteen years.

"It is our highest climb," her father said. "You nervous?"

Leda shook her head. "I'm ready," she said. "You?"

"You know I am." He winked and squeezed her shoulder. The faded red of his scarf matched the reds and browns in his plaid shirt. Her father had style. Panache. Even his scarf told a story.

Leda took another swig from her water bottle: most of it was gone. She had brought extra to drink while they waited.

"What's going on?" Her father could be annoyingly persistent at times; he hadn't become the chief physicist at Green Solutions, the company racing to be the first to develop the latest in battery storage, for no reason.

"What do you mean?" Leda screwed the lid on her bottle, her gaze sliding from her father's.

"You seem subdued," her father said. "You were more excited when I dropped you at the airport."

Tears pricked Leda's eyes. She managed a half smile. "Must be a combo of jet lag and altitude."

"You've never been a good liar. But I'll let you slide this time."

Leda pressed a quick kiss to her father's cheek. She loved her pop. That's why the thought of his betrayal was so hard to believe. She would ask him about it tonight in their pup tent. He would tell her the picture wasn't her mother, and everything would be good between them. They could tackle Mt. Kilimanjaro concerned only about the extreme altitude.

Leda surveyed the many groups waiting to register for the climb. She had overheard hikers talking when she went to the bathroom. Some already knew each other and were part of large families or were friends. Her gaze wandered over the family who were part of their group, her eyes lingering on Wyatt. He leaned casually against the railing as if he were waiting for nothing more urgent than the local bus. Blond streaked his longish brown hair; his olive skin giving no doubt that the streaks were from time spent outdoors. His hiking clothes looked natural on his lean frame, even the knife resting on his hip seemed to fit, although Leda could imagine snickering at another man who did the same. Leda didn't remember the other hikers' names; she vaguely recalled Wyatt and the other young man were brothers climbing the mountain with their parents. The young woman hung on the other young man's arm. A large diamond flashed on her finger. They must be newlyweds. Who else would wear diamonds on a climbing trip?

"David's signaling us." Her father's words snapped Leda out of her reverie. Their lead guide, a stocky man of average height, was gesturing for them to join him at the open window of the ranger station. The two slung their daypacks over their shoulders and hurried to meet him. The Californians crowded behind. David pointed to the space where they were to register. Her father wrote his name and date of birth, scribbling his passport number without looking at the official document. He had always been good with numbers. Leda copied the numbers from her passport to make sure they were correct. *"Twendai? Ready?"* David said. *"Pole* (po-lay), *pole* (po-lay). Slowly, slowly." And he set off across the parking lot.

The high sun warmed Leda's shoulders, and she began the climb feeling as if she were at the beginning of a roller coaster ride with the same butterflies in her stomach. They passed the abandoned Land Cruisers, isolated now in the empty parking lot.

The asphalt ended abruptly at a rutted dirt road. Trees heavy with lichen draped like lace curtains shaded the wide path. Leda wondered if they would see any other wildlife besides the monkeys. She had read about wandering elephants, but knew most of the wildlife had disappeared from the forest because of illegal homesteads. She still peered through the dense undergrowth hoping at least a water buffalo might be hiding amidst the greenery. It would be a welcome distraction from thinking about the moment she would show her father the picture of the blond woman who looked so much like her mother.

Chapter 5

David led the group while Erik Ngala walked behind the last person. David had worked with Erik before and knew him as a reliable fellow Chagga. This was the first time he had seen Erik on the trail since the terrible death of his nephew, a young porter. It was tragic how a storm had roared across the mountain with freezing winds and rain so those who didn't have proper clothing shook to death. Erik usually worked as a lead guide, but agreed to be assistant guide on this trip. David thought about this for a moment, curious about why the older man would accept a junior post. Lead guides earned more. But David couldn't worry about Erik's choice. A man's business was his own.

David was glad the Americans were starting to come back to the mountain. Tips had been low since the embassy bombing and 9/11. Europeans were not used to tipping, and more than once he had been handed one large Euro at the last camp and told to split it with the porters. The porters grumbled when that happened and tended to run faster down the mountain to the exit gate, being less careful with their loads. David had a reputation for honesty among those who worked on the mountain, but it wasn't often that he traveled to Moshi and the bank where he could exchange the large bill for smaller ones. Then, it could be weeks before he saw the same porters as each could be at various stages along the mountain or on any of a number of ascent trails. Most were also supporting families and made the trek as often as they could many not taking more than one or two days off between trips, some running to the gate in the early morning with one load, only to join another group headed up the mountain that same day.

The Americans in this group seemed in good spirits. Most of their gear looked expensive and new, the paint on their trekking poles was not even nicked. The father of the sons laughed a lot. A full sound that echoed in the quiet. His body took up a lot of space but so far he had not appeared to have trouble hiking. David had seen the mother's eyes before she covered them with her sunglasses. She had many lines that radiated from them and a permanent crease between her eyebrows. She must worry a lot. Or maybe she smoked cigarettes. Hikers sometimes lied about their habits, but the mountain had a way of breaking secrets. Their two sons had thick brown hair like their father must have had before the gray took over. One had the same hulking build as his father, but the other was slender and shaped more like a Masai. The young woman was married to the big son. Her face was very tan and she had gleaming white teeth. Her smile reminded David of a small peeled banana.

David's first impression of the dark-haired young woman was of her carelessness in losing the granola bar to the monkey. He would remind her and her father not to litter along the trail. He disliked seeing wadded up tissue and plastic wrappers discarded among the ferns and trees. The trash was even more bothersome at the higher elevations where the delicate tundra fought for survival every day. It didn't need to wither and suffocate because of the thoughtlessness of foreigners.

David waited by a log while the group took turns squatting or standing behind a bush – depending if it were one of the women or one of the men. Another Chagga guide had asked him once if he thought it was funny that they toiled like Masai boys – but herding tourists instead of cattle. A Masai guide had overheard them, and boasted that the Chagga would always be second best at herding. David supposed that might be true, but the Chagga were known rivals of the Masai and had always excelled at farming and whatever else they put their minds to while the Masai were known for wandering and marrying lots of women to do all the work.

When he learned that the Americans had visited a traditional Masai village, where the chief's son charged tourists lots of money to sit inside the smoky mud and stick huts, David, of course, brought them to a place where a round Chagga hut with a peaked thatched roof had been re-created. Too bad the girl and her father arrived later. They could have learned something useful as well. Unlike some of the Masai, no Chagga lived in the traditional manner anymore. An old man in a cardigan and a neatly ironed shirt told the family stories of when the Chagga first came to the slopes of Kilimanjaro. How they played a trick on the residents they found – the pygmies – tortured them and chased them away. "But don't worry," the old man said, "you can still find the pygmies with their big, ugly heads in the jungles of the Congo." David could tell the tourists were bothered by how the old man talked about the pygmies with their big heads. He had heard stories about how the Americans were careful not to make insults. He supposed that was why they were taking turns right now hiding behind the bush, while the rest chatted and pretended the ones behind them weren't doing something that back home would be most personal and private.

In the old days, when the white men first came to the Chagga's land, the Chagga Chiefs would take their wealth and send them home empty handed. Or, they might take their wealth and hold them for ransom, doubling their earnings. The white men had finally overpowered the Chagga, taking their land from them. But the balance of power was changing. The national park rules said the climbers must hire guides and porters if they wanted to reach the mountain peak. Those who were too cheap to pay for excellent guides and porters ran the risk of paying the steep price of failure or possibly death. But those who wanted success hired guides like David and were happy to give him even more money after they reached the summit. Most were generous with their fives, tens and twenties which didn't seem like much to them, but was more than enough to pay his children's school fees and to buy new books and uniforms each year. Maybe he would have enough this time to surprise Grace with a gift like she had surprised him with the coat.

The tall son moved to a spot near David. His hair was longer than his brother's and messy. His movements were fluid like a cheetah. Wyatt had spent a lot of time today talking with David, asking him about his family. David was polite. Everyone knew the Americans were big tippers, but they also could be awkward about being taken care of.

David had let the cheetah son go ahead on a particularly steep, narrow spot with the excuse that he wanted to make sure the mother, who was trailing behind, was okay.

He reached out his hand to her and helped her up a deep step. When she put her hand in his and thanked him – *"asante-sana"* - he knew she was one of those American women who didn't mind assistance. You could never be sure: some American women wanted to prove they were strong. But David would remember this mother's gratitude, and would help her often.

Now, the mother patted the tall son's arm. She spoke in a low voice to him, but David heard her say she was glad he was on the hike. The bigger son stood by the log where his wife was busy stretching.

Finally, the big American father finished behind the bush and ambled to the clearing. He grabbed his daypack, slung it onto his back, and then slapped the tall son on his shoulder as he passed.

"Got a confab going Wyatt?" The father's voice was all boom and chuckle. "Let's get this show on the road." And he lumbered up the trail.

"Don't mind my husband." The mother spoke to David.

David didn't mind. He knew the large man wouldn't get too far ahead. The trail and the altitude increased steadily, and a pace that would seem slow at a lower elevation was almost too fast on Mt. Kilimanjaro.

Chapter 6

Leda paused in a small clearing among the giant trees, ferns and tangled vines to catch her breath. Other hikers must have stopped here; Leda couldn't imagine any other reason for what was no more than a brief open space of trampled mud on the side of the trail. A thick moss-covered log did a poor job of defining the clearing's edge. Vines crept along its base. Her father forged ahead. Based on how the day had gone so far, it would take her father awhile to figure out she wasn't close behind. Her father had clipped his music player to his belt and inserted his earplugs from the start. Right now he was probably striding along to a Van Halen guitar solo. His taste in hard rock often surprised people, but Leda knew she would find her pop working furiously in his home office when she heard the loud strains of Rush, Led Zeppelin or Jimi Hendrix thunder down the hall.

Leda preferred to listen to the natural sounds along a trail, whether the rustle of the wind in the pines or the trickle of a meadow brook. So far she had heard nothing along this trail but the occasional birdcall and her own muffled footsteps and labored breathing. She had seen no animal life; she was careful to avoid the occasional swarms of red biting ants that scurried at the base of some trees. The dank smell of mud and wet wood that never dried permeated the jungle in the muted undertones of old perfume. The hiking group had spread out along the steep steps built with sticks, the family keeping together and adopting a slower pace with David while Leda and her father went ahead with Erik. So far they hadn't seen other hikers on the trail, only boot prints filled with muddy water.

In the clearing, Leda sucked water from the plastic tube near her mouth. Her two-liter water pouch might be running low, and she swung her pack from her shoulders to check. Erik came back down the trail looking for her. He helped her refill the pouch from the extra water bottles she carried in her daypack. It was difficult to gauge Erik's age. He and David were both a little bit taller than her and stocky. Erik wore a faded ball cap pulled low on his forehead, but Leda could still see lines creasing his skin. Like David, Erik smelled of sweat. Leda felt embarrassed at first of her deodorant and hotel soap smell – she knew from previous travel it was usually Americans who were concerned about body odor.

"*Habari*? How are you?" Erik's English was careful. "You are hungry?"

Leda shook her head. She was full of water.

"You must eat," Erik said. "Food is good for the fuel."

Erik pulled a clear plastic box from his pack and handed it to her.

Inside was a white-bread sandwich cut in half, a large piece of roasted chicken, a hardboiled egg, a juice box, a cellophane wrapped stack of tan rectangular cookies labeled energy biscuits, a triangular shaped pastry and some foil- wrapped chocolate. Leda could have made three lunches out of the amount of food. She was considering which item to eat first when her father strode into the clearing.

"You all right?" His voice was loud. Leda gestured towards his earplugs. Her father removed them, and plopped on the log next to her. They had enjoyed many conversations on similar trailside logs, but today Leda was mute. She un-wrapped the chicken and took a huge bite.

Erik dug into his backpack and produced another box for her father. It was quiet in the clearing. A cloud passed in front of the sun, darkening the small space so that the light was more like the near twilight shadows of the jungle trail. Leda shivered.

"Erik, you want some?" Leda held out her white bread sandwich. She gestured for the guide to sit on the log on the other side of her, but he shook his head and held up something that looked like a piece of flatbread made out of cornmeal. She supposed it was African food.

"What's this?" Leda held out the triangular shaped pastry from her box.

"Sambosa."

Leda bit into the pastry. It was filled with a delicious mix of roasted vegetables. She was beginning to feel better. She pocketed the energy biscuits for later.

She knew this trail would be harder than others they had tackled, but she couldn't believe it had taken four hours to hike three miles. They had another three miles to go until the night's camp for a total elevation gain of almost 4,000 feet. Leda knew it took longer to hike mountain trails than it would to walk around the neighborhood, and this trail was particularly steep. But, she was surprised at how slow they walked, and how out of breath she was.

Leda hoped to catch glimpses of Mt. Kilimanjaro and its snowy cap as she walked, but the forest was too dense. On the ride from the hotel, the peak had been wreathed in clouds. Last night, she arrived too late to see it. Now, she closed her eyes and imagined pictures she had seen of the majestic peak. She found it easier to achieve her goals if she could visualize them. But the picture of the blond woman intruded behind her closed lids instead of the summit.

"A penny for your thoughts," her father said, startling Leda so that she opened her eyes.

Did he really mean it? He might think it was the worst penny he ever spent. Leda swallowed the last of the *sambosa*. She felt it travel in an uncomfortable lump all the way down to her stomach. Maybe this was a good moment. She could tell her father about visiting the cousins, the picture and the mix-up about Natalie Whitby. Her pop would set everything straight. They could laugh about Russell and Eleanor and continue up the trail.

Just then, the young California couple lumbered into the clearing. The two settled on the log close to Leda and her father.

"That looks good," the young woman said nodding at the open lunch boxes.

Leda's father smiled. "It is."

The young woman reached her hand across to him. "I'm Jen. This is Chase. And I've forgotten your names."

"Dr. Phillip Stanton." Her father wiped a crumb from his lips. "My daughter, Leda."

"A doctor. How convenient. Just in case. You never know...." Jen's words ended in a chuckle.

"Simply a doctor of physics," her father said, holding his palms up in what Leda knew from experience was meant to be a humble gesture.

"My mistake," Jen said. "But that's okay. Wyatt can handle all the first aid emergencies."

"Are there lunches for us?" Chase said. He cast a hungry look at the boxes open on Leda and her father's laps.

"David has your lunches," Erik said.

Jen grabbed her stomach and groaned.

Leda pulled out the packet of energy biscuits. "You can have these," she said.

Chase laughed. "Ignore her. She's a drama queen."

"I'm not." Now Jen was laughing. Chase wrapped his arms around her and the two slid off the log onto the dirt, Jen squealing and giggling. The cellophane package crinkled in Leda's hand. The rest of the group entered the clearing as Chase reached out a hand to help Jen from the ground. Leda returned the energy biscuits to her pocket. Names were exchanged again, although Leda needed no reminding of Wyatt's.

Gail doffed her daypack and sank down next to Leda. "Lunch already?" she said. "No wonder I'm hungry." David distributed the lunch boxes from his pack. The log tilted when Tom sat, and even more so when Jen and Chase added their weight. Wyatt settled on the ground. Leda stood and offered her spot, but Wyatt waved her back. He appeared comfortable, his long legs crossed, his hair brushing the top of his dark sunglasses. Leda felt shy under his steady regard, and she slid back into place next to her father. Gail patted her knee, and Leda remembered the way Gail had touched Wyatt at the previous stop. All of a sudden she was twelve years old again watching her sobbing best friend being comforted by her mother and feeling a raw ache for the mother she never knew. The mother who Leda had thought was dead all these years. Could she have been wrong?

*****

David accepted the small green hard candy the young woman offered. He would save it in his pocket for his son. If Jen gave him another later, he would hold that one for his daughter. The family lounged in the clearing, taking a long time with their lunch. The father and daughter and Erik had continued up the trail a while ago.

"We are climbing very far today," David said. And every day, he thought. For a family with two grown sons, they hiked very slowly. It was common for the foreigners to meander the first day: everything was new and many were not fully prepared for the constant uphill. But they would adjust or fail in their quest of achieving the summit in the six days allotted for the ascent.

David gestured for the family to take the trail ahead of them. The path was clearly marked and well traveled by hikers, guides and porters and they couldn't get lost. He had heard tales from his father of lions roaming as high as the Shira Plateau – the camp where they would stay tomorrow – but he had never seen one. Maybe they moved like spirits through the camps at night. But it was still the day. They were lucky it was not raining. He had guided many groups through the forest when the rain was steady, the trail a muddy stream, the climb a slog in rain gear that steamed. Today, the trees shaded them from the sun, but it was warm enough to walk without jackets. David had seen a ray of light strike the young woman's bare arm when she offered him the candy, briefly turning it gold.

Right now, it would be best for him to fall in behind the mother. Perhaps he could speed the family up if he kept moving gently closer and closer to her heels.

Chapter 7

Leda could feel Erik at her back and it was enough to get her moving a little faster. She sucked on a hard bit of lemon candy.

More clouds gathered, and the day grew darker. Leda took off her sunglasses and hooked them in her shirt collar. Soon, Erik suggested they put on their rain gear. Leda and her father stepped to the side of the trail and lowered their daypacks. She was putting on her waterproof pants when the rest of their group passed.

"*Jambo.*" Leda greeted each. They already wore their rain gear. All had zipped their jackets and pulled up their hoods except for Wyatt. Now, without his sunglasses, Leda was struck by how his grayish green eyes looked like the lichen. The breeze played with his hair.

Leda ducked her head, and balanced on one leg to pull on her pants. She teetered, and lurched onto the trail colliding with Wyatt. Somehow he steadied her and the two managed to stay upright. Leda muttered an apology, and disentangled herself from his grasp. Leaning against a nearby tree trunk, she succeeded in tugging her pants on over her boots. She was zipping her jacket when it started to drizzle. The family was just disappearing around the bend.

"You could have leaned against me," her father said. "You always have before." Her pop's voice sounded wistful.

Her father always had been a great supporter of hers; there was no denying that. Leda adjusted her hood, wished she could don her sunglasses again so her father wouldn't see the tears misting her eyes. Erik waited further up the trail, his bulging pack on his back.

Leda prepared to step onto the trail, but her pop beat her to it. They had enjoyed a good-natured competition on past hikes, and her father held out his arms to prevent her dashing by. She was in no joking mood though and simply fell into step behind him.

The gentle drizzle soon became a constant rain, and the lichen drooped. Walking on the trail became like sliding on muddy ice, the tree roots that crisscrossed their route grew slick. Leda was glad she had her trekking poles to steady her when the soles of her boots grew thick with mud and no longer provided any grip.

Erik led at a steady pace. Her father stayed behind him, and the three climbed in a tighter clump than they had earlier. Leda was careful not to stab her father's calves with her trekking poles while she worked to keep her balance. At some points, it seemed as if she slid back two paces for each step she took forward. She was beginning to drag again. The rain was relentless, a constant drumming on the already sodden branches of the giant wild poplars. The lichen was more gray than green, the ferns on the forest floor drooped. The camp must be just ahead. Leda's hopes were raised at each bend, but were dashed when the tents did not appear. They had moved steadily closer to the rest of their group, and she could make out Gail's huddled shape, her daypack a water- darkened lump under her waterproof coat.

"Anyone in moderate shape can climb Mt. Kilimanjaro. I am in moderate shape. I am in better than moderate shape." Leda's thoughts were repetitive. Like a marathoner blocking out all other thoughts except those that propelled her forward. Sweat wet her armpits inside her waterproof jacket.

Her father slid in front of her, and almost lost his footing. His trekking poles were in his duffel and probably already at camp. Of course, her father didn't think he needed trekking poles while hiking on the slick trails of the rain forest!

"Watch out!" The words of warning flew from her mouth.

It was like a slow motion scene from a movie. One minute her pop was upright, and the next, his boot was slipping out from under him, his arms were wind milling and his fingers were splayed. Leda jumped to the side to get out of the way. The inevitable was already in motion. There was no way out but for her father to wind up with his face in the mud. But what Leda didn't expect was to be caught up in his plunge. Her father's waterproof outfit was wet, and it became like a sled – a sled that snagged the edge of her ankle and brought her down. And she fell on her butt with a whap. The fall jarred her spine. She felt it at the base of her skull. There was nothing to do but sit in the mud, the rain a curtain of water, rivulets sneaking into a space where her hood gapped from her cheek.

Her pop laughed like the fall was intentional and all in good fun. People often said he had a wry sense of humor. He was the one who would post a workplace sign warning people to escape a fire first and tweet about it later. But Leda didn't have the patience for his humor right now, wry or not. She was shaken. She breathed deeply through her nose, blew the breath out through her lips. Leda felt an unexpected longing for her mother. Or at least the mother she imagined she could have had. Tears started.

"Are you needing help?" Erik asked.

Her father waved him away. Gail's concerned face appeared over Erik's shoulder.

After more sliding and slipping, her pop held onto a low tree branch and pulled up. He reached out a mud-stained hand to Leda. "It's official now. We've been baptized on Mt. Kilimanjaro."

Instead of taking his hand, Leda grabbed a glob of mud and flung it at her father, connecting with his already muddied chest. She scrambled to her knees, planting her hands in the mud to push up, and managed to dash past him before he could retaliate. Her pop probably thought she flung the mud ball as a joke, but Leda had fired because she was frustrated and confused about her mother. She was mad about the niggling doubt that said her pop was a liar. Now she ducked, and her father's mud ball flew over Erik and splattered the side of Gail's face.

Leda burst into embarrassed laughter at her father's misfire – a laughter verging on tears. The altitude forced her near hysteria into sputters and finally hiccups.

Her pop looked horrified, and he rushed past Erik to offer his profuse apologies to Gail. She was gracious in her forgiveness refusing the extra bandana he pulled from his pocket to wipe away the mud. She rubbed at the streaks with the back of her hand until the rain-washed most of it away.

"We must continue," Erik said, "if we want to reach camp before dark." He set off up the trail and the two followed at a quicker pace so that the entire group was hiking together. Although they continued to slip and slide, no one fell again until Erik couldn't recover from a misstep. He gathered himself up with great dignity, and continued hiking making no mention of the streak of mud that slashed like an arrow across his backpack.

*****

David stopped at a wide elbow in the trail. The bedraggled group gathered around him. "We are very close to the camp," he said.

After so many times up the mountain, David was adept at reading body language. And he knew his group was having a hard time. Particularly the large American son. His shoulders seemed more rounded than they had at the start. The quieter father hadn't bothered to do a good job of wiping the mud from his skin after his fall. David didn't know why his daughter threw mud at him. But that was the way of daughters. They were hard to understand. Sons were better. But David couldn't worry too much about the father and daughter. They were Erik's concern. It was too bad the skies had opened and gushed water. It was never good to have such difficulty on the first day. It could set the mood for the rest of the trip. And then no one would be happy, even if they reached the summit and his tips would be low.

He remembered the earlier interaction with the American mother, and he went to her side.

"You are fine." His tone was gentle.

"This rain." Gail sighed. She pulled a damp tissue from her pocket. It looked like she meant to wipe her face with it, but she chuckled and put it back. "That won't do any good. Are we having fun yet?" Gail directed her question to the group huddled in the wide space.

Her husband smiled. "Best time ever."

The two exchanged a warm look. The young brother and his wife were holding hands. The tall son stood to the side – alone. No one wanted to take a break and go behind the bushes with blue-colored berries or the large ferns. All said they were anxious to keep going and get to their dry tents. They snacked while they walked.

David thought about the rain and what it meant for the trip. It wasn't unusual for there to be rain – they were walking through a rain forest. But it didn't downpour like it was now too often. Usually a few showers, just enough to make the trail muddy and interesting. No one wanted a straightforward hike. That was boring. A simple trail up the mountain would not lead to a big tip. There had to be some obstacles to overcome. Some hurdles that David was good at helping his clients climb over. But this much rain could make people stop and not want to keep going. He had heard stories of other clients who gave up on the first day. Thankfully, the father and daughter only suffered from being covered in mud. Some hikers slipped in the mud, got hurt and had to be carried down the mountain without ever reaching the first camp. What bad luck that would be. He could hear the group slipping and sliding behind him and he was torn between speeding up to reach camp before too long and risking a serious injury. So instead he did nothing. Just continued pole pole up the mountain, praying to God this trip would be a safe one.

*****

The clouds parted and the moss steamed under the watery sun. Everyone stopped to unzip and remove the waterproof outfits. It wasn't cold, and Leda's neck was slick with sweat. Water dripped from the leaves of every tree and bush and fern in the thickly wooded space, and it almost seemed like it was still raining. The camp had been "just around the next bend" for close to an hour now. So when Erik pointed and asked if Leda could see the tin roof of the ranger's hut, she didn't quite believe him. But the next corner revealed the simple hut squatting on a knoll. They followed the trail that wound up to the top of the knoll, and then climbed the wooden steps into the hut. Two planks were nailed against the wall as a rough bench. The hut was empty – not even a spider's web hung in the corner - but a logbook was open on a bar-like structure also built of planks. Leda had heard beer was sold at some camps, and she almost wished a bartender would appear with a foaming glass of amber liquid in his hand. Almost, because she knew it would not be a good idea to drink alcohol on a high altitude climb.

"I sure could use a cold beer," her father said. Leda swallowed, and took a swig of her water.

"We have tea at camp," Erik said. He gestured for them to sign the book.

Leda signed her name, registering her presence at the camp. She didn't stop to think that the logbooks were probably used to keep track of those on the trail, just in case someone went missing. The rangers could turn back to her page, skim down the signatures and say. "Oh yes. Leda Stanton was here on July 8. Look where she signed her name. This is where we need to start our search." Leda was tempted to relax on the bench next to Gail, but before she could, Wyatt sat next to his mother.

The rest signed their names, and then all descended part way down the knoll and wound through a series of camps that dotted the edge of the rain forest, each with a varied number of pup tents of different colors and one larger tent. Some had a narrow tent off to the side. Leda peeked into one and saw a portable camp toilet. Giant poplars dripping with lichen and water as well as bunches of low bushes disguised the true number of campers and tents, but the group walked awhile further to reach their own site.

Their camp – a cluster of four florescent orange pup tents, a large tan tent and an even bigger forest green tent - was set up in a small opening ringed by scraggly bushes. Twilight shadowed the small site and a man stirring a blackened pot over a smoky kerosene stove. Another man poured water from a yellow plastic jug into a deep round plastic basin.

"Tea is ready." Erik said, indicating the forest green tent. A porter appeared beside Leda holding a square plastic pan of water and a small towel. Vapors curled from the basin. Leda dumped her daypack by the pup tent she would share with her father. The porter offered her a bar of soap, and she dipped her hands in the warm water. Washing had never felt so wonderful. She pushed back her sleeves and scrubbed all the way to her elbows. She splashed water on her face. When she looked up, she saw the summit for the first time. It seemed to glow a warm pink in the setting sun. The spectacular sight thrilled her; the summit was even more beautiful than in the pictures. Leda watched as the sun's rays diminished and the snow deepened to a dark purple, the trees surrounding the camp became black silhouettes. The water droplets on her skin chilled, and Leda shivered. She pressed the rough towel she had been holding to her cheeks.

The temperature dropped with the setting sun. Leda ducked into the large green tent hoping it would provide some warmth. The light was dim. Once her eyes adjusted, she could make out a rectangular table covered with a red and black-checkered cloth. White folding chairs crowded around the table. The family was already seated, the men's backs touching the tent wall. They passed a bowl of popcorn. A plate stacked with brown cookies was in the center of the table next to a basket of cocoa mix and assorted teas. Leda's father entered the tent after her. He pulled out her chair as if they were sitting down to a formal dinner. Leda sank onto the chair. She had never sat on a chair before while on a hike, and the feeling of an actual chair on the slopes of Mt. Kilimanjaro was very relaxing. Gail passed the teas and hot water. Soon Leda was munching on a ginger cookie in between sips of cinnamon apple tea. The tent felt a little warmer than outside, but Leda imagined it was because of the heat rising from the hikers gathered around the table.

"Forget what I said about a cold beer." Her pop cradled a steaming mug in his hands. "A cup of cocoa, a bowl of popcorn and a chair. Who could ask for more?"

Not even Leda could disagree with the sentiment. She didn't notice the locket hung outside her shirt, having slipped unnoticed from its hiding place while she washed.

Chapter 8

At dinner, candlelight pooled on the plastic tablecloth, flickered on the platters heaped high with deep fried fish, vegetables in curry sauce, slices of white bread and mango. Gail bowed her head before she ate, but the others started eating their broth. All were still wearing their fleece jackets, but some had opened the front zipper. Rain gear was spread to dry outside over the top of their pup tents. Tom's chair was backed up against the tent wall, his face almost hidden in shadow. He and Gail hunched in their chairs as if sitting up straight was too much of an effort. The younger hikers passed the plates of food. David was at the end of the table near the tent flap.

Conversation was sparse.

"Hope it stays clear."

"That rain was killer.

"David, will be it clear tomorrow?"

David shrugged. "Most likely," he said. "Although one can never predict the weather on Kilimanjaro." He spooned the last bit of soup into his mouth.

"Have you seen the toilets?"

"Don't get me started."

"This is not an appropriate dinner topic." Gail set her spoon on the table with an emphatic thump. "Please pass the vegetables."

Forks scraped. Scraped against teeth.

"The toilets are just holes."

"Really small holes."

Gail's lips tightened.

Tom sat up straight. "I'm going to do something about the toilets," he said. "There must be someone already working on the problem. I'll get the company behind it as soon as we get home." He forked a heaping serving of fried fish into his mouth.

"What about the ones we saw earlier," Gail said, " in the villages?"

"Those too," Tom said. Gail patted his arm.

"One day down, five more until the summit," her pop said. Now that the mud was washed off his face, his skin glowed ghost-like. It could be the candlelight. Oregonians often were pale. He was probably tired, and still jet-lagged. Leda didn't feel in such tip- top shape herself. The tea had provided a quick energy boost that soon vanished. "Let's see, we hiked six point two miles, and gained three thousand nine hundred fifty feet." Her father sounded professorial. He had taught physics at the community college once while Green Solutions looked for more financing. "What's the plan for tomorrow?"

Leda plopped a heaping serving of vegetables onto her plate.

After tea, she had set up her tent, pulling her sleeping bag from its small stuff sack and fluffing it out over her sleeping mat. She was leaning forward to smooth the head of her sleeping bag when she noticed the locket dangling from her shirt. She clasped the necklace to her chest, feeling like she had been caught even though her father wasn't in the tent. There wasn't room enough for both of them to set up their sleeping bags at the same time. Leda wondered if he had noticed the locket at teatime. He hadn't said anything. Leda slipped the locket back under her shirt. She arranged her airplane-sized pillow and her duffel. Then, checking to make sure the locket was still safely hidden under her shirt, she left the tent so her father could set up his sleeping bag.

"Leda?" Her father's voice drew Leda back to the dining tent. "The plan for tomorrow?"

Leda pushed the trekker's guide she always carried towards her father. She forgot about the photo of the blond woman hidden in its pages. Her pop shot her a puzzled look and opened the book as if that had been his plan all along. "Shira Hut, three point eight miles, climbing two thousand seven hundred fifty feet to an altitude of twelve thousand six hundred feet."

"Wyatt has that book," Chase said. "He's read it cover to cover." The Californian appeared as pale as Leda's father. Must be the candlelight.

"Nothing else to do on the airplane," Wyatt said, speaking to his brother.

Leda studied Wyatt's face. His skin looked the same as it had earlier today - healthy. He raised his eyes, his glance catching hers, and he smiled. Leda gave him a shy smile before returning her attention to her plate of food.

"Leda's read it a million times," her father said, "and many others about the mountain." Even Leda could hear the proud note in his voice, and for the first time, she cringed wondering what the others thought. "Her favorite is the journal of a woman who reached the summit in the early 30s."

Leda finished her vegetables and cut into a piece of fish.

"It's always been our dream to climb Mt. Kilimanjaro." Her father wouldn't stop talking. "Please pass the mangos."

The battered fish formed a dry lump in Leda's mouth; she chewed and chewed on the lump but somehow it never seemed to get small enough to swallow. She looked up from her plate. Chase, Wyatt and her father waited for her to speak. She pointed to the lump in her cheek, and kept chewing. The other three had been talking amongst themselves at the opposite end of the table, their voices a steady murmur but now the tent was silent. Leda could hear the movements of the cook outside, the clang of pots.

"So this is a father/daughter trip?" Gail said. "Your wife is very understanding."

"I'm widowed," her father said.

Leda coughed as the fish went down her windpipe. Everyone stared at her while her face reddened. Her eyes watered. Her father patted her back. She reached for her cup, managed to swallow some water and raised her hand to indicate she was fine. Earlier, in London, she hadn't even thought that if the picture was of her mother it meant her mother had abandoned her. Now, the possibility of her mother's abandonment hit her with a cruel force and her stomach harbored nausea like she had never experienced. Dickens was right. The poets had got it wrong. It was not the heart that broke, but the stomach that clenched. Dickens argument made perfect sense to her now, sitting on a folding chair in a foreign land, eating dinner with strangers; perhaps she didn't even know her own pop as well as she thought she did although what he said was true. The Natalie Whitby in the picture was dead. Whether she was Leda's mother still needed to be determined. Leda remembered the photo in the trekking guide, stuck between the pages chronicling the early explorations of the mountain. How could she have forgotten when she slid the book across the table to her pop?

"I'm sorry," Gail said.

"It's not recent." Her father cut the mango slice into smaller pieces, and then forked one into his mouth. Leda kept her eyes lowered, hoping the photo wouldn't betray its hiding place.

"I'm afraid our family is here because I insisted on it," Gail said.

"And we're footing the bill," Tom said in between bites of fish. Gail elbowed him.

"We're celebrating," Gail said. "We've made it through forty years of marriage, and I figure we can make it another forty if we can survive this climb."

"Hope it's easier than wallpapering together," Tom said.

Gail laughed and smacked his shoulder with a playful slap. Tom planted a quick kiss on her cheek.

Something about their interaction didn't sit right, but maybe Leda was primed to expect the unthinkable worst now despite her hopes otherwise. Wyatt watched his parents as well – his arms folded across his chest, his chair tilted back against the tent wall. The upper half of his face was in shadow, but his lips were pressed tight – an expression eerily reminiscent of his mother's disgust when the earlier dinner conversation had turned to the mountainside toilets. Leda finished her dinner, and pushed her plate aside. The platters were empty. It was completely dark outside. She stifled a yawn. Wondered what the time was.

"8:30." Wyatt's statement surprised her. "It's 8:30. You looked like you were wondering the time."

"And I'm ready for bed," her father announced. He stood and waited behind Leda's chair. When she made no move to leave, but held out her cup for more water, her father left without saying anything, thankfully leaving the trekking guide behind. The others straggled out behind him until Wyatt and Leda were alone.

"Long day," Wyatt said. He rested his foot on the rung of the chair where Leda's father had sat between them during dinner. She nodded. "Rain didn't help." Despite his words, he radiated energy, the candlelight wavered on his cheekbones and his eyes seemed to sparkle. He was attractive in a wild sort of way, and completely different from Henry, her father's assistant. Leda imagined Henry with the glow of a computer screen on his face. Right this moment he probably was staring at his monitor, hoping to solve a difficult problem before her father returned to Green Solutions. Her father didn't know yet his attempt at getting the two together had failed. They had nothing in common besides her father, and Leda knew Henry asked her out because her father wanted it.

"The hike doesn't seem to have affected you at all," Leda said. "You look the same as you did this morning." Heat rushed up her neck as she realized how her words sounded. She reached for the trekking guide, pulling it close.

"Leda's an unusual name," Wyatt said. "Is it from the Yeats' poem?"

"It's German." Leda was glad for the subject change, but surprised Wyatt asked about the poem.

"So you've thought about climbing Mt. Kilimanjaro for a long time?"

"The dream thing?" Leda said.

Wyatt nodded. "What's that all about?"

"My father and I've talked about this mountain since I was a little girl," Leda said. "It's almost taken on fairy tale proportions." Her smile was wistful. "The king and his only child tackling the impossible together." The tent flap fluttered in the wind. "Have you ever noticed that mothers are missing in fairytales?"

One of the porters cleared the platters, silverware and cups from the table, handing them out the door to someone waiting outside.

"I was more into Harry Potter," Wyatt said. "His mother and father are dead."

"Makes you wonder," Leda said.

"Parents can be a pain in the butt." Wyatt moved his foot and leaned on his forearms, his upper body closer to Leda. "Is your father feeling all right?"

"Why do you ask?" The warmth returned to her neck and she lowered the zipper of her fleece so the night air could cool it.

"His skin looked a little gray."

Leda remembered how white her father's skin had looked in the candlelight. But so had Chase's. "He's probably just tired."

"Has he hiked at altitude before?"

"Plenty of times," she said. "Could be jet lag."

"You know him better than me."

Wyatt pushed back from the table and stood. "Shall we? I think the porters sleep in here." He held the tent flap open for Leda. She stood, but couldn't seem to let go of the back of her chair. She wished they could stay in the dining tent longer. Now that the moment of truth was here, the time she had been waiting for all day to talk alone with her father, fear held her in place. How well did she know her father? What if the photo was of her mother? Leda could be jumping into something she wasn't prepared to face.

"Is your tent set up?" Leda said.

"Want to see?"

Leda knew how dumb her words sounded but she hadn't been thinking when she blurted them out. She felt the heat in her cheeks, and she was sure she was blushing like a schoolgirl. "Just making conversation," she said. She grabbed the trekking guide, bent under Wyatt's arm, and swept out of the tent. Wyatt followed her into the night.

"Just joking." Wyatt's teeth flashed in a smile Leda could see even in the dark. "We hardly know each other."

Several shapes huddled nearby. Leda realized they were probably the porters waiting to clear the table. She clicked on her light. "We have six more days to fix that," she said. At his quizzical look, she added, "for the ascent and descent." Inside, she groaned. When had she developed diarrhea of the mouth? "Good night." Leda headed towards her tent before she could say more stupid things, Wyatt's good night trailing behind her.

Chapter 9

The pup tent was dark. Leda could make out the lump of her father in his sleeping bag. His duffel was shoved to the end of the tent by his feet. His boots rested nearby.

Leda crawled into the tent as quietly as possible. She did her best not to bump into her father in the tight space. She had to squint at the tiny numbers of the padlock that secured her duffel: theft could be an issue on the mountain. She carried stacks of small bills and her passport in a money belt, as did her father. Leda froze at the sound of groaning coming from the sleeping bag next to her. All of a sudden, her father flung the bag from his shoulder, sat up and grabbed his coat. He was in a hurry. Leda moved out of the way so he could pull on his boots and dash from the tent. His pounding feet vanished in the direction of the outhouse. Leda remembered Wyatt's question about her father's health. As far as she knew, her father had never suffered from altitude sickness before. He had always been the picture of health on their many hikes in the Cascades and the Columbia Mountains.

She peered out the flap. Lights flickered in the nearby pup tents. She could make out figures moving around inside, but couldn't tell who was in which tent. With her father gone, Leda checked the pages of the trekking guide for the photo. It was still safely stuck between the same pages. She slipped the guide into her daypack, and picked up her roll of toilet paper. She might as well visit the outhouse although she dreaded it. She could empathize with Gail's disgust. Leda adjusted her headlamp, and stepped outside. Erik appeared at her shoulder seeming to materialize out of the night.

"Oh," Leda's hand flew to her chest. "I didn't see you."

"That's because I'm black as the night," Erik said. His smile was quick, and gone in a flash. "Breakfast at 7:30. We have a small day tomorrow, but best to reach camp before lunch."

"Sure. Sounds good."

"Your father? He is okay?"

"I think so." Leda looked down the path to the outhouse. Was her father okay? Maybe she should check on him. But Erik hadn't left. Did he have more to say? She swung back towards him. She could barely make out Erik's features. Leda had lowered the beam of her headlamp so it wouldn't shine in his face. She shifted, switched her toilet paper to her other hand. "Is there something else?"

"We will climb out of the forest tomorrow," Erik said. "You will see the mountain top at Shira Camp."

Leda felt a dark figure behind her. She whirled. It was her father.

"You're jumpy," he said.

"You would be too if I sneaked up behind you."

"You've been in a sour mood all day," her father said. "You feel okay?"

"Fine," Leda said. "And you?" She lifted her chin so that her headlamp lit up the lower half of his face. When she tilted her head further back, her father shielded his eyes from the light. "You left the tent in a hurry."

Leda couldn't remember a time when she had seen her father seriously ill. He often said he had the constitution of an ox combined with the stubbornness of a mule. She could attest to the second part. She narrowed her eyes and tried to see past the shadows on her father's face, to see what Wyatt and Erik had noticed.

"Nothing a good night's sleep won't cure," her father said. He reached out and touched the locket that hung outside her shirt. Leda lowered her head and the light. The locket must have slipped out while she was rummaging around in her duffel. "Where did you get this?" he said. His voice sounded odd. "In London?"

Her father had given her an easy out. She could make up a story about buying the locket at a street fair.

But she plunged ahead with the truth, something about her father's hidden face giving her the courage she had lacked before. "I've had it a long time," she said.

Her father didn't speak or move. He waited. Now, Leda could feel a tension in his waiting. She was hyper attuned to his moods like an antenna built to sense his wavelengths. She had been that way for as long as she could remember. She took a deep breath.

"I found it in your closet." She raised her chin to meet his, her headlamp shining full in his face. He looked surprised and then disappointed before he shielded his eyes from the light.

"You had no business being there." His voice was soft and cool, and in an instant, Leda was reduced to feeling like a small child who didn't quite measure up. She lowered her head, ashamed. Her father spun on his heel and stalked back to their tent.

Leda couldn't do anything but watch him walk away. She didn't know when Erik had left, apparently slipping away as quietly as he appeared. When her pop asked about the locket, Leda told him the truth. She hoped he would talk to her about it, of course she would apologize for taking it, and then she could show him the photo. But now, she realized her hopes had been foolish. Why would he react any differently than he always had? Leda sighed. If her father was upset about the locket, she didn't know what he would do if she showed him the photo. Dejected, Leda continued to the bathroom. She tripped on an exposed root, and almost fell to her knees. Adrenaline coursed through her body, her heart pounding. She proceeded down the path with more caution, taking several deep breaths to calm herself. But the altitude spoiled her plan, and the deeper she breathed, the more it hurt.

      The condition of the toilet had been unexpected when she first visited it this afternoon. It was nothing like the pit toilets she was used to at other campgrounds: four wooden walls and a slanted ceiling enclosing a space large enough for a short bench with a toilet seat. Those toilets didn't flush either, but usually enough chemicals were dumped down the hole to keep the smell bearable between cleanings. Here, on Mt. Kilimanjaro, the walls and the roof were similar, but there was no bench or toilet seat to sit. People were expected to squat over an open rectangular hole in the bare, wooden planks. Leda was sure the hole wasn't any bigger than a paperback book: a small target missed more often than not. And the stink was not disguised by chemicals. She wasn't looking forward to visiting the toilet at night. Too bad physical necessities couldn't be avoided like uncomfortable discussions about photos and mothers. Held off until a more convenient time and more sanitary setting. A headlamp was a definite necessity – nothing should be set on that floor. Maybe it would be better when the interior was shadowed, and all the soiled planks couldn't be seen. She would keep her light away from the shallow hole that she had glimpsed this afternoon – it didn't look like it had been cleaned in months. The door was open a crack, signaling nobody inside. Still, Leda knocked and asked. Pressing her lips together, holding her breath as long as she could, she stepped in, swung the door closed, lowered her pants and squatted.

      Leda couldn't get back outside fast enough. The door banged behind her. She finished zipping and fastening her pants outdoors. She scrubbed her hands with antibacterial lotion, and vowed to visit the bushes near the tent during the night if needed rather than returning to the outhouse. She was more careful on the way back to camp. A complete stillness hung over the darkened camp. No campfires were allowed; the trees would be gone now with all the hikers passing through if each site had a crackling fire. The thick tree canopy cast darker shades and shadows; the moon tonight provided a thin light. A rustling in the nearby thicket quickened Leda's steps. Probably just a miniature antelope or maybe a bush pig. More frightened of her than she was of them. In her haste, she didn't see the two men talking at the edge of their camp.

      Leda unzipped the flap. Her father was in his sleeping bag, his headlamp off. She hesitated a moment, nervous, but he remained still with his back towards her. She scooted inside on her butt so she could remove her muddy boots without getting the tent dirty. Boots off, she slid onto her sleeping bag and exchanged her clothes for the long underwear – top and bottoms - she planned to wear as pajamas. They had been told they could pack only thirty- five pounds in their duffels, and Leda's snacks made up most of that weight.

At this fairly low altitude – close to 10,000 feet – Leda didn't need to zip her sleeping bag. She settled against her pillow and closed her eyes. She wondered if her father was awake. His comment about the locket had thrown her. But she had to know the truth about the photo. Her pop must know how much she missed her mother. She and her father had many heart to heart talks in a dark tent on other hikes; talk of the trail behind them sometimes grew more serious. Her earlier misgivings faded. This was her Pop. She knew he loved her. Tears leaked from the corners of her eyes, trickled down her cheeks. She cleared her throat. "Pop?"

Her father's sleeping bag rustled, and then he groaned. This time he didn't bother with his boots, but dashed out into the night in his wool socks, leaving the tent unzipped.

Cold air wafted in. Leda shivered. Wiping away the moisture on her cheeks, Leda snuggled deeper into her bag. Yawned. She ached with a bone deep exhaustion - the shock of her meeting with the cousins, her anxiety on the flight from London and last night's sleeplessness – had kept her awake. Now, her limbs felt heavy. Her eyelids drooped, and she fell asleep. Sometime in the night, she woke, donned her boots, slipped out of the tent and squatted in the bushes. Her father didn't seem to have moved while she was gone. She watched the steady rise and fall of his sleeping bag, before she slid back into her own. Maybe all he needed was a good night's sleep. They could talk tomorrow. They still had most of the mountain to climb.

*****

Erik stood outside the large tan tent, his gaze fixed on the dark mountain peak outlined against the starlit sky.

"She's a cold one," he said when David stopped next to him.

"We must never forget it," David said.

"Colder towards those that can least afford it," Erik said. "Like Stephen." He gestured towards David's warm coat. "Not all are so fortunate."

"A terrible tragedy," David said, "to lose one so young. How is his father?"

"He suffers."

"And you?"

Erik was silent.

"Maybe it's too soon for your own return to Kilimanjaro."

"A lazy man can't support his family," Erik said.

David held out the money he had been carrying. There had been no time at the Machame Gate to give Erik the three U.S. five dollar bills. "Stephen's," he said. "From our last trip together. Please give them to his father."

Erik snorted. "Fifteen U.S. dollars. Is that what a Chagga man's life is worth?" He balled the money in his fist, and then shoved it in his pants pocket.

David was silent. Kilimanjaro mountain guides were among the highest paid and best educated in the region. In fact, not many of the educated could find jobs that paid as well. The guides must be good English speakers and trained in recognizing high altitude symptoms. For the duration of the trip, a guide held a client's life in his hands. Porters didn't need to speak English, and the competition for the jobs was fierce among those who could hold up under the physical challenge. Fifteen dollars U.S. tip for a shorter five-day trip was a generous amount in a country where many existed on a dollar a day. Erik knew that. Still, he was human and rightfully mourned his nephew's untimely death during a brutal mountain storm.

"The company should have sent his family $28 in pay," David said.

"They sent half. Because he didn't work the whole trip." Erik's tone was bitter.

There was no point in arguing with Erik. David shifted his gaze to the dark tents.

"How are the father and daughter doing?" David said.

"Well," Erik said. "They are in good shape."

David had seen the father run for the outhouse. The man might be in good shape, but the altitude could play unexpected tricks on anyone.

"You should pay more attention to the young son," Erik said. "The big one."

Had he missed something? David didn't think so, but it never hurt to listen to an elder.

Chapter 10

A porter delivered a steaming cup of coffee to the pup tent early the next morning and minutes later a warm basin of water. Leda could get used to this. First, a table and chairs, and now a fresh cup of coffee handed through the tent flap. Her father must have gotten up earlier. His rumpled sleeping bag was empty. She wondered if he felt better this morning. Leda sipped her coffee and thought about the day ahead. She felt refreshed, ready to tackle whatever the trail had in store. This morning, she was confident she could approach her father with deliberation and delicacy. He wouldn't catch her off guard again. Sitting with her legs warm in her sleeping bag, she didn't feel as desperate. Instead, hope blossomed inside her. Her father would listen to her reasonable questions, he would answer them, and both would be satisfied. Leda would start by apologizing for looking in his closet, for taking the necklace and keeping it all these years. He would understand she had acted out of teenage angst. She drained the last of her coffee.

Setting aside her cup, she got out of her sleeping bag. The morning was cool. Leda dressed quickly, braiding her hair as best she could and pulling on a wool cap. She didn't have to look in a mirror to know her hair was a mess. And she didn't plan to look in a mirror the entire trip. She never did on a hike. Of course, it was usually just Leda and her pop. They had never traveled with a group or a guide before, always packing in their own gear, setting up their own tents and cooking their own food. In a burst of activity, her heart lighter than it had been since London, Leda stuffed her sleeping bag, rolled her mat and packed her duffel. She grabbed the empty coffee cup and her toilet paper roll and ducked out of the tent. The last person she expected to see was Wyatt.

"*Habari za asubuhi?*. How is the morning?" Wyatt sounded as cheerful as his phosphorescent orange wool cap. "Sleep well?"

"Surprisingly," Leda said. She adjusted her dull gray cap. There was nothing she could do about her coffee breath. At least coffee breath smelled better than morning breath. And why did men always look so good when they camped? There was something about unshaven cheeks that was just so well…manly. "Nice hat."

"One of my best thriftstore finds," he said. "Mind if I walk with you?" Wyatt indicated the toilet paper roll in her hand. "I was headed that way myself."

No secrets around here, not even when it came to trips to the toilet. "Sure, why not?" Leda heard her father's laughter coming from behind the dining tent followed by another's. Her father must be feeling better. She could set that worry aside.

"Sounds like our fathers are getting along," Wyatt said.

"I suppose that's good." Leda fell into step beside Wyatt.

Wyatt's laugh had a dark edge to it. "You make that sound like a question."

"Well…we are going to be spending a lot of time together," Leda said.

"I hope so."

Leda shot him an embarrassed look. "Not everything I say is an innuendo."

"I didn't think it was." Wyatt widened his eyes as if protesting his innocence.

She laughed because she didn't know what to say. Wyatt obviously was a flirt, and an attractive one. But, she felt awkward around him. She wasn't used to feeling unsure of herself. The two walked in silence to the outhouses. Wyatt wasn't around when Leda stepped back outside. She headed to the campsite alone.

Her father was deep in conversation with Erik outside the entrance to the dining tent. He wore his sunglasses even though the area by the large tent was shadowed, the early morning sun still low. He appeared to be arguing with Erik about something, but their voices were quiet, and Leda couldn't hear them until she got close.

"You are sure about this?" Erik said.

"Most definitely," her father said. He disappeared into the dining tent without acknowledging her presence. Erik left, and Leda followed her father into the tent. He didn't hold out a chair for her this morning, but plopped into a chair between Gail and Wyatt. Leda shrugged her shoulders.

Porridge steamed in a tall metal pot in the center of the table. Platters of toasted white bread, eggs and mangos rounded out the meal. A basket of whole bananas seemed an afterthought. Her father ladled a good-sized helping of porridge into a bowl in front of him. Leda asked Gail to fill her bowl.

"Sugar?" Wyatt offered the basket of blue packets. Her father emptied several packets onto his cereal and dug in seeming to relish the thick mixture.

Leda helped herself to the eggs and some mangos. She was curious about her father's argument with Erik. He avoided her gaze, breaking off chunks of white bread, and popping one at a time into his mouth until the bread was gone. Leda wondered if he was still upset about her getting into his closet so long ago, and the fact that she wore her mother's locket. She hadn't bothered to hide it today. The gold heart glinted proudly on her shirt.

"That's a pretty necklace," Jen said. She wore small earrings, tiny as the tip of a pen. Leda had seen them sparkle in the sun yesterday when they started. "Is it special?"

"It was my mother's," Leda said. She meant to speak casually, but her voice seemed to wobble. She pointed to her neck and drank some water as if the tremble in her voice was due to a dry, scratchy throat.

Leda's father chose a small, unpeeled banana. After a few bites, he pushed back his chair and stood. "I better pack my duffel. Erik wants them outside so the porters can break down the tent."

"Mine's locked. Can you put it out for me?" Leda asked. Her father didn't answer, but ducked through the open flap. She watched through the opening as her father tossed his uneaten banana in the bushes, before disappearing into their tent. His action was not at all like him. Her duffel was shoved outside. Leda ate her breakfast, and drank another cup of coffee anxious about what would happen on the trail today. Her earlier optimism had flown.

*****

David gathered his group by the open door of the dining tent. It was a fine morning; the sky was clear above the kerosene smoke caught in the top branches of the skinny poplars. He drew in a deep breath of fried ham and damp earth.

"Habari za asubuhi. How is the morning?" David said.

"Nzuri." (Good)

David was pleased with his group's hearty response. Everyone seemed to be in happy spirits. They had gotten ready very quickly this morning; he could feel the eager energy pouring off of them.

All the locked duffels were piled near some rocks. Porters had refilled each hiker's water supply for the day, and the group's daypacks leaned against a tree trunk. Gail adjusted the strap on her brimmed hat. Tom twisted and snapped his trekking poles into the proper position.

"Our climb today is shorter," David said. "It is possible to reach Shira Camp by lunch."

Gail smiled. Yes, David thought, it looked to be a very good day indeed.

The porters stood in a loose group near the dining tent. Most had taken off jackets, sweaters or sweatshirts and wore them in a loose knot about his waist. One stepped towards David and spoke to him. David nodded.

"They want to give you a morning song," David said. "To help you get up the mountain."

One porter started singing and dancing, the rest joined in, some trying to outdo others with their fancy dance steps. They clapped. Some lifted their knees high. Others bent and whirled and shook. Although their steps were not the same, they appeared to be performing in unison. David hid his smile behind his hand. Porters didn't always perform a morning dance and song on the Mt. Kilimanjaro trail: he hardly ever saw one. David appreciated their efforts – he didn't mind taking the extra time in the morning. He could tell the hikers liked the performance. Gail's feet were moving. Soon, Gail and Jen joined the dancers, the porters encouraging them with smiles and nods. Even Tom moved his feet. Physical condition was important for reaching the summit: a high spirit even better.

The younger son and the young woman's father left for the outhouse. David remembered Erik's warning about the young son. He would watch him most carefully today. The older son and the second young woman stood apart, the dancers separating them. The song ended with shared laughter among all the dancers. David nodded at the porters, and then headed up the trail. He could hear the dancing energy in the hikers' light steps behind him. Some guides didn't appreciate ideas from the porters, but David welcomed this mornings'. He hoped the porters would do the same every morning. Now that the dance was over, the porters would pack up the tents, cooking supplies, table and chairs, kerosene jugs, water and luggage, and jog past the hikers on the trail. All would be ready when the group arrived at the 3840 meter Shira Camp.

*****

The group wound its way through the larger camp, leaving the skeletal poplars and giant heathers behind. Hikers were already on the trail. Porters who balanced huge plastic-wrapped bundles on their head, shoulders or back toiled further up the mountain.

Soon, Wyatt, Chase and Jen forged ahead with Leda, her father and Erik while David walked with Tom and Gail. Leda's father inserted his ear buds right away. "I need an energy boost this morning," he said. Leda figured his battery couldn't last much longer. He would need a charge soon. But her father surprised her when he plugged his IPOD into a flat black rectangle hanging from his daypack. "Solar power." He smiled and kept walking. There was not a cloud in the sky.

Her father's quick pace of the morning slowed the higher they climbed. By this time, Leda had fallen in behind him, hoping for a moment of conversation. The others surged ahead with David. Leda felt like a racing engine stuck in first gear, but she didn't push past her father, instead contenting herself with soaking in each new view of the white-capped Mt. Kilimanjaro summit above the foothills. Her spirits rose as they climbed. It was as if the beauty of the summit encouraged her. She would stand on top of it later this week; she would solve the mystery of the woman in the picture before the climb was over. The tree line was well behind them, and now the path led through tussock grasses dotted with thick trunked trees like many -branched palms sporting bouquets of green spiked succulents. Two hours or so later, they reached the foot of a twenty-five foot high rock cliff where the others had gathered for a break.

*****

Erik perched on a high boulder a few meters away from the rest of the group where the hikers leaned against boulders at a slight indentation in the path. David moved to join him.

"He doesn't look good." David nodded at the youngest American who sat with his shoulders slumped, his attitude worn. His unshaven cheeks looked like the dirty gray ice fields on the summit, and he nibbled without enthusiasm on the corner of a energy biscuit. David was grateful Erik had told him to observe the large young man.

Erik finished the last energy biscuit in a pack. He stuffed the cellophane wrapper in his pocket.

"Is he determined to summit?" Erik said. He brushed the crumbs from his hands and prepared to jump down.

David thought through the symptoms of serious altitude sickness. Swelling around the eyes was one indication. The American wore sunglasses, so David couldn't tell how bad his symptoms were. The American mother stood close to the young brunette woman, her head tilted as if she were listening very carefully. David tried to remember the young man's attitude on the trail yesterday, but he couldn't. He didn't know what the young man thought about reaching the summit. The older guide was correct: strength of will could overcome illness if the illness wasn't too bad. He would keep his eye on the young man. The brunette's father seemed to be struggling as well, but not as badly.

David jumped from the boulder, and walked with Erik towards the *wazungu* – white people. Sometimes David thought about the first meaning of the word – people who roam around aimlessly. The word the Chagga used to describe the early foreign explorers. It was good to remember. This group needed him to reach the Kibo summit.

Erik would stay back with the father and daughter. If the father got worse, David knew he wouldn't see the father and daughter at the next camp. Erik would insist they head back down the mountain. The group gathered their daypacks and started their scramble up the steps carved into the cliff. It wasn't long before David's group pulled ahead, and Erik's group was lost behind a bend.

*****

Her father rested against a boulder without protest. Leda sank onto the semi- flat spot of a nearby rock. Clumps of grass sprouted amidst the broken lava. A steady stream of hikers wound up the steep rock steps cut into the cliff above them. This was definitely a different kind of wilderness experience. Usually, Leda and her father only saw the occasional hiker on their trips and more often than not were the only ones on the trail. Her father opened a pack of energy biscuits stacked in cellophane. He still wore the ear buds.

"Want one?" Her father offered her the packet of sand colored cookies. Leda assumed he was talking over his music.

Leda shook her head. She bit off another piece of her granola bar. Drank some water. "Hard going this morning," she said.

"Good, never been better."

Leda pointed to her father's ears. He pulled out the ear bud closest to her.

"I was talking about the trail," Leda said. She tucked the crumpled granola wrapper into her daypack.

"No monkeys here," her father said. "But always good to be trail wise."

Her father's compliments made her feel good; they meant he noticed her. He approved and that meant he loved her. Now, Leda knew she was forgiven for the locket transgression. How easily she could fall back into their old comfortable routine, but somehow this time the compliment chafed.

"I doubt the first climbers cleaned up," Leda said. She was thinking about the journal she had brought chronicling the climb of the first woman to summit.

"They didn't care about the environment then," her father said. "Considered themselves masters of the earth and all that moved on it." He finished his energy biscuit.

"I don't see any evidence they were here."

"It's the lack of evidence," her father said, "you know that. Where are the wild animals? The elephants? The lions? My god, it was probably someone in the first group that killed the leopard Hemingway wrote about." Biscuit crumbs trembled in the salt and pepper stubble on his chin. "No one has seen a live leopard up that high since."

"If they shot it," Leda said, "wouldn't they have their porters carry the carcass back down the mountain so they could stuff it and show it off to their friends? It lay undisturbed at the edge of the ice field for years."

Leda didn't realize the others were listening.

Wyatt spoke beside her, quoting Hemingway's story, "no one has explained what the leopard was seeking at that altitude." He popped a peanut M&M into his mouth. "Someone snapped off a frozen ear as a souvenir," he added. Leda couldn't help but laugh at the thought of a frozen leopard's ear thawing in someone's pocket. She could tell from Wyatt's grin he meant to lighten the mood. He didn't understand the way it was between her and her pop.

Her father harrumphed behind her.

Leda turned back towards her father. He held his hand over his mouth. She couldn't tell if he was disgruntled Wyatt interrupted or if he wasn't feeling well. "You okay?" Her father kept his hand up. After awhile, he sipped some water.

Gail held out a sandwich-sized plastic bag. "Would almonds help?"

Her father's smile was faint. "No thank you. You're very kind," he said. Somehow the crumbs had fallen from his chin and onto his kerchief. Leda mimed brushing crumbs from her own neck, and her pop shook the crumbs free from his kerchief.

Chapter 11

A thin mist hung over the cliff face. The mountain created its own climate. It was such a large volcano jutting unexpectedly out of the plains, almost as if God wanted to play a joke by burying an enormous rhinoceros skeleton and leaving its horn exposed for humans to climb. Even the winds couldn't help but be distracted by the protrusion and often were diverted from their course and deflected up its slopes.

Many pictured Africa as hot and Africans as half-dressed. Kilimanjaro was just south of the equator, but David rarely wore short sleeves when he was on the mountain and never wore shorts. In the course of seven days, a Kilimanjaro hiker could experience tropical rain, hail, sun, snow, and sub-freezing temperatures. David had never been to the Ngorongoro Conservation Area, a crater where wild animals roamed in Tanzania, but others who guided the *wazungu* on safaris there had told him it was often cold.

David scratched a spot on his lower back where a mosquito had bit about a month ago. The original bump disappeared in a few days, but a new one grew and was becoming painful and tumor-like. Sometimes mosquitoes deposited the tiny egg of a botfly with their bite. Now, David might have to leave the group to get the botfly larvae filled growth cleaned out. These things never happened at convenient times.

He did have one porter who could speak a little bit of English on this trip. The young man was responsible and could fill in as an assistant guide. Still, David would hate to leave even if it was just for a couple of days. But there was no point in worrying.

Worrying never got you very far. Grace was good at it, so he usually left all the worrying to his wife, who spent all her time at home anyway. All he could do was continue to walk, pray to God and hope the botfly stopped growing and causing pain.

David turned his attention back to the trail and his family of followers. They had already spread out on the steep climb up the cliff steps in a rhythm many hiking groups naturally established, the more aerobically fit pushing ahead, a gap steadily increasing between them and the others. Although it wasn't always the younger ones in the lead, in this case, two of the three younger family members hiked close behind David. The older Americans and the youngest son rested at a bend further down. David stood aside so the others could pass and waited. The fast ones would stop when they got tired or hungry.

From his vantage point on the cliff, David could see Erik and the father and daughter working their way slowly uphill just below the American parents and their son.

*****

Leda led her father. He had yielded the spot in front about an hour ago. The color of his complexion had improved to a faint pink, but it was clear he was still in a battle with the altitude. She could hear it in the plodding of his steps. Physically, Leda felt fine. She inventoried her body: no headache, no nausea, but short of breath. Her fleece jacket was zipped against the chill. Her father continued to wear his ear buds, but Leda couldn't be certain his solar charge still worked. When she talked to him, he shook his head and pointed to the ear buds. Conversation wasn't easy anyway. The rough trail was too narrow to walk side-by-side, and other hikers were constantly passing. Or at least they used to constantly pass. Maybe their slow pace had dropped them back behind even the stragglers. Now, Erik walked behind her father, his presence encouraging her father onward to the camp. This morning's urge to walk faster, the frustrating sense that her father's pace was holding her back was gone, replaced by a need to help him, if only by staying close. Erik wouldn't let her father continue if he really were sick. Leda was sure her pop would feel better after a long afternoon nap, and completely recovered after tea.

Then, she could explain to him why she searched his closet. She could talk to him about the hole inside that had never gone away since her mother died. They would have a long talk, and he would reassure her all was as it had seemed her entire life. He would recognize Leda was an adult now, and could talk with him in a reasonable manner about everything. Yes, he would say, it was a terrible tragedy her mother died at such a young age. He would tell her he understood why she looked through his closet for something from her mother, and why she kept the locket. He would explain he wasn't mad she searched for relatives. He would apologize for the horrible shock she received in London, but he would assure her the blond woman in the photo wasn't her mother. The raw pain of his own loss would be evident in his eyes, and they would understand each other. A horrible thought formed. What if her father was so sick, he had to go to a lower altitude and abort the climb? They had always said the other should keep going if that happened. But Leda didn't know if she could stand being abandoned by her father now.

Leda's memories of her mother floated like the mist on the cliff. Was that her mother's shoulder she slept on? Her mother's face leaning over her crib? Her tears that wet Leda's neck? Leda had a dim recollection of toddling down a shadowed hallway searching for her mother, compelled by a need she couldn't fully understand. Near the end of the hall was the open doorway to her parent's room. A dim light from the door smudged the hallway carpet. Leda had the faint impression of pausing at the edge of that light of her mother sprawled face down on the big bed, her body shuddering with sobs. Even though she was just a child, Leda felt at her core something deep and uncontrollable and frightening. She didn't remember if her mother saw her trembling in the doorway. Her memory ended with the crumpled hem of her mother's dress and her bare legs drooping off the edge of the bed.

Chapter 12

At the top of the cliff, the trail meandered into a rock- strewn valley. Single trees with misshapen arms, the five meter high giant senecios, and lobelias, the three-meter high herbs with flower spikes like huge forefingers pointing heavenward, clustered near the stream at the valley's bottom. David never lost his admiration for the plants' hardiness and ability to adapt to the mountain's harsh conditions. Some varieties of the plants could only be found on Mt. Kilimanjaro's slopes. American hikers told him the senecio trunk looked like a hairy palm tree trunk. They all had different ideas about what the green sprouting at the end of the branches looked like. David forgot the pain of his bump when he considered the multiple branches and forks of one giant senecio. And he paused to extol the plant's amazing qualities.

"Its age is plain for all to see," he said. "Another tree hides its years and a man can only guess by its size. The age cannot be known until the tree is cut down and it is no longer a tree, but wood for a house or a cookfire.

"But a senecio is proud to be old on Kilimanjaro. Look at me, it says. I am a survivor. The forks in each branch tell how old the senecio is. Each fork represents twenty five years."

In a way, his Chagga ancestors were like the senecio. Hardy, adaptable. They had come from another land, and expelled the pygmies. His father had taught him how to survive. How to be a man who thrived in harsh conditions. One day, David would be old and still living in the foothills of Mt. Kilimanjaro. Maybe his son would be a mountain guide, a fork in the ancestral branch.

David continued along the trail, leading the family across several streambeds. He helped Gail scale a series of boulders scattered with gravel and squeeze past some rocky outcrops. From there, the trail became almost level across the Shira Plateau, a landscape of broken shale and clumps of everlastings, low plants with daisy- like flowers.

*****

Leda didn't know a morning could be so long. Her sock had wrinkled on her right heel. It rubbed her skin and bothered her, but not enough to stop and take off her boot.

The three stopped for lunch in a valley unlike any Leda had ever seen. She was used to the lush valleys of the northwest, the thick grass and abundance of wildflowers, trees mobbing the slopes, water so plentiful it virtually went unnoticed. Now, Leda studied the sparse palm- like trees Erik told her were senecios. He said the plant with the leaves pointed like spears at its base and the large thimble like growth was a Lobelia. Yesterday, they hiked through a lush rainforest with giant ferns and trees dripping with lichen, and today – just two miles higher – they climbed in the open with only the hardiest of plants scattered among the jumbled rocks.

Erik provided the same meal as the previous day – white-bread sandwiches, a piece of cooked chicken, a hard- boiled egg and a *sambosa*. The lunch was too much yesterday, but today Leda ate everything. Her father sat with the box open on his lap for a while, and then picked at the chicken and the egg. Leda urged him to try the *sambosa*. He did without comment or complaint. It was quiet in the rocky valley, except for the occasional high-pitched cry of some birds flitting about.

Her father peeled the bread from his sandwich. He broke off a piece, and put it in his mouth. Leda watched as he worked on the bread, the lump moving from one cheek to the other. His swallow seemed forced. He took another bite, smiled at her with his lips closed. Leda prepared herself for a long wait, however long it took her father to eat his lunch. Erik re-filled her water supply from an extra bottle he carried. Her father held out his water bottle for more.

"You're being extra nice," her father said.

"Am I?" Leda bent to pull at her sock, to tighten her bootlaces.

"Somehow I get the feeling I'm the fatted calf," he said. "Yesterday you threw mud at me, and now you're encouraging me to eat."

Leda was silent, her head bent over her boots. So he hadn't thought the mud ball she threw at him was a joke after all.

"Is it the altitude or is something else going on?" Her father chugged some water. "If you won't talk, I'll have to speculate. Are you mad I didn't go to London with you?"

Leda straightened.

"Because I wanted to," her father said. "The project came out of nowhere."

Leda sighed. She had heard the same excuse before, but her pop always did take time for their annual climb and he usually chose a location where he couldn't be reached.

"I'm sorry I went in your closet," Leda said.

"Leda girl," her father said, his voice a heavy sigh. "I'm sorry you did too." He put another piece of white bread into his mouth. His jaw worked as he looked off into the distance. He spoke around the bread. "How long have you had the necklace?"

"I found it when I was thirteen," Leda said.

"And you've had it all these years without telling me?" Her father shook his head.

"I could tell you didn't like to talk about my mother," Leda said. She could hear her voice begin to break, and she swallowed some water and closed her eyes. She noticed the foreign smells of Mt. Kilimanjaro – the unknown seasonings in her father's sambosa, maybe curry and onions, the hint of floral from the Lobelia, the suggestion of ash in the wind. She needed to stay calm. If she didn't, Leda was afraid her father would withdraw. She had seen it before when she lost control of her emotions. She didn't remember what caused her to sob or yell: it could have been anything – the imagined insult of a classmate, the beginning of puberty, the absence of her mother. Every time, her father's body would go still and his expression go flat. It was like she threw a rock into a pond, but the rock simply sank without making any ripples. She didn't know where her father went at times like that, and it scared her that one day he might not return. Leda felt the beginnings of the raw spot on her heel where her sock had rubbed. She might have to take off her boot after all.

"I thought you were done asking me about her," her father said. "I thought we had moved on." His voice sounded sad.

Leda wanted to worry the necklace, but her fleece jacket was zipped high on her neck and she couldn't reach it. Instead, she drank more water. Her father did the same, finishing up his lunch, balling up the empty paper and foil wrappers and snapping closed the lid on his plastic box. A small brown bird with a short white tail landed on a rock just behind her father. Standing bolt upright, it emitted a loud piping call.

"I'm surprised you're wearing the necklace now," her father said. "After all these years."

Leda's throat felt full of cotton. All the careful words she planned to say vanished from her brain like they had never existed. She stared at her father – dumb. Then, out of nowhere, an enormous sense of loss welled up inside her, deafening her so all she could hear was the rapid beat of her heart. She pressed her hand to her lips. Dropped her eyes to the toes of her boots. This was not how she planned to talk with her pop. All she could do was shake her head in silence. She felt her pop's hand on her shoulder. She could only imagine his expression, and she refused to look. Her father's hand fell away. Leda took some deep shuddering breaths.

"You were limping earlier," her father said. "Do you need to fix your boot?"

The moment to speak, to talk with her pop about London had passed. "It's fine." Leda's voice sounded choked.

"You sure?" her father said. "You don't want to get a blister at this stage."

"It's fine." Leda stood and paced around the lunch spot. "See?"

"You are ready to go?" Erik said. Both Leda and her father looked at the guide, Leda feeling as if Erik appeared out of nowhere. She had lost track of him. "Your boot needs fixing?"

"My boot is good." Leda grabbed up her daypack and looped the strap of her trekking poles over her wrists.

"Don't be stubborn," her father said. "You're the one who'll suffer for it."

Leda left the small clearing. She couldn't listen to her father's advice now: even if he was right.

Eventually, Leda slowed and they resumed their pre-lunch pole pole pace, taking their time easing past several large boulders and climbing up and over rocky outcrops. The trail didn't lend itself to further conversation. Leda's thoughts were scrambled. Her wrinkled sock chafed the spot on her heel, constantly reminding her of her poor choice not to fix it when they stopped for lunch. Her skin felt raw. She refused to stop, seized with an uncontrollable urge to get to camp. She did her best not to limp. Every once in a while, they would round a bend and gain a full view of the looming summit. Leda always paused as if she was drinking in the view, but she also tried to sneak her hand down to her sock and yank it smooth.

They wandered for a silent hour across a plateau of solidified lava kicking up dust and gravel and the occasional chunk of shiny black obsidian. Then, they came over a slight rise and into a patch of more level ground where hundreds of pup tents were staked. Scrub brush dotted the outer edges of the camp, while giant heathers with tall slender trunks and stunted grasses were scattered among the tents. Erik led them to their campsite. Her father wasted no time stripping off his boots and crawling into the tent where he fell asleep on the mat he hastily unrolled. Leda dropped her daypack. She headed to the outhouses. Four women waited in line by the closed door of one. The other door banged in the wind. A small rectangular hole was cut in the center of that outhouse floor. The planks were clean. A mop and bucket leaned against the outer wall.

"Why are you waiting?" Leda asked the last woman in line.

"This one's got a seat," the woman said, nodding at the closed door.

Leda got in line.

Chapter 13

The mist had cleared. Leda stood on a shale outcropping just above the tent where her father still slept. God, she was a chicken. The summit seemed to mock her. It wasn't hiding now, but towering full-shouldered above her appearing closer than it actually was. Erik had told her about 400 were camped on the plateau tonight. A temporary tent village, boiling pots and all that would pack up and move on in the morning. She imagined the same number would set up camp the following night, and so on throughout the year – at least during the good climbing seasons. With the basic creature comforts at hand, a shelter, a warm sleeping bag, food and a western style toilet, it was hard to remember the mountain was wild. Of course it could be conquered, it was only a matter of a strong will. If only she felt so sure about talking with her pop.

Leda tried to imagine the area in the early 1930s when the woman from the journal and her party camped nearby. A wild lion had run through their camp. The men scared it off with their guns, and although they had tracked it through the day, they had never found it or seen it again.

The wind carried hints of ginger from the night's approaching dinner. Leda zipped her fleece, slid her gloved hands into her pockets. She had doctored her heel earlier, cutting a piece of moleskin to cover the raw patch. She barely noticed it now.

Pieces of shale slid and clattered, footsteps approached.

Wyatt's down jacket was open, but he had replaced the kerchief he usually wore pirate style on his head with his wool cap. "You're deep in thought," he said. "Worried about summit day?"

Leda shook her head. "Not really."

A gust of wind cut through Leda's fleece, and she shivered, burrowing her chin deeper into the fuzzy collar. Wyatt shifted his position to block the wind. He made a very nice shield, and Leda relaxed.

"Where's your dad?" Wyatt said.

"Sleeping."

"You two having fun? The hike living up to the dream?"

"I don't know if fun is the right word," Leda said. "As for the dream." She let her words trail off.

The wind snatched Wyatt's chuckle. "Fun doesn't quite describe it does it?"

Leda smiled. "Let's just say I'm appreciating the challenge."

Wyatt indicated the summit. "I don't know if its because we're in Africa or because Hemingway wrote about it, but Mt. Kilimanjaro possesses a certain mystique." Wyatt waved his hand in a sweeping arc to indicate the hundreds of tents pitched in the camp. "Something's drawing all these people."

"What about you?" Leda said. "Why are you here?"

Wyatt started to speak, and then hesitated. "Off the cuff, I would say a free trip." He laughed. His teeth were very white against his tan skin. His beard was growing in darker than the streaked blond of his hair. "You heard my mother. We're celebrating my parents' 40th anniversary. Family togetherness and all."

The two stood silently for a while considering the summit. The snow glowed a perfect pink blush in the rays of the setting sun.

"I'm probably like most everybody camped in those tents," Wyatt said. "Mt. Kilimanjaro. The Roof of Africa. Somehow it's both an exotic challenge and romantic."

"That must be why your parents picked it for their anniversary celebration," Leda said. The two shared a comfortable laugh.

"Most people would throw a party," Wyatt said. "But my parents aren't like most people." A muscle twitched in his jaw. Wyatt appeared lost in thought, his gaze held by the summit. The wind shifted and swirled around them, and although they were within shouting distance of the camp, Leda felt as if they were further away, and not standing on a simple rocky outcrop just above their campsite. Wyatt appeared to belong in the rugged landscape. It was easy for Leda to imagine him in the early climbing party. She pictured him scouring the surrounding plateau for signs of the visiting lion, and she felt inexplicably safe. His gaze slid to her face. "They say lions used to be spotted here," he said.

Leda blushed that he had caught her staring at him. She wondered how he knew what she had been thinking. She fiddled with her zipper. Pretended to pull it higher. "I have the journal of an early climber with me," she said.

"The little red book you were reading this morning?"

Leda nodded. "A lion ran through their camp here."

"What I wouldn't give to see the mountain then," Wyatt said. "Back when it was wilder."

"You think its tame now?"

The sun had sunk lower, and now the summit seemed a pearly white. "Disneyland turned the Matterhorn into a little kid's roller coaster ride," Wyatt said. "Mt. Kilimanjaro seems on track to becoming the celebrity fund-raiser poster child. And how many down there" - Wyatt indicated the myriad of tents – "are making a point for their 40th or 50th birthday?"

"That doesn't mean it's tame," Leda said, "just because we haven't seen a lion."

"No, but perception can triumph reason." Wyatt burrowed his hands into his pockets. "And to answer your question, no, I don't think it's tame. We can train, eat well, wear the appropriate clothing, but in the end, the altitude could defeat us or the mountain could whip up a storm that sends us packing." The wind rattled the thin branches of a scraggly bush nearby. For the first time, Leda noticed the absolute stillness of the landscape, the absence of any animal life. The small brown birds she had seen flitting about earlier had disappeared. Not even a raven soared on the wind currents overhead. "You're shivering," Wyatt said.

Leda hated to leave. It was easy to talk to Wyatt, and to look at him. But the wind was biting. "I should get my warmer coat," Leda said. The two scrabbled down the shale-strewn slope to the camping area. Her father emerged from the tent wearing a down jacket and wool cap pulled low on his forehead. He stretched his arms over his head. Their camp's pup tents were clustered just beyond him. The wind snapped the flap of the larger green tent. "See you at dinner." Wyatt passed her father with a nod. Leda's gaze followed Wyatt until he disappeared into the pup tent staked next to theirs. Her father's voice drew her attention.

"Where have you been?" her father said.

"Just enjoying the view." Leda ducked into their tent. The still stuffed sleeping bags, duffels and mats littered the tent in haphazard fashion. She arranged her mat, and spread her bag bringing order to her side of the small space. Digging in her duffel, she pulled out her down coat. She quickly wrapped a wool scarf around her neck. She had learned last night the dining tent would provide cover from the rain and a break from the wind, but little shelter from the cold.

Leda was surprised her pop still waited by the tent almost like a guard. The wind had whipped his face into a state of ruddiness. She thought he would have gone to the outhouse or something.

"Feeling better?" she said.

Her father nodded.

"Dinner's just about ready," she said, sniffing the gingery scent of broth, even stronger here than on the shale outcropping. Just a few feet away, the cook stirred a huge pot on the kerosene stove.

"For the first time, I'm starving," her father said. The two joined the rest of their group entering the dining tent. Like the first night, the hikers helped themselves first from a large pot of steaming broth. Leda cupped her hands around the warm bowl, letting the steam waft over her face. Dinner was chicken, rice, crepe-like pancakes, fruit and white bread. Her father seemed to have a hearty appetite. He filled his plate with a heaping serving of rice, pancakes and chicken and dug in. Leda did the same. Talk around the table was desultory, and mostly involved chatter about the weather and the western style toilet. Feeling stuffed, Leda leaned back in her chair. She was content for the moment to be silent, to listen to the rest eat and talk. Everyone sauntered out of the tent about the same time.

Stars filled the night sky like milky clouds.

"The Southern Cross," her father pointed to the sky, "can't see that in Oregon." The group ambled a short distance from the camp. Jen and Chase dropped behind holding hands. Leda found herself walking between her father and Wyatt.

"The heavens declare the glory of God," Gail said from behind Leda, "The skies proclaim the work of his hands."

Leda's father said, "The light we see and call stars actually began its journey hundreds of years ago." His tone sounded professorial. He must be feeling better. "So basically, what we see now happened in the past."

"My point exactly," Gail said.

No matter the point of view, the past was exactly Leda's problem. The past – an unexpected past to be sure – had traveled, no hurtled through time into the present raising unsettling questions. Was the woman in the photo her mother? Had her mother abandoned her? Or had her father stolen her? Leda took a deep shuddering breath. .

"Amazing sight." Wyatt's voice seemed to come out of nowhere stopping the retort Leda knew her father was ready to give to Gail. "There's Orion's Belt."

"An asterism, part of the Orion Constellation." Leda could hear the competitive edge in her father's voice. He added, "Leda's boyfriend is well versed in the stars."

Leda felt Wyatt's gaze on her. "I'm going to the tent," she said. "I'm cold."

"Think I'll stay up awhile," her father said. "I spent all afternoon in the tent." There was a pause as Leda hesitated. "The fresh air feels good," he added.

Leda clicked on the headlamp dangling on her chest like a necklace. There was no point in reminding her father about his unpacked sleeping bag. A disordered tent had never bothered him in the way it did her. Her walk back to their camp was brisk. A light moved in the tan tent, and she could hear voices inside murmuring. Leda unzipped the pup tent. She unlaced her boots, set them by the door. After stringing the headlamp up as an overhead light of sorts, Leda set to work organizing her father's side of the tent. She worked quickly within the narrow confines of the space, scooting on her knees, fluffing both sleeping bags so the down was no longer compressed, arranging them so their heads would not be on the downward slope when they slept. Putting the tent in order felt good – lining up the sleeping bags, arranging the duffels at the foot of the beds and her small pillow a final touch. Leda adjusted her headlamp and made a final trip to the outhouse. When she got back to the tent, she called out to her father in a low voice. She didn't want to unzip the tent while he was changing. Hearing no answer, Leda opened the tent flap and crawled inside. Her father still hadn't returned. Leda changed into her long underwear. Settling on her sleeping bag, Leda risked a look at the trekking guide, flipping the page open to where she had last seen the photo.

It was gone.

Chapter 14

Leda did her best to squash the first rush of panic. The photo probably slipped out of the book and was laying somewhere in the recesses of her daypack. A thorough search of her daypack turned up crumpled tissues, lip balm, discarded wrappers, sunscreen, waterproof pants and anti-bacterial hand lotion. Maybe she had put the photo in her duffel and forgotten. Leda pawed through her as yet unused thicker layer of long underwear, two pairs of clean wool socks, a small plastic bag with her brush, toothbrush, toothpaste and deodorant and numerous uneaten granola bars. Her toilet paper rolled unnoticed into a shadowed corner.

She was still searching for the photo in her duffel, running her hand along the sides and bottom when she heard the murmur of approaching voices. The wind had stopped, and she could distinguish her father's voice and Wyatt's. She remembered her father's words earlier about spending the afternoon in the tent. Had he found the photo?

Her eyes shot to his duffel. Leda felt a moment of panic. Without the photo, what proof did she have her mother hadn't died in Oregon? Leda had to remind herself the photo proved nothing – yet. She crawled over to her father's side of the tent and unzipped his duffel, cringing at the imagined noise of it. She paused. Listened. The voices were silent, and she held her breath. Then, her father spoke, Wyatt answered, the conversation continued. Leda exhaled. She slipped her hand inside the duffel. The pinpoint light of her headlamp seemed to cast more shadows inside the heap of her father's stuff than illumination. She was feeling her way through his snacks, her fingers sliding over the wrappers when he spoke at the closed tent flap, "You decent?"

Leda jumped at his quiet voice. She imagined him bent at the waist, his lips hovering just by the zipper, not wanting to disturb the sleeping occupants of the tents no more than two feet away.

Leda withdrew her hand with a guilty rush. She zipped his duffel closed, wincing at the sound. "Give me a minute," she said. Crawling back to her side of the tent, Leda rushed to restore order. She was breathing hard when she slipped into her sleeping bag. She couldn't put off asking her father any longer about whether the London cousins told her the truth, picture or no picture. She didn't know why she had gotten into her sleeping bag. But she pulled the edges up over her shoulders and close to her ears.

"Ready," she said.

When her father entered, Leda faced the tent wall on her side so he could change. She listened as took off his boots, and struggled out of his coat in the small space.

"This yours?" he said.

Leda's heart pounded. Was it the photo? She risked a look over her shoulder. Her pop was holding a roll of toilet paper.

"Mine's in my coat," he said.

Leda turned her head back towards the tent wall. "Just toss it in my duffel." She closed her eyes.

She listened again as her father moved to unzip her duffel. The tent grew silent. Leda could hear the faint stirrings of the hundreds of others in the camp or maybe she just imagined it. Then, her pop spoke, "What's this?"

Chapter 15

Leda knew before she looked what her father held; a strong premonition raised goose bumps at the base of her neck. Her father's voice had that tone. It was a tone suggesting he had removed himself to a place she couldn't go. It was the tone that went along with the unruffled pond look. She had taken a couple of psychology courses in college, and she was pretty sure the tone and the look had something to do with his upbringing. His family didn't live nearby, but Leda knew from random visits over the years his family was loud and boisterous and given to "excessive displays of emotion." That was how her father described them after they returned to their homes in a far away state.

His mother seemed to suffer the most from these excessive displays. At first, Leda liked the way his mother whisked her into her ample arms – encouraging Leda to give her gram a big hug. She liked the way gram smelled of rosemary and sage. It made Leda think of the earth, and she snuggled deep into her gram's stomach. She was just a child. But as she grew older, Leda noticed a strange expression on her father's face whenever his mother slung her arm around his shoulders. He seemed to disappear inside himself, his jaw going slack and his eyes becoming an even lighter shade of hazel. Even the toes of his shoes seemed to turn inward. After a while, Leda felt an equally stilted awkwardness in her gram's embrace. It seemed only natural at the time she would adopt her father's shuddering distaste of excessive emotion – happy or sad - to show her solidarity with her pop.

Now, Leda shuffled around in her sleeping bag, and turned to face her father.

He pinched the photo between the index finger and thumb of his right hand. The pinpoint force of his headlamp shone through the thin paper and dispersed into a larger circle on the wall of the tent. His eyes were pooled in shadow, the tip of his nose caught in the light, his lips and chin hidden in darkness.

Leda rose to a sitting position, draping her sleeping bag like a blanket around her shoulders.

"It's a photo," she said. She hadn't meant to state the obvious. Those were just the first words to blurt out of her mouth. She wondered how he had found it when she couldn't.

"I know it's a photo," her father said. Now he spoke with the calm, collected voice of the well-studied director, and former professor - so well-modulated even those seated in the back row, like her, could hear and understand.

Sometimes, Leda felt sad when her pop talked in professorial tones to her. She imagined other fathers speaking more warmly to their daughters. But then, she would feel guilty. Maybe she was expecting too much from her pop. Maybe she was wishing he acted more like a mother.

"Why do you have it?" Her father's cap was gone. Leda saw it tossed onto his sleeping bag. His hair was tousled. He leaned back on his heels, his pants still on, his feet in his gray wool socks with the reinforced toes.

Leda took a deep breath. It didn't matter that her pop had the photo, that somehow he had found it. This was her pop. She could trust him.

"I got it in London," she said, "from people who might be relatives."

Her father stayed silent.

"They thought, they said it was a picture of my mother." Leda's words came out in a rush now. "The woman in the picture is Natalie Whitby, and I wasn't sure. I wanted to ask you. I mean, she looks like my mother but older." Leda's flood of words stopped as abruptly as they had begun.

"Relatives in London?" her father said.

"You said my mother was from England. I found them through an ancestry website."

"I thought we were happy. I thought I provided a good life for you." Now his voice was heavy and his shoulders slumped. "Why do you feel the need to search for more?"

The all-too familiar guilt seeped into Leda. She had hurt her pop. "You're great," she said. "The best."

Her father held the picture in both hands now, his head bowed as he studied the woman's face. His face remained shadowed so Leda couldn't even begin to guess what he was thinking.

Leda ventured a question. "Does it look like her?" Her voice sounded small even to her. The questions she really wanted to ask, the ones that haunted her and that fear kept her from speaking aloud were: Is that my mother? Have you been lying to me all my life?

"Tell me more about these relatives," he said, continuing to study the picture.

"They live in London. Their neighborhood doesn't look English at all." Leda knew she was talking in a circle, but she couldn't seem to stop herself. "It was hot, not how I pictured England. Their names are Eleanor and Russell. Brother and sister." Did she imagine it, or did her father shift when she mentioned the names? "Their father's brother was the brother of my great-great grandfather or something like that."

Her father finally let go of the photo, and it drifted and settled like a white feather on the foot of Leda's sleeping bag, the woman's face hidden against the slippery material. Leda waited. Her heart slowed, her breathing almost stopped. She hardly knew what she waited for. Did she still possess a tiny bit of hope her pop wasn't a liar? That he would dismiss Eleanor and Russell? That he would logically explain away the striking resemblance and shared name of the woman in the photo and her mother?

"And how are they?" he asked. "Are they in good health?"

"You know them?" Leda said. The question came on a burst of breath full of unresolved doubt.

Her father sighed. For the first time since he held the photo, he looked at her. Leda was blinded by his headlamp, and she threw up her hand to shield her eyes. Her father clicked off his light and the tent was plunged into darkness.

"I did," he said. Leda's pupils were still adjusting from being flooded with light. She couldn't see her pop. His voice seemed disembodied his words hard to believe – at first. Until they forced their way into Leda's mind.

"You know them," she said. Now, her tone was accusing. Her eyes were beginning to adjust to the darkness, and she could just make out the dim form of her father hunched at the end of her sleeping bag. Any guilt she had hurt her pop disappeared in an instant. She leaned forward with a sudden movement and snatched the photo. "It's her. My mother. Isn't it?" Her voice was louder than it needed to be given the tight quarters of the tent, but she was beyond caring. "Isn't it?"

Her pop's nod was faint, hard to make out in the darkened tent, his whispered yes fragile as a thread.

"How could you!"

His betrayal pierced Leda, and a violent shudder shook her. The sleeping bag had slipped from her shoulders when she grabbed the photo, and she was exposed, her thin long underwear shirt her only protection against the frigid temperatures. She crossed her arms over her chest, hugging herself. Leda saw her father raise his hand, and she wondered how he could possibly explain what he had done. But before he could, a man's voice penetrated the tent's nylon walls.

"Keep it down." The voice came from the tent to the right of theirs. "We're trying to sleep."

Leda hadn't known the others long enough to be sure, but she guessed the voice was Tom's. Whoever, it was, the request sent Leda's father to his sleeping bag. He climbed into the bag without taking off his pants.

"I could have known her," Leda said, her voice lower. "I could have spoken to her. But now it's too late. She really is dead."

"I'm sorry."

Leda strained to hear her father's voice. "Is that all you have to say?"

"For the moment, yes." Her father pointed to the tent wall indicating the people sleeping, or trying to sleep, in the nearby tent. He rolled onto his side with his back towards Leda and pulled his sleeping bag up over his shoulder.

Leda wanted to pound on his back with her fists. She wanted to shake him. But she did none of those things. It would be useless. Her pop wouldn't budge. He would simply become more and more unreachable.

"We can talk tomorrow," he said, his voice floating over his shoulder. "When you're calm."

"I'm calm," she said, knowing she was lying. Her father ignored her.

"You're wearing your pants," she said, hoping to needle him into a response. He didn't move. Instead she just heard the voice next door – "Shut it already!"

"You shut it!" she said.

Leda thought she heard muffled laughter from the tent on the left of theirs. Her father's figure remained still. Leda tucked the photo of her mother under her pillow and, after a brief moment, slid into her sleeping bag. Why had her pop lied to her all these years? Why didn't he want her to have a mother? Didn't he know how much she needed one? Tears streaked her cheeks, and wet the soft material of her bean-filled pillow. In the blink of an eye, Leda's life had become as foreign as this mountain. Her father's side of the tent was quiet, and she imagined he had fallen asleep. She felt a sudden urge to flee from the tiny space she shared with her pop. She thrust aside her sleeping bag, grabbed her down coat and left the tent.

Outside, the camp was dark. The hundreds of hikers and porters and guides slept in their tents oblivious to the canopy of thick stars. Leda had never felt so alone in her life. She was afraid her tears would freeze on her cheeks, and she dabbed at them with the back of her bare hands. She stood not far from the little tent, having come out without her boots or her headlamp. She didn't dare move too far away. How would she find her way back if she wandered among the narrow corridors of the tent village, each one mined with unseen ropes holding the tents fast? She remembered the cliff not too many steps ahead where the long-drop toilets clung to its edge.

The bulk of the mountain rose behind her. Leda swiveled. The summit, so spectacular at sunset, created an enormous black space in the star strewn sky, as if someone had taken a pair of scissors and cut out its mountainous shape from a piece of paper full of sparkles. Leda burrowed her chin into the collar of her down jacket, and thrust her ungloved hands into its pockets. Her tears had stopped, and she inhaled deeply through her nose. The night air was dry. No animals rustled in the dark. No wind stirred the low, sparse bushes on the nearby slope. She waited outside until the space became too big for her, the absolute quiet and bone deep cold driving her back to the small tent where her father slept.

Chapter 16

The botfly continued to be bothersome throughout the night. David couldn't sleep, and he had seen the younger American brother vomit in the nearby rocks many times. There was nothing to do, but go to the doctor and get the botfly larvae scraped out. From the size of the tumor, David would probably need several stitches to close the wound. He was no good as a guide now – not as long as the botfly insisted on distracting him.

Chase must get to a lower altitude as soon as possible. It was the only way to cure his sickness. So, it looked like the two of them needed to head down the mountain. It was too bad Chase was so sick, but the facts were the facts and now David could help him down the mountain and make sure he got safely to his hotel. And Erik could take over as the lead guide – for a little while. David had called for the truck while it was still dark. If David and Chase got an early start for the road, David could be back guiding the group within two days by taking the shortcut.

The sky lightened. A light hail had fallen in the night, and frosted the tops of the tents. David zipped his warm jacket. He shook the water containers to break the thin sheet of ice on the top. Then, he refilled his water supply, bringing extra for Chase. He stowed snacks and lunches in his daypack. Chase would feel like eating again at a lower altitude. The two of them could reach the Mweka Gate by tonight. The hike to the road would take about one hour, and the truck ride down the rest of the day.

Porters moved around the camp, purifying water from the nearby stream, getting breakfast ready, and breaking down their own tents. David intercepted Erik on the way back from the outhouse.

"Shikamoo," David said. His breath was like a puff of smoke. Erik nodded. *"Marahaba,"* he said.

"The young American must go down the mountain," David said.

"He has a strong will," Erik said.

"A strong will is important," David said. "But might not be enough." He had not expected Erik's resistance, but he would not question the older man's knowledge and experience. Often these bumps could be overcome with patience and skill. He tried a different tactic.

"A botfly is growing under my skin," David said, "and needs scraping. I'm going down the mountain this morning. You could take over as lead."

Erik slid his hands into his pants pockets. He had zipped a windbreaker over his wool sweater. A brief shadow of emotion flickered over the guide's face. His mouth worked but he remained silent. David remembered their conversation at the Machame Hut. Perhaps Erik was not ready to be lead guide. But David had to make the offer. It was only right given Erik's status as assistant.

"Elihud will be here to help you," David said. Elihud was a porter David had worked with before. His English was not good, but he knew a few words, which was more than the other porters.

Erik picked up a stone from the ground and worried it in his hand. David waited. Finally, Erik swung back his arm and threw the stone. It tumbled in a high arc through the air before flying out of sight beyond the mountain's edge.

The young American woman, Jen, emerged from her pup tent. She hadn't put on a jacket or shoes, and she hurried in her wool socks to where the two guides stood. She grimaced when she stepped on a sharp rock, but didn't stop until she reached them.

"I'm worried about my husband," she said. "Can you take a look at him?"

David followed her to the tent. She stepped aside so he could put his head through the open flap. Erik leaned over his shoulder.

"Chase." David spoke sharply to get the ailing man's attention. "Wake up."

The man struggled to a sitting position. It was evident from his pale skin and the swollen pouches under his eyes that he was suffering from a serious case of altitude sickness.

"How do you feel?" David said.

"He threw up constantly last night," Jen said.

David continued to observe the young man, as did Erik.

"Dizzy," Chase said. "I feel dizzy." He lay down as if he balanced a dozen eggs on his head.

Erik and David backed out of the tent. Jen folded her arms across her chest and shivered. "Well," she said. "What do you think?"

She was an American, and her impatience didn't surprise David. Jen began hopping from one foot to the other.

"Your husband must go down the mountain," David said. "Otherwise it will not go well with him."

Jen shivered. "I should go with him,"

David considered the young woman. She looked to be in perfect health. He imagined the tips slipping heedlessly through his fingers. His children not having enough fees for school.

"You want to reach the summit?"

"Yes, but…"

"Your husband is safe with David," Erik said. "I will stay with you and the others"

David was surprised by Erik's comment, but he didn't allow his emotions to show on his face. Instead, while he waited for the young woman's decision he prayed she would stay.

Jen hopped. She wrapped her arms more tightly across her body. She sighed and gazed at the peak. Long minutes passed away. Finally, she said, "I'll talk to him."

"We must leave right away," David said.

The young woman nodded, and then disappeared into the tent zipping the flap closed behind her.

Chapter 17

Leda woke up. Her father was out of his sleeping bag, fully dressed and sitting by the tent flap his boot in his hand.

"Sneaking out?" she said. Leda sat up. She rubbed the sleep from her eyes, and stifled a yawn. She hadn't slept well. Vivid dreams troubled her throughout the night, but now she couldn't remember a single one. All that was left was a feeling of something dark touching her.

"I'm simply going to the bathroom," her father said. He pulled on his boots and began lacing them.

"And then you're coming back? So we can finish our talk?"

"Is that what you want?"

"Of course!"

Leda's father tied his bootlaces into a bow, and then turned and looked at her. "I'm happy to discuss things with you," he said.

He didn't say it, but his tone implied he would be happier if she were rational.

Leda raked her fingers through her hair, pulling the mass of curls away from her face. A shadow fell across the tent flap. "Coffee?" The porter's voice came from outside.

"I'll be here with the coffee," Leda said.

Her father zipped open the flap and left. "Back soon."

Leda set the coffee on the tent floor. She dressed warmly, pulling a long sleeve shirt over her long underwear top and her hiking pants on over her long underwear bottoms. She needed her fleece jacket even in the tent. She would put on her down jacket and wool cap and gloves when she went outside. Leda braided her hair while she waited. She raised one of the coffee cups to her lips, savoring the warmth and the heavenly smell. She was nearly done drinking it when her pop returned. He scooted into the tent, not taking off his boots or zipping the tent flap.

"Before you start," he said. "I want you to know I never lied to you about your mother."

"You let me think she was dead," Leda said. "That she died in Oregon."

"Those were your assumptions," he said.

"Which you never bothered to correct."

"I had my reasons."

"What possible reason could there be for keeping me from my mother?" Leda set her plastic coffee cup down with a thump. The tiny puddle of liquid in the bottom splashed against the sides.

"It was for your own good." Her father's voice was calm, but perhaps with an underlying tinge of sadness. He picked up his cup and turned his face away before Leda could see if the emotion reached his face. "You were just a toddler really."

"I'm an adult now," Leda said.

Her father swallowed his coffee in a single gulp. Leda could only assume it was lukewarm as he didn't choke or gasp. "Can't we just leave the past in the past?"

Before Leda could answer, their fellow hikers paused in a clump outside the tent flap. Leda could see their legs through a gap. Her father reached to hold the tent flap open and peered out.

"Is he really that sick?" Tom said.

"David thinks so." It was Gail's voice. "I hope he'll be okay."

"He should stick it out," Tom said. "He's strong."

"David knows what he's doing." Gail said.

"He's the expert," Wyatt said.

"Maybe I should go with him." Even Leda could hear the worry in Jen's voice. She wished the group hadn't interrupted her conversation with her father. Now, her father levered himself out the tent and joined the others.

"What's going on?" he said.

Leda grunted in frustration. The apparent crisis outside the tent had provided her father with an excuse to escape her questions. She scooted to the tent flap and crawled out without her boots or down jacket. Somehow her pop had maneuvered his way to the other side of the knot of hikers. She frowned at him, but didn't succeed in getting his attention.

"David's taking Chase down the mountain," Gail said. "He's suffering terribly from altitude sickness."

"Heard him vomiting all night," Tom said. "Between that and some people talking, it was hard to sleep."

Leda shot a look at her father. He pressed his lips together.

Gail touched Tom's shoulder and spoke in a soft voice. "We're all sorry he has to leave."

Tom looked at Wyatt, and shook his head.

"I bet you wish it was me leaving," Wyatt said.

Gail spoke, "He didn't say that."

Wyatt's mouth twisted in disbelief. "Whatever you say Mom." He shrugged his shoulders. "Chase would want you to stay Jen."

As if on cue, Chase appeared stumbling behind David. His skin was pale underneath the rough beard on his cheeks and jaw. He wore sunglasses and a wool hat pulled low on his forehead. "You should stay," he said to Jen, his voice weak. "I'll be okay once I get off this damn mountain."

"You sure?" Jen rushed to hug his arm.

"Mom will kill me if you leave." Chase touched his lips briefly to Jen's cheek. Before anyone could argue, David turned and led Chase through the maze of tents.

"Pop?" Leda's voice was a question. She tilted her head towards the pup tent inviting him to return to their conversation.

"Breakfast is ready," Erik called to the group from the door of the dining tent. "We have a long day ahead."

Leda's father shrugged his shoulders as if he was helpless to do what he wanted, and followed the other hikers to the dining tent. Leda watched the group go. Would her father ever satisfy her need to know about her mother? For the moment, he was her only option for concrete answers. Eleanor and Russell hadn't told her much of anything. She had hardly known what to ask at the time. The picture was a shock, and Leda stumbled out of their home vacillating between thinking the photo was of her mother and denying the possibility it could be. Maybe she needed to try a new tactic with her pop. Leda ducked back into the pup tent, pulled on her hiking boots and down coat before heading to the dining tent.

The rest of the group was already gathered around the table. Every one still wore his or her coat. Gail cupped a steaming mug of tea. Leda squeezed into a chair near Tom. Her father sat at the far end of the table surrounded by Wyatt and Jen.

Leda served some ham from a platter onto her plate. "I'm sorry Chase had to leave," she said.

Tom sighed and stabbed a piece of ham from the platter with his fork. "It sure surprised me," he said.

"Why is that?" Leda didn't really care, her mind was busy figuring out how best to get her pop to talk, but minding the niceties never hurt.

"He's a strong kid," Tom said. "Makes more sense that it would be me."

"Really?"

"We all have our secrets," Tom said. "Maybe I'll let you in on mine before the trip is over."

Tom's comment made Leda feel awkward. Was he referring to her conversation last night with her pop? She didn't know what to say, so she simply passed Tom the pineapple. She was happy when Jen spoke. "We agreed if one of us got sick, the other would keep going, but I didn't think it would happen."

"We'll look out for you," Gail said. She patted the younger woman's hand. "You're part of the family."

Leda felt a prick of jealousy at the older woman's actions. She imagined her mother's touch, and she looked to the end of the table where her father talked with Wyatt. The two had steaming bowls of oatmeal in front of them, plates heaped with scrambled eggs, ham and pineapple. Apparently, her father had gotten over his bout of altitude sickness unlike poor Chase.

Chapter 18

Leda perched on a rock. Her braid was covered with a buff, a stretchy piece of fabric sewn in a circle; she wore gloves and her waterproof jacket over her fleece. She felt optimistic about the day ahead. It was useless to pepper her pop with questions now. In the rush of emotions last night and this morning in the pup tent, she had forgotten the lessons she had learned over the years. Her pop responded well to rational dialogue. Hadn't she convinced him to let her spend the night at Lindsey's when the other girl's parents were out of town? She told him the two were working on a class project. Which was true for the most part. He didn't need to know that the class project was a party for the graduating seniors. Her father had been busy with his own research at the time but Leda was sure her rational argument won the day, not his distraction with solving battery circuitry.

Leda surveyed the vast camp. Porters hustled among the tents, packing up tables, pots and food. They folded the damp tents of those hikers who were already on their way. Her own small camp was a hive of activity, her duffel and sleeping bag waited outside her pup tent.

After breakfast, Leda retreated to this rock and opened the journal her father had bought for her, all part of her plan to show her father how rational she could be. Nowadays, hikers could choose from six different routes up the mountain. It was difficult to know the route this woman – Emily Parker- had followed. Leda knew she had been inspired by Gertrude Benham's ascent to the crater rim in 1911, although Benham was not officially recognized for her efforts. The words in the journal were sparse. Emily noted breakfast, tea and dinner and the local animal and plant life. Leda flipped the pages of her guidebook, and compared the two. The work kept her busy. It distracted her from thoughts about her parents. Today they would climb to the Lava Tower at 15,000 feet, and then descend to the Barranco Valley at 12,950 feet, a total gain for the day of about 350 feet from the camp at Shira Plateau. The nine miles of up and down was to help them adjust to the altitude. Earlier, Erik said the cook would serve a hot meal at Lava Tower. Hot food was easier to digest at higher altitudes.

A flurry of activity caught Leda's attention, and she glanced up from her books. Their porters were gathered in a loose group by the dining tent singing and dancing.

Again, they all did something different, some moving their entire bodies, knees high, elbows flying, while others wiggled their arms and hair. But somehow they looked cohesive, and just like yesterday their energy was high. The porters appeared carefree in their dance, but Leda wondered if they harbored any resentment over this morning's questioning. A hiker from a different group had reported a missing camera, and all the porters from each camp were asked about it. The camera wasn't found.

Jen and Gail danced to an entirely different rhythm nearby. Leda imagined Jen moving with a more fluid grace in a sports setting, perhaps on a volleyball or basketball court, she was tall and long-limbed. Gail appeared to be disco dancing or maybe doing the twist, in any case, she moved her thin body with abandon. Gail waved to Leda. "Join us," she shouted.

Leda smiled and shook her head. She closed her book, sliding it into her daypack along with the journal.

By this time, several porters had enveloped Gail, with her waving arms and carefree smile, into their dance, weaving and spinning around her. This morning, Tom shuffled his feet at the edge of the group. Leda's father stood still next to him. Leda wondered if the day's trail would provide an opportunity for her to talk more with her pop. She hoped she wouldn't have to wait until tonight. Privacy was hard to come by in the tight quarters of the camp. She narrowed her eyes at Tom. There was no doubt Tom was the one who told her to shut it last night. She tried to remember whose tent was on the other side of theirs, the tent where she thought she heard laughter. Leda felt a quiet presence at her elbow. It was Wyatt adjusting his daypack, and staring at his own father with lowered eyebrows. Leda had a faint memory of Wyatt ducking into the tent on the other side of theirs or was it the next tent over? She couldn't be sure.

Erik gathered the group for the day's hike and set off in the lead. The group hiked quietly, settling into the day's climb. The trail crossed a wide- open expanse of scattered bits and pieces of volcanic rubble. Large clumps of everlastings seemed to thrive on the rocky terrain as well as scruffy looking shrubs, some taller than Leda. The trail was thick with other hikers.

Leda struggled to get into the rhythm of the morning's pace. The trail started steep, and kept going up. The breathing was more difficult than yesterday's. Leda kept reminding herself the whole point of the day was to get to a higher altitude, to help her body adjust so she could make the final push on summit day to 19, 340 feet. Tom and Gail fell behind. Leda congratulated herself on keeping up with the faster group of her fully recovered father, Wyatt and Jen - until the porters moved past, some almost jogging, the white and green plastic covered bundles on their heads swaying.

The pace was difficult to maintain, and with the constant passing of those who were slower, and being passed by those who were faster, Leda gave up trying to talk with her father. Neither commented on the woman who wore diamond studs. Or the man dressed in camouflage. Climbing Mt. Kilimanjaro was a far cry from the privacy and away from it all feeling of their other hikes. She doubted the cooks even hid the food at night from wild animals like she and her pop usually did in bear boxes or bear canisters. Eventually, Leda's group climbed above the gray and white clouds ringing the summit. Her heart pounded, her breathing was hard. Leda had never been higher than the clouds before except in an airplane. Then, she usually was asleep behind the drawn shade. The clouds looked like fat pillows.

"Is that Cheer Bear?" Jen pointed and laughed. Only Wyatt joined her. The two stood comfortably together, almost like brother and sister. The pause provided welcome relief for Leda to catch her breath. She stopped next to Wyatt, the top of her head reaching his shoulder. She and her father were of average height. The two liked to joke their stature was the only average thing about them. Today, her pop looked slight next to Wyatt and Jen. Leda turned her gaze to the scenery.

In the close distance, Mt. Meru thrust its peak above the cloud sea.

"It looks like we're almost as high as Mt. Meru," Wyatt said. "And it's close to 15,000 feet."

"No wonder my chest hurts," Jen said. "That's not Mwenzi?"

"We'll see Mwenzi on summit day. It's one of the three summits on Kili."

"Three summits?" Jen said. "It's so confusing."

"Don't worry, we're only climbing to one – Kibo," Wyatt said.

Jen kicked at his boot.

"Chagga legend says two of the sister summits fought," Leda said. "Mwenzi and Kibo." When Wyatt looked at her, Leda felt compelled to add more. "I read a lot. I like to be prepared."

"Who won?" Wyatt said. Gail and Tom reached them, stopping for a breather. Tom mopped his brow with a cloth handkerchief.

"Kibo, of course," Leda said. "She beat Mwenzi over the head with a big piece of firewood because Mwenzi was too lazy to get her own."

"Thus Mwenzi's jagged appearance," Wyatt said.

"How come the oldest always wins?" Jen said. She poked Wyatt in the arm.

"Not always." Wyatt shot a look at Tom.

"What about the third summit?" Jen said.

"Shira? I don't know any stories about it," Leda said.

Jen aimed a camera at a smiling Tom and Gail. Mt. Meru appeared to be floating in the background.

"How about you two?" Jen asked Leda and her father. "Want me to take your picture?"

Leda looked at her pop. She wondered if he was thinking of all the pictures they had taken together on different trails, all the photos crowding the top of her dresser, the one photo of her mother sitting alone. She thought of the picture of her mother tucked into her guidebook again. Her mother was alone in that picture too. Leda opened her mouth to say thanks, but no thanks. She didn't want any part of photos with her pop until he answered her questions. But then she remembered her optimism of the morning, her determination to act with cool logic.

"Sure," Leda said. She handed the camera to Jen and moved to the side of the trail. Her pop was slow in joining her. The two stood close, but not together.

"Smile," Jen said. Leda tilted the corners of her lips. She wondered if her smile looked as fake as it felt. Was her pop smiling? Leda wasn't feeling at all rational when Jen handed her back her camera. She took her time returning it to her daypack. Her father was already headed up the trail with Tom, Gail and Jen. Wyatt waited for her.

Chapter 19

The trail was wide, the ground even so Wyatt could walk beside Leda.

"So, you read a lot," Wyatt asked. "You must be either a student, an editor or maybe a teacher."

"A speech therapist," Leda said.

Leda considered him. Black sunglasses wrapped around his eyes. A bandana covered most of his hair. The constant wind ruffled the sandy brown pieces loose on his neck. "Jen said you could handle the medical emergencies, so you must be a doctor."

"Nope, a lifeguard."

She guessed he was in his late twenties. "Isn't that a seasonal job?" Leda said.

Wyatt said. "I save lives year round."

Leda dabbed at her dripping nose with a wadded tissue. Silent. She remembered Wyatt quoting Hemingway. She had thought he was more of an intellectual, at least a teacher or scientist like her and her pop. Leda and her pop made a game of pegging people. She would have never guessed Wyatt was a lifeguard.

"I have a college degree." Wyatt shook his head and smiled. "Don't know why I felt the need to tell you that. I suppose your boyfriend's working on his PhD."

"My boyfriend?" Leda said.

"I thought your dad mentioned someone."

Leda's laugh was a huff of breath. "He is working on his PhD, but he's not my boyfriend. He's one of my father's research assistants. My pop set us up but it didn't work out."

"Keeping secrets from your dad?" Wyatt grinned.

"Apparently it runs in the family." Leda's voice was grim. She held the wadded tissue to her nose.

"What's that supposed to mean?"

"Nothing."

The two walked in silence for a while.

"Why a lifeguard?" Leda said.

"Are you really interested?"

"I've never met a lifeguard before. Only those who worked at the local pool in the summer."

"Was one your high school boyfriend?" Wyatt said.

Leda laughed. "Only the one training for astronaut school."

Leda was feeling better, and the two climbed at a more rapid pace than the others, soon overtaking Tom and Gail. Wyatt sped past them. Leda hurried to catch him, her competitive juices flowing even though she was panting from the ever -thinning air.

"Walk with us," Gail said, her breath punctuating her words.

Leda moderated her pace. Her breathing slowed. The other members of the group, including her father, were not too far ahead. She could catch up with them later. Here, the rocks seemed more jumbled. The grasses and flowers still present, but fewer in number.

"It must seem strange," Gail said. "Old folks like us climbing."

"You're not old," Leda said, "certainly younger than my father."

"We're not too far off in age," Gail said. "Did your mother hike?"

Leda took a swig from the tube of her water supply. The group with her father pulled steadily away.

"I don't know," Leda said. "She died before I got to know her." Was there a hitch in her voice? She could blame it on exertion, but now her pace was slower she wasn't feeling out of breath. Did her mother hike? Leda didn't know. Did she even like the outdoors? Maybe she was more of an indoor person who quilted or painted or arranged flowers or something. Leda applied lip balm. She knew her mother was a university student when she met her father. She knew her mother graduated with a degree in Greek mythology and history – of all things – and she gave birth to Leda a short month after. She knew her mother was beautiful. In those rare moments when Leda's father talked about her, he described her mother "like a golden-haired goddess in one of those legends she was always reading." So maybe her mother didn't quilt or arrange flowers. Maybe she hid in a window seat, feet curled under her and read. Maybe she was a dreamer. And now Leda knew more of the story, she realized her father hadn't been commenting on her mother's looks at all. He was using her mother to illustrate the folly of escaping into myth. The problem of acting impulsively.

Leda could no longer hear Gail and Tom lumbering behind her. She looked ahead on the trail where the track quite clearly continued its steady climb along an open ridge. The long line of hikers from the morning had spread out over the trail, and only two groups were still in sight. She couldn't see the rest of her group. They hadn't been that far ahead had they?

"Leda." Wyatt's voice was behind her and to the left. Leda swiveled and noticed a clump of lava rock mounds for the first time. Wyatt stood next to one that was taller than him. Gail and Tom were headed to where the others had gathered, veering off from further down the trail. Leda had left them behind, speeding ahead with her thoughts.

The lava rock mounds – large boulders perched on narrower pillars of smaller stones held together with mud - provided a shelter of sorts from the wind. Orange and yellowish-green lichens clung to the rocks, glowing spots of color against the gray.

Leda expected her pop to make a comment about her getting ahead of the group, but he said nothing. He leaned by himself against a thin pillar, perfect for one. Jen moved over on the rock she shared with Wyatt, creating a space for Leda. Erik handed out the now ubiquitous energy biscuits. Leda squirreled away the cellophane wrapped package of the stacked, bland cookies, tucking it in her backpack. She noticed Wyatt did the same.

"Not your favorite?" she said.

"You're not ripping into yours," he said.

"My emergency stash," Leda said.

Leda opened a sandwich -sized bag of trail mix, bits of dried bananas, almonds, shaved coconut and chopped dates, she had put together for the trip. Her father tossed handfuls of the same mix into his mouth. Wyatt munched on almonds and M&Ms; Jen chewed a cereal bar. Everyone seemed to have different ideas on what would power him or her up the mountain. Gail and Tom joined the group, settling against a nearby rock. Jen had taken off her gloves, and her gold wedding band was brilliant in the sun. Must be a newlywed. "How long have you been married?" Leda said.

"Seven months," Jen said. She looked dejected as she bit off a chunk of the cereal bar. "Maybe I should have gone down the mountain with Chase."

"You'll only be apart a few days," Wyatt said.

"It already seems like forever." Jen finished her bar and wadded the empty wrapper into a ball.

"Spare me," Wyatt said.

Leda remembered her earlier thought that Wyatt and Jen acted like brother and sister. "Have you known each other long?"

"Since we were kids." Jen threw the wrapper at Wyatt. "And you've always been a sour old maid."

Wyatt snorted. He picked the wrapper off the ground and stuffed it in his jacket pocket.

"You have something against marriage?" Jen said, her tone challenging.

"Nothing against yours," Wyatt said. He tossed a handful of M&Ms and almonds into his mouth.

"Just marriage in general?" Jen asked.

"I can see I'm alone here," Wyatt said. His gaze swept the group, "Except for Phillip, but he was married once. Even Leda's probably rushing to the altar with her boyfriend." Wyatt winked at her, but then she glimpsed her father's startled face and inhaled a date. It stuck in her throat. She could feel her cheeks reddening as she coughed and hacked. Wyatt patted her back until she exhaled the wrinkled fruit into the palm of her hand.

Chapter 20

Leda's eyes were watering when she regained control, her nose running. She reached into her daypack for some toilet paper to dry her face.

"You okay?" Gail said. "Have some water."

Leda stood. "Think I'll head behind those rocks."

"Watch your step," Jen said.

Leda thought Jen's warning was about the rough terrain, but her meaning became clear when Leda reached the backside of the rocks. Toilet paper and human waste littered the ground. The cluster of large rocks was rare on this portion of the trail, and obviously a popular stopping point for many hikers. Leda was careful to put her used tissue in a small plastic bag she could throw away at the next camp.

The rest were ready to continue on the trail when she returned. Her pop stepped towards her, staking his claim on her company. Leda could tell from his expression he was eager to talk with her. Wyatt apparently had done her a favor by joking about her marrying Henry. He had broken through her father's wall in a unique way she hadn't considered. She should thank him, but Wyatt was already heading up the trail behind Erik.

It wasn't all that long ago her pop encouraged her to date Henry. He probably wanted to warn her about the dangers of rushing into marriage with someone she hardly knew. And now she thought about it, hadn't her father known her mother for only a few months before they married? She always thought their story hugely romantic: love struck couple falls madly in love, marries after a whirlwind romance, mother tragically dies a couple of years after giving birth leaving a grief stricken husband and father alone to raise the child. The truth – what little she knew – was vastly different. Had her parents divorced? Had her mother given custody of Leda to her father? Leda swung her daypack on, and slipped the wrist straps of her trekking poles over her hands. The trail was wide enough for her father to walk beside her. The constant blowing of the wind whisked the loose edges of Leda's coat, and the ends of her father's bandana waved like miniature flags.

"Isn't it a bit soon to be talking marriage with Henry?" her pop said. When it came to her life, her father liked to get right to the point. Leda wished he would extend the same philosophy to her questions about his life with her mother.

Leda said, "You and mom got married after a few months. I always thought you were happy."

Her father cleared his throat, "we were."

"For how long?"

"What difference does it make? What happened in the past should stay there. We're talking about your future."

"Pop," Leda said. "I can't move forward without knowing about my past."

"Some things are better left alone."

"Why did she leave?"

"All you need to know is she loved you."

"It's not enough." Leda said. "I needed to hear it from her. You stole that opportunity from me. You kept me from knowing her." The wind made her nose run. Or was it the dust? Her lips were stained with snot, her cheeks with tears. Her tissue was nothing more than a disintegrated mess that felt like lint. Still, Leda lifted it to her nose. She didn't bother to wipe her cheeks. The two continued to climb, not more than twenty feet behind the others.

"I'm sorry," her pop said.

"That's what you said last night," Leda said. "Can't you give me anything more?" Leda stabbed the tips of her trekking poles into the ground, but the dirt was hard and she barely made a dent.

"No."

The single syllable was as unyielding as the dirt. Frustration filled Leda, and she felt like she might explode. She sped up. She didn't care that her heart raced in the thin air at 13,000 plus feet or that her breathing was shallow. Leda pulled away from her father, not slowing until she caught up to the other hikers in their group. She walked next to Wyatt. Her heart felt as if it would jump out of her chest it pounded so hard from her exertion.

"What's up?" Wyatt ambled along, treating the steep climb and the increasing altitude like a stroll along the beach. Leda waved her hand in a signal that she couldn't talk. She held the crumpled tissue to her nose.

"You should make a snot rocket," Wyatt said.

"A what?" Leda panted. She could still feel her heart thumping against the wall of her chest, but it no longer felt like it would burst.

"A snot rocket. Close one nostril like this," Wyatt demonstrated with his index finger, "and blow onto the trail."

"That's disgusting."

"No more disgusting than that tissue."

"I suppose you learned that in lifeguard training." Leda sniffled, resisting the urge to dab at her nose with the tissue.

"I've done it a time or two in the ocean." Wyatt's teeth flashed.

Now Leda's stomach cramped. The nausea had come out of nowhere.

"Let's change the subject," she said. Leda tipped her head at the three in front of them. "Does your family travel together often?"

"Not since we were little," Wyatt said. "But we made an exception for this."

"That's right. Gail and Tom's wedding anniversary."

Leda's parents had been together for two years at the most. She had never seen pictures of their wedding. Her father didn't store a lot of photographs.

"You all seem to get along," Leda said.

"All the world's a stage, and all the men and women merely players; they have their exits and their entrances."

"A lifeguard who quotes Shakespeare." Leda did her best to ignore the pit settling in her stomach.

"You think I spend all my time reading first aid manuals?"

Leda's tissue was beyond useless. She could let snot stream down her lips and drip off her chin or she could take Wyatt's advice. She pressed her index finger to one nostril and blew. It worked.

"A speech therapist who makes snot rockets."

Leda joined Wyatt in his laughter.

Chapter 21

Now the group was strung out along the trail, Jen walking ahead with Tom and Gail. Leda refused to look behind to see where her father was. Erik hiked a little bit ahead of them all. Lava Tower appeared not too far away. But by now, Leda had come to realize distances in these wide-open spaces could be deceptive. True, Lava Tower might be less than a mile away, but above 14,000 feet in altitude, it could take more than an hour to hike that far. From here, the tower looked like a dark rock mass with a squarish top, almost like a stout black chimney that had melted. The exposed slopes of the Western Breach provided a dramatic backdrop. So far, the weather had cooperated, and although everyone still wore their jackets zipped and some wore gloves and hats, the sky was blue with only a few thin clouds. Besides the persistent wind, the mountain was silent, void of animal life or chatter.

A sudden wave of nausea attacked Leda, and then disappeared. These waves had been hitting her the past couple of miles. She found she could control the worst of it by inhaling through her nose and blowing out through her mouth. The maneuver wasn't easy. Liquid either dripped from her nose or back into her throat. What if she became sick, like Chase, and had to be sent back down the mountain? She banished the fleeting thought. Negativity could ruin her hope of reaching the summit if she allowed it to take root. Mind over matter would get her through this. Would the same attitude help her sort through the hurt of her father's refusal to talk? The confusion of her mother's leaving? The shame of not being wanted? More negativity pressing her down, slowing her until she plodded along the trail, moving like she carried a heavy sack of rocks on her shoulders.

"You been to San Diego?" Wyatt said.

His question startled her out of her thoughts. Leda swallowed hard.

"Is that where you all live?" Leda said. Her voice sounded breathy.

"Just me," Wyatt said. "Do you live close to your dad?"

Leda inhaled deeply. The nausea fled. She said, "I live with him."

"I can't imagine living with Tom," Wyatt said. "Five hundred miles is as close as I want to get."

The two hiked in silence. Leda's nausea came and went at unexpected moments, her nose continued to gush and her breath ran short. This trail was the hardest she had ever experienced. She would never have considered making a snot rocket before, and, now, when she had to pee, she simply squatted behind a low shrub near the trail. It wouldn't take a genius hiking by to figure out what she was doing, her back, head and shoulders were not hidden.

When she returned to the trail, Leda spoke to Wyatt as if their conversation had not been interrupted by a long period of silence, "I'm moving out when this trip is over." The nausea wave returned, and she rode it a little while, skimming along its surface before it vanished.

Wyatt said nothing. It was almost as if she were brainstorming out loud.

"I'm not sure where I'll go." Leda drank some water. She couldn't live with her father if he refused to talk with her about her mother. She couldn't imagine sitting across the kitchen table from him, drinking coffee or eating dinner as if nothing had changed. Maybe she would move to England. Find out more about her mother. Her father must not be the only one who could give her answers. Afterwards maybe she would move to California. She could take up surfing. All these strange thoughts must somehow be related to the thin air. She knew people got light-headed from lack of oxygen.

Not too far in front of them, Jen sang a song about bottles of beer on the wall. Yes they all must be feeling the effects of the higher altitude. All except Wyatt who continued his loping pace with no apparent ill effect.

"Tell me about San Diego," she said.

"Thinking of moving there?" Wyatt said.

"Maybe." The nausea vanished. Leda increased her pace, digging her trekking poles into the dirt and striding with what could be considered a small bounce – given the altitude. "You could teach me to surf."

The Lava Tower had seemed to be close, but a few rises still stood between its base and them. There used to be snowfields at this altitude, but now a few scattered ice fields and snowfields outlined the shadowed crevasses further up.

"See the porters?" Wyatt sounded cheerful.

Leda was glad for the excuse to stop, and she swept her eyes along the slope of broken rocks. Wyatt held her shoulders and turned her so she faced a little more to the right.

"Just up there."

Leda followed his pointing finger. Two porters, one wearing highlighter green pants and the other a shocking blue jacket, picked their way down what looked like a thin trail. They balanced water jugs on their heads.

Leda watched them descend towards the Lava Tower. Wyatt's hand still rested on her shoulder. Leda made no move to step away, but shifted her focus to his fingers. She imagined a pianist would have fingers like Wyatt's.

Wyatt noticed her gaze and removed his hand. "They're dirty. Didn't bring a nail file." His laugh was self-deprecating.

"Do you play piano?" Leda said.

"You feel all right?"

Wyatt's tone had changed. Leda imagined he was speaking to her in his lifeguard voice. "Maybe a little light-headed," Leda said.

"Anything else?"

"Kind of sick." The nausea had returned, and she had a heavy feeling of fullness. She could see her father just ahead on the trail with Tom and Gail.

"We're almost there," Wyatt said. "A hot lunch should fix you up."

The porters had pitched the dining tent between the tower and the Western Breach. Taut ropes kept the tent from blowing away. A weathered plank outhouse was nestled in some rocks opposite the tent.

"Picture time!" Jen organized everyone into a group shot, and showed Erik how to use her camera.

It was dim in the tent after the dazzling sunlight. The folding chairs were crowded around the table. The smooth tablecloth, the silverware and plates all seemed surreal in this moonscape. Leda sank into a chair feeling worn. She removed her gloves, but kept her jacket zipped. With the flap closed, most of the wind was blocked, but the cold seeped through the thin material of the tent. Gail and Wyatt took the chairs next to hers. Gail's knee knocked against Leda's every so often, and Wyatt's arm pressed her elbow. Leda welcomed their huddled warmth. Her pop sat on the other side of Gail. Although he was only a chair's length away, for the first time in her life, Leda felt separate from him.

The cook passed platters of food through the flap, heaps of roasted chicken, potato salad and sliced mangos. Leda took her time with the ginger flavored soup: the warm broth settled her stomach. She picked at the other offerings. She opted to fill her mug with plain hot water. She never knew unflavored, steaming water could taste so good, be so satisfying. Gail sipped on a mug of hot water as well.

"It's what homeless people do," Gail said. "I worked at a downtown coffee shop once."

Leda didn't know how to respond to the comment. Not too long ago, she would have assumed Gail worked at the coffee shop when she was in high school or college. Now, Leda figured Gail might have worked there any time in the past few years.

She joined the others in passing around the platters of food and eating. The constant wind rattled the tent reminding Leda of the fragile shelter around them, the inhospitable environment outside the thin walls. Gail pointed her fork at the empty chair by the tent flap.

"I wonder where Erik is," Gail said. David had always eaten in the dining tent with them, but Erik had not come to the tent.

"Did you see the porters carrying water?" Wyatt said. "That's the Umbwe route. Three climbers were killed on that route."

"What happened?" Leda said.

"A rock avalanche while they slept," Wyatt said. "Another hiker and some porters were seriously injured."

Leda shuddered. She knew climbing Mt. Kilimanjaro was a risk, but she was in good shape and didn't believe it would be a life-threatening risk for her. But a rock avalanche could happen anytime and kill anyone.

"Now your mother won't be able to sleep at night." Tom chided his son.

"It was a rare occurrence," Wyatt said. His voice was stiff. "Besides, we're not on that route. It's the most dangerous and difficult on the mountain. Hardly suitable for our party."

"You worry too much Tom." Gail sipped her hot water. "I'm sure that happened a long time ago."

The tent flap opened and Erik stepped inside.

"Feeling good?" Erik said

Gail patted the empty chair next to her, but Erik shook his head, clasping the chair back with his hands instead.

"Very important to eat," Erik said. Leda felt his gaze on her, and she ripped off a bigger chunk of chicken with her teeth. Wyatt refilled her mug with hot water. Leda attributed his action to his lifeguard training, but still she thanked him with her smile.

"Is the trail up the Western Breach open?" Wyatt asked Erik.

"Machame Trail best for the success. Many ups, little down." Erik moved his hand to demonstrate his words.

"So the rock slide closed that trail?" Wyatt said.

"Not permanent," Erik said. Erik's face looked pinched. He muttered something about Kilimanjaro Leda couldn't understand, and then ducked out of the tent.

Chapter 22

The hike to the road took longer than David planned. The young American was very weak and needed help. Rays of sunlight peeked over the summit to their right, but the trail remained in shadow. When he looked back, David could see Chase's breath, constant short puffs that came and went like the mist on the mountain. David encouraged the man to drink lots of water. Now was also a good time for Chase to chew on the energy biscuits. The mild flavor always tasted good to those who were sick. David was happy the wife kept hiking. Even if the young man was done, David felt sure his parents would be generous tippers if his wife did well. The parents treated her like their own daughter. In his many trips up the mountain, David had noticed the women often did better in the high altitude than the men. His wife had never climbed the mountain. Still, David knew Grace could do it if she wanted.

Even when they stopped to rest, the young American didn't speak. David wasn't insulted. He knew the man struggled. The whites weren't that different from the Chagga or the Masai. David had learned from his many trips up the mountain all men – no matter what country they came from – did not like to appear weak. The young man worked hard to disguise his sick feeling from his wife. Now, Chase didn't work as hard, but David could tell he was still pretending. Chase chewed only two of the energy biscuits in the pack. David saw him crumple others behind a rock when he thought the guide wasn't looking. David didn't say anything. The American was his client, and it wouldn't be polite to point out his weakness unless it threatened his life.

David carried both daypacks slung on his left shoulder. It was necessary to keep them from rubbing the botfly pestering his lower back. The bump was growing larger, and it took great effort not to touch it. Chase hadn't asked about carrying his own daypack. He didn't seem aware it hung from David's shoulder. When Chase looked like he needed a drink of water, David would stop and help Chase squeeze water from the drinking tube into his mouth. They had walked for more than an hour, the rim of the sun squatting on the mountain's shoulder, when Chase finally spoke, "How much further?"

The question told David much. "We are nearly there," he said. He held out his hand to help Chase down a rock step, but the American ignored it. His knees buckled.

David grabbed his elbow to stop him from falling. "Just rest," David said. "There is no hurry."

At the road, the Land Cruiser was not yet there. David squatted by the side of the road. Chase sat with his legs crossed. He rested his chin on his palms. A black raven, its feathers tinged purple in the sun flew overhead; its cry was harsh. In a bold swoop, it landed on the road and stared at the men. The ravens were like hyenas, except they scavenged after men instead of lions or cheetahs, picking around the campsites for trash.

Sometimes the ravens made David think of an old priest he knew. All dressed in black with a white circle at his neck. The priest and the bird had very large noses. And when the two stared, people sometimes got scared. David didn't. He knew the priest meant no harm. David wondered if the raven would come near. As soon as he thought it, the bird hopped closer. The raven, and the priest, also had something else in common. Both liked to eat. Now, the bird glared at David. "Give me food!" it seemed to say. David held out his hands, palms open. The raven should have stayed near the Shira Camp with its brothers. There was always plenty of trash at the sprawling camp. The bird skipped closer. Chase moved into a crouching position. David shouted at the bird to scare it away.

The truck came with a swirl of dust, surprising the raven so that it burst from the road with a guttural squawk. David stood and slapped his palm on the door. The raven flew in the direction of Shira Camp

The American pushed up from the ground, dusting off his coat. Coughing. David opened the rusted door of the Land Cruiser for him. Chase didn't need an invitation to get inside. David was ready to boost him into the cracked seat in the back. But the American moved faster than he had all morning, as if the back seat of the truck was the softest couch he had ever seen. David supposed it did look good to someone as sick as Chase. David climbed into the front, and the truck began the long drive back down the mountain. At the first big bump, David grunted in pain. The driver slowed, his eyes a question. David waved him on. He couldn't get this botfly scraped soon enough. He leaned forward so his back wouldn't hit the seat again.

Several hours passed before the American spoke. The skin around his eyes was no longer swollen. David noticed the empty water bottle on the seat next to Chase.

"You're going back?" Chase said, "To the mountain?"

"Yes," David said. "Tomorrow night I will be with the group."

"Who's leading the group? Erik?"

"He is a good guide. He has many years on the mountain."

"He makes me nervous," Chase said. "He's too quiet."

David could see the worry in the other man's eyes now he wasn't feeling as sick.

"Your wife is safe with Erik Ngala," David said. "I would ask him to guide my own wife on the mountain."

"Has your wife climbed the mountain?"

"She has no interest."

"Maybe I should have let Jen come with me."

"Sir, do not worry," David turned his body so he faced the back. A sudden bump made him grip the top of the seat. "Your wife is well taken care of."

Chase sighed and leaned his head back. "I suppose it's useless to worry now."

Rain pelted the Land Cruiser, the hard drops spurting dust on the hood. Soon, the dust became small streams of mud. The Land Cruiser slipped and almost spun off the road. The driver held tight to the wheel. Many times, David thought the truck might hit a thick poplar, but the driver steered well. Giant cobwebs of lichen and thick tree branches brushed the sides and top of the truck. Rain slapped the windshield. David was glad his group had not hiked through such a storm in the rain forest. The American slid on the back seat, banging the door with a thump. After, he gripped the strap that hung from the roof. No one spoke again until the Land Cruiser stopped in front of the hotel.

"Will someone take me to the Mweka Gate?" the American said. "I'd like to be there when my wife returns."

David nodded. "The truck will come get you." David reached to open his door. He wanted to help Chase from the back, but the American got out before David swung his door open. The two stood on the dirt road for a while. Finally, David handed Chase his daypack. Still, the American did not leave.

"Your wife is safe," David repeated. "She is strong and will do well."

"We're newlyweds," Chase said. "Not even married a year."

David stood with the young man. He remembered the first year of his marriage to Grace: they couldn't get enough of each other. But the mountain didn't care about lovers. The drive to survive and summit usually overcame even sexual desire. David considered the young man. Now he was at a lower altitude, he stood straighter. Yes, he would miss his new wife down here.

Chase nodded. Slinging his daypack on his shoulder, he climbed the short stairs to the hotel lobby. His steps were pole pole, his shoulders round. David could only guess the young man was thinking about his lonely bed for the next four nights.

David climbed into the Land Rover. He must get to the doctor this afternoon. The botfly could wait no longer.

Chapter 23

Erik placed Gail and Tom at the front of the group, followed by her father. The descent was rough with some rock ledges to step down at first. A porter who spoke a few words of English walked behind Leda at the back of the line.

Leda felt better after lunch. The nausea seemed to have disappeared, at least for now - she crossed her fingers where she was holding her trekking poles. She didn't want to jinx her current good fortune. Wyatt ambled with his hands in his pockets just in front of her. Gail and Tom definitely were setting a slower pace. The wind didn't seem as persistent; they were dropping into a less exposed side of the mountain. It would be downhill for the rest of the day to the Barranco Valley camp, not good psychologically knowing all they had gained before lunch would be lost, but Leda would keep her focus on the logical reason for the descent.

"You think Chase's okay?" Jen stopped just in front of Wyatt. Leda paused on the rough stone step just above him.

"Sure," Wyatt said. "I bet he's feeling better already."

"I can't stop worrying," Jen said.

"The best cure is to get to a lower altitude," Wyatt said. "They're probably already in the rain forest." Wyatt sounded confident in his knowledge. Jen must have thought so too as she turned and started walking again.

Leda levered down the stone step using her trekking poles barely missing whacking Wyatt's ankle. "Sorry," she said.

Wyatt stopped and faced her, "Why are your fingers crossed?"

Leda laughed. "Guess I'm a little superstitious about getting sick and being sent down the mountain."

"I felt kind of sick before lunch," Wyatt said.

"Are you trying to make me feel better?"

"Why would I do that?" Wyatt smiled, and kept walking. Leda thought she heard him whistling but the sound was so faint she couldn't be sure.

Leda thought about the declaration she had made to Wyatt about moving out. It wouldn't be easy to do or to tell her pop about. Both had looked forward to living in the same house again even if it was only for a few years while she paid off her student loans. And, she had always thought she would settle in the Portland area. The thought of moving elsewhere was scary.

"Are you groaning?" Wyatt said.

"Sorry, I didn't mean to," Leda said. Wyatt paused as if he was waiting for her to say more, but she waved her trekking pole in a gesture meant to keep him walking.

It would be easy to rely on her father for free housing, but she couldn't stay with him while she continued searching for answers about her mother. She would have to do it behind his back, and it wouldn't be right. His refusal to talk wasn't going to stop her. She wasn't satisfied with his apology or his plea to leave the past alone. She felt a touch of nausea again, but she couldn't be sure if it was from the altitude or fear of the unknown future. Reaching the summit of this mountain would be the best thing for her. If she lost her courage about moving out or searching for answers about her mother, she could simply tell herself "I got to the summit of Mt. Kilimajaro, I can do anything." Of course, she might still be able to get more information from her father, and then she wouldn't have to move.

"Now you're laughing," Wyatt said. "What's going on back there?"

"Do you have a dog?" Leda said.

"No, do you?" Wyatt had slowed to walk beside her.

"I always wanted one after this lady came to our elementary school," Leda said. "One of her dogs visited hospice patients, and the other one, the one with only three legs, visited vets in the hospital. It sounded so cool. Plus, I wanted a dog to sleep with me at night."

"Why didn't you get a dog?"

"My father said the dog would miss us when we went hiking."

"You couldn't take the dog with you?"

"It didn't occur to me."

The trail narrowed and Wyatt was forced to move in front of Leda. He turned his head to talk to her, and nearly tripped.

"Keep your focus in front," Leda said, her tone light. "I wouldn't want you to fall."

"Surely you jest." Wyatt leapt down a rock and skittered on the gravel nearly losing his balance. Jen jumped out of the way acting as if Wyatt had come close to knocking her over. It was all Leda could do to keep from laughing harder. "See," he said, "I'm fine."

Now, the rocky trail required concentration but not enough to keep Leda's mind from wandering.

She wondered what had attracted her father to her mother. She tried to remember if her pop had ever told her or if she had ever asked. Leda had lived with the myth of her mother's early death for so long, it was hard now to separate fact from the fiction she had imagined. She did remember how old she was when she decided her father was lonely. It was at her tenth birthday. Their celebration was clear in her mind, as was the piece of molten chocolate cake the restaurant waiters brought to the table lit by a single candle. Leda thought her father looked sad. She was positive he kept looking at the laughing couple sharing a dessert two tables over. If he wouldn't do anything about getting a new wife, Leda would do it for him.

It seemed like providence when Leda walked into her fifth grade class that fall and saw her teacher. Miss James was so pretty with her perfect sheet of long black hair and her sky blue eyes. They had learned about descriptive writing in fourth grade. Miss James had a butterfly tattoo on her left ankle. Leda saw it on the day Miss James forgot to wear a Band-Aid or a sock. For two whole weeks, Leda didn't turn in her homework. She pushed a boy on the asphalt playground. Miss James called her father and a parent/teacher conference was arranged. It was better than a blind date. Leda couldn't believe it when nothing happened except she was grounded for the rest of the month.

So Leda didn't get Miss James for her mother. And all the time she had been scheming about Miss James and her father, Leda's mother had still been alive.

Leda sipped her water, and looked up at the sky. A few clouds hastened towards the summit. She could smell the dust on her clothes, dust that smelled dry and volcanic. Giant senecios and lobelias seemed to spring magically from the rocks – a lush, but scattered forest compared to the barren slopes she had just hiked, and it boggled her mind that plant life could thrive at this altitude. "I'm in Africa," Leda thought. She felt a rush of elation that she was here. She even forgot for the briefest moment about figuring out how to get her pop to tell her more about her mother.

"You're quiet," Wyatt said.

"Still thinking," Leda said.

Wyatt nodded and continued his easy stride, not changing his gait whether he was stepping down a rock ledge or simply hiking along the trail. He looked loose and natural in his worn pants and boots. Effortless. Jen bounded along in front of him seeming to have no fear of the rough terrain. If the gravel sent her skidding, she merely righted herself and kept going, until she put her all her weight on a teetering rock. Before she could jump from it to the next one, the rock came rolled loose. Jen's feet went out from under her. Her arms wind milled. She lost her balance, her daypack pulling her backwards. It looked like she was going to take a nasty fall. Leda cried out. She was certain the back of Jen's head was going to smack the rock ledge behind her. There was nothing Leda could do but watch. She was too far away.

Chapter 24

Wyatt rushed forward. Leda wasn't sure how, but one second Wyatt was sliding, the dust swirling around him and the next the two were in the dirt Wyatt's hand gripping the back of Jen's daypack. Leda hurried towards them.

"I thought you were going to be knocked unconscious," Leda said.

Tears streaked Jen's dusty face. "That wasn't fun," she said.

Leda held out her hand. She helped Jen to her feet.

"I miss Chase," Jen said.

Leda dug in her jacket pocket for a tissue. "I'll stay with you tonight if you want," she said. She handed the other girl the clean tissue.

Wyatt held out his hand. "What about me?"

"Why would she stay with you?" Jen sniffed and patted her face.

"I was asking for a hand up," Wyatt said.

Jen's laugh sounded rough after her tears. "Don't forget how long I've known you," she said. "Watch out for him."

"Warning noted." Leda held out her hand to Wyatt. The warmth of his fingers reminded her of his hand resting on her shoulder earlier, and she blushed at the contact. Wyatt stood easily. He could have gotten up on his own. He held her hand longer than necessary but Leda didn't mind. The three continued down the trail, Jen being more cautious than before. Still, they soon caught up with the older members of the group.

It wasn't long before Gail tripped. Again, Wyatt sprinted forward. For all his bulk, Tom moved faster. His hand under Gail's elbow, steadying her before Wyatt could reach her. "I've got her son," Tom said. "No worries." Wyatt held up his hands, mumbled something about only trying to help. But Leda remembered the way he looked at his father this morning. Wyatt resumed his place just in front of her, and she sensed a different energy from him than before. His stride no longer easy, instead each step emphasized with a puff of dust.

The altitude decreased, their pace grew faster. Soon, Wyatt and Leda passed her father, Gail and Tom. Jen chose to stay behind. Leda thought about hiking with her pop again, but it was so much easier now to be with Wyatt.

Leda followed in his wake wondering what it would be like to be part of his family: to have a mother who stuck around to tuck you into bed at night, to hug you when you were sad, to ask you about your day. Leda and Wyatt were still close enough to hear the others - Tom's voice rising above the rest, his words indistinct. He must have said something funny, because Gail's laughter rang out, bouncing down the canyon in little ripples.

"Gail seems happy," Leda said.

"Does she?" Wyatt plowed down the trail and rounded a pile of boulders. The going was getting rougher, the path snaking up and around and down sometimes just above a rocky streambed where a thin line of water trickled and sometimes crossing over the streambed only to curve back across. Now, the others were further behind. Leda scrambled to keep up with Wyatt. He stepped down a gravel-strewn rock, sliding but staying on his feet again with the ease of a professional ice skater. Leda hesitated, and then plunged after him. The forward motion was too much for her. She instinctively thrust out her hands to cushion the inevitable fall. Her trekking poles flying out behind her. But Wyatt grabbed her hand, and held her steady. Neither moved quickly to separate.

"Thought I was going down," she said. She pressed her other palm to her chest. "My heart's racing."

"Want me to carry those?" Wyatt indicated her trekking poles with his free hand.

"I'll put them in my pack." Flustered she had gripped his hand for so long, Leda let go and fumbled with her poles, trying her best to collapse them. But the dumb lock refused to snap open. Unlike her father, who would have taken the poles from her, Wyatt calmly watched her futile efforts. Leda finally admitted defeat, and asked for Wyatt's help. He moved the lock easily and stowed the shortened poles in her pack.

"Last night you asked why I was here," Wyatt said. The two continued along the trail at a slower pace, the porter following behind. "I wasn't entirely joking when I said because it was a free trip. My mom was desperate for me to come. So I guess you could say I'm whoring myself out."

"That's an odd way to put it," Leda said. "My father paid for my trip as a gift."

"Do you feel bad about that now?"

"What do you mean?"

"You're not hiking with him," Wyatt said, "and I heard you yelling at him last night." Wyatt hopped down another small rocky ledge, turned to help Leda. "It was hard not to hear you." His words almost sounded like an apology.

Embarrassed, Leda brushed his hand aside. Squatting and bracing her palm on a rock, she managed to slide onto her feet. "Sorry," she mumbled.

"No worries," Wyatt said. "I don't get along with my dad either."

"We get along," Leda said. "Or at least we used to."

Wyatt was silent. Leda imagined he was waiting for her to explain, but instead she huffed her way along the path, kicking aside loose stones. One bounced and hit the side of Wyatt's boot, but he acted like he didn't notice. He never stopped moving. She could hear the porter close behind her; he smelled like he and his clothes had been up and down the mountain many times.

When Leda didn't say anything, Wyatt continued, "Tom hasn't been happy with me for a while. Ever since I took a fulltime job as a lifeguard."

"But why did you?" Leda said. "You have a college degree."

"That's what he said." Wyatt stopped abruptly, so that Leda stepped on the back of his boot. Fortunately, the porter was further back. Wyatt turned so he was facing her. "Have you ever read Thoreau?" Wyatt didn't wait for her answer. "Thoreau called the ocean a wilderness. Snakes, bears, hyenas, tigers – and lions – vanish as civilization approaches. But the most populous and civilized city can't scare a shark from its wharves. That's what Thoreau said. The ocean is our last untamed wilderness. And I like helping people."

"Couldn't you find another job that would encompass your passion?" Leda said.

"I didn't know elitists hiked," Wyatt said. "And I was beginning to like you." Wyatt shook his head and continued along the trail leaving Leda standing with her mouth open. Wyatt liked her? She closed her mouth and hurried after him.

"Hey, wait up." Leda panted in Wyatt's wake. "I'm sorry. Really."

Wyatt slowed a little. A brief widening of the trail gave Leda the opportunity to walk beside him. "Am" a breath 'I' another breath "forgiven?" Leda said.

"I'll think about it."

The trail narrowed between two boulders again, and Leda was forced to fall behind. In the ensuing silence, Leda thought back over their conversation. Wyatt had quoted Thoreau. Had she really said encompassing and passion in the same sentence in response? Crap. She sounded like her pop. She would apologize again and hope Wyatt forgave her.

Shadows crept down the right side of the canyon, and worked their way across the trail. It seemed as if she had been hiking forever, lunch in the dining tent a lifetime ago. All Leda wanted to do at this point was reach camp. Her body had entered what she called the robotic phase about an hour ago, her arms and legs moving with a will of their own, her mind in a haze.

Just ahead, four people rested at the edge of the trail. The hikers' clothes had a fine layer of dust just like Wyatt and Leda's. Wyatt, Leda and their porter walked by with a *jambo* and a nod. Leda couldn't help but smile when she saw the energy biscuits in the others' hands.

"Do you want to stop?" Wyatt asked when they were past.

"I'm fine," Leda said. Rest stops were good up to a certain point, and then they could actually make starting all over again harder. If she stopped now, she might collapse and never go again. And then how would she get to the camp? Maybe Wyatt would have to carry her. Ha. Now that wasn't a bad thought. Her smile at the picture of Wyatt carrying her was wide.

"Have I told you how glad I am you're here?" Wyatt said.

Leda's heart gave a girlish flutter. "You don't even know me."

"Just walking with you is keeping me civilized."

"So you would become a savage without me?"

"According to Tom, a lifeguard is a mere step above," Wyatt said.

The two snacked as they walked, Leda dipping into her energy biscuit reserves, sharing with Wyatt, thinking about what he'd said. It was difficult to puzzle it out, when her brain felt encased in cotton.

Chapter 25

Finally, the orange pup tents came into view. Leda couldn't imagine a more welcome sight. The tents were staked on a small dirt hillock dotted with towering senecios. An infinite valley of purpled hills provided a dramatic backdrop. The whole setting reminded Leda of pictures she had seen of a desert oasis. She imagined she was as happy as a desert caravan would be to arrive after a long dry journey. As soon as she dropped her daypack by her tent, a porter appeared with a plastic basin of steaming water. Wyatt disappeared, Leda assumed to his own tent. She dipped her hands in the warm water, rubbed them and splashed her face. Luxury on the slopes of Mt. Kilimanjaro. Was that an oxymoron? Leda was about to take off her boots and climb into her tent when she remembered her promise to Jen. Her offer to spend the night with Jen hadn't been entirely selfless. A night separate from her pop might show him how serious she was about finding out more about her mother. Leda peered into the other two tents. When she found one with a single duffel and sleeping bag, she gathered up her own stuff and brought it over. Then, she took off her boots and crawled into the pup tent. She unrolled her mat. Stretched out on it. Who knew two inches of air could provide such a nice cushion? Leda closed her eyes for a nap.

The other's arrival in camp woke her. She thought she heard her pop asking Erik about her whereabouts, but she stayed sprawled on the mat. Jen crawled into the tent.

"Thanks for staying with me," Jen said.

"No problem." The two began setting up the tent.

"Are you going to tell your dad?"

"Later."

"He's asking about you."

"He'll survive." Leda was careful in organizing her side of the tent, smoothing her sleeping bag and placing her pillow just so.

"Everything okay?" Jen had finished with her side, and sat cross-legged on her sleeping bag. She took off her baseball cap and straightened her ponytail.

"Yeah. Sure." Leda looked sideways at Jen. The other girl shrugged her shoulders.

"If you want to talk…" Jen let the words trail off. She stopped fussing with her hair and stretched out on her sleeping bag. "This feels like heaven." She closed her eyes.

Leda climbed out of the pup tent just as the rays of the setting sun left the uppermost branches of the senecios. Her pop hurried to intercept her on the way to the toilet. It looked as if he had been waiting for her to emerge.

"You're staying with Jen?" he said.

Leda continued towards the toilet, forcing her father to fall into step with her.

"She misses her husband," Leda said.

"So you're just helping her out?"

"What else would it be?"

"You're not avoiding me?" her father said. "Because it's felt that way all day."

"That's funny," Leda said. "Because it's felt like you've been avoiding me." Leda stopped. She faced her father, the wad of toilet paper clutched in her hand. "You know what I want."

"I do," her father said, "but what you want isn't going to do anything but cause pain. And what father would want to cause his daughter pain?"

"I'm twenty four," Leda said. "Don't you think it's time I knew the truth?"

"Sometimes truth is not the best course."

Leda stared at her father in the blue shadows of the canyon. The two stood next to the toilets, their nasty odor a jarring note in this otherworldly place of distant purple hills and dimly lit valleys and unfamiliar trees towering over them like spiky redwoods. Her pop stood with his arms folded across his chest. Whether he was protecting himself from the gathering cold or the ghost of her mother, Leda couldn't tell. Leda saw it was useless to argue. She turned on her heel and entered the toilet, letting the door slam on her heel.

Dinner was quiet, the usual hot broth followed by platters of spaghetti and pineapple. Her father had not waited for her outside the toilet. Leda couldn't blame him. The toilets stunk. Now, he sat next to her, but seemed distant. It was a familiar feeling for Leda, but one she usually experienced in Oregon. Then, she knew his mind was occupied with work. She had never felt so far from her pop on a mountain trail.

As a distraction, Leda observed Wyatt's family. She no longer had to wonder why Wyatt kept his distance even while he was sitting at the same table. Gail appeared pensive as she sipped her hot water. Even Tom was less boisterous than usual, talking about turning in early tonight. Erik made a brief appearance to announce the morning departure time. A puff of freezing air came into the dining tent when he opened the flap. The sheltered spot in the valley was at about the same altitude as they had started the day. They wouldn't know if they had really accomplished what they set out to do – getting used to the altitude - until later when they reached the summit base camp, and then attempted the summit. Leda recognized a certain ironic parallel in their day's walk to her own emotional roller coaster. All the ups and downs of her thoughts about her parents seemed to have brought her no closer to a resolution but one – she was determined to move out.

Wyatt walked with her from the dining tent. "No star gazing tonight?"

Leda shivered. "Too cold." She tipped her head back. "But the stars seem brighter."

"They do."

Silence enveloped them as Leda looked upward. Her body tingled with the knowledge of Wyatt's presence by her side. Eventually the cold became too much for her, and she stamped her feet to warm her toes turning her gaze from the sky to Wyatt. He had his eyes fixed on her. They no longer seemed green like the lichen, but a darker shade more like the senecios in the starlight. Wyatt leaned towards her. Leda's pulse jumped in her neck. His lips touched hers, and then he pulled her closer. She didn't resist, but gave herself fully to the kiss. She was no longer cold by the time they broke apart. She lingered in his embrace.

"I should be getting to my tent," Leda said.

"Hope you're warm enough," Wyatt said.

Leda laughed. "I'll be plenty warm. I'm sharing a tent with Jen." She disentangled herself from his arms, and headed to her tent. Even though they had descended during the afternoon, they were still at high altitude. That's why her heart beat rapidly. Okay, maybe it wasn't the altitude; maybe she was developing a camp crush on Wyatt. What was the harm in that?

The sound of a zipper being drawn with a firm hand caught Leda's attention. Had it come from her pop's tent? There was no way to be sure. She wondered if he had seen her with Wyatt.

Chapter 26

Leda woke the next morning with a slight headache. She wiggled one arm out of her sleeping bag for her water bottle, and downed what was left in it. A layer of frost covered the ceiling of her tent. She didn't wait for the morning coffee to crawl out of her sleeping bag. Braving the cold, she stripped off her long underwear shirt and pulled on a form fitting sleeveless top. Leda grabbed the still warm long underwear, yanking it back over her head, thrusting her arms through the sleeves. Her down jacket came next. The material was cold, and she shivered. She debated whether to keep dressing or to get back into her sleeping bag. Like every morning and evening there would be no campfire, a new direction for a country struggling with deforestation. Leda pulled her hood over her head and slid back into her sleeping bag. Jen slumbered in her bag. The other girl had talked and mumbled in the night. Leda couldn't understand her words, but she figured Jen was missing her husband.

Leda lay against her small pillow thinking with nostalgia of the African hotel they had stayed at before the trip. The hotel had not had a lot of comforts, and Leda complained about the trickle of hot water in the shower, the rooster that crowed off and on all night, the mooing cow and the small, hard bed. There had also been a strange screeching in the night the hotel workers said was a monkey. Now, the hotel seemed like Eden.

After three days without a shower, Leda could feel the dirt on her body. Her scalp itched. She welcomed the morning bowl of warm water brought to the tent by a porter. At least she could clean her hands and face. The splashing water woke Jen. She sat up with a groan.

"Good morning," Leda said.

Jen grunted.

Breakfast in the dim dining tent was quiet. The sun had not yet reached the small knoll where they camped, and the group huddled around the table in their warmest coats and hats. Leda wished her pop good morning, and even managed to brush a kiss on his cheek. His rough beard prickled her lips and reminded her of past hiking trips. She loved him, but was still mad at his stubborn refusal to tell her more about her mother. She was at a loss about what to do next. It was a new feeling for her: her pop a puzzle she couldn't figure out.

"You sleep okay?" he said to her.

"Sure," she said. "You?"

He nodded. Leda doubted anyone was fooled by the charade. She pulled out a chair and sat down.

Her headache was gone, but she didn't feel hungry. Even so, she ate a heaping serving of porridge, scrambled eggs and toast. She drew the line at the sausage, not even able to watch as Wyatt had a second helping of it. The sausage looked suspiciously like miniature hot dogs – a food she studiously avoided even at home.

After breakfast, the morning routine was established. Gail and Jen danced with the porters. Tom edged closer to the dance group each day. Leda couldn't see her pop, but figured he must either be packing up in the tent or at the toilet. Today, Wyatt joined Leda on her rock. Leda held Emily's journal open, but she was having a hard time focusing on the pages. Wyatt hadn't said anything about last night's kiss, and neither had she. Still, his presence next to her signaled a change in their relationship. It made her nervous. What exactly was she doing with this Southern California lifeguard? She felt a definite attraction to him, but she hadn't come to Mt. Kilimanjaro looking for romance.

Leda snuck a glance at Wyatt. He seemed to be in another world, his gaze held by an indiscernible point somewhere in the indistinct distance. Today they would scale the 1,000- foot Barranco Wall, which was close to vertical in some places. Leda flipped to the corresponding pages in the journal. "Arrived at Barranco Valley under heavy clouds. Rain began at dinner. Hasn't let up. Still waiting to continue. Barranco Wall said to be difficult. Impassable in rain." Leda already knew the next page chronicled those who suffered broken bones on the wall's slick rocks.

Frost glistened in large ice crystals on the pup tents and gilded the giant senecios. The sky was a clear blue. Leda had packed away her down jacket, but wore her fleece and gloves. The group would drop into the Barranco Valley and hike a short way before reaching the base of the wall. The trekking guide said splotches of red paint sketched a zigzag route up the cliff nowadays, avoiding the most difficult sections, showing hikers the footholds and handholds.

"So did she say how she made it up the wall?" Wyatt said.

His voice startled Leda. She had finally relaxed enough to ignore him while she studied the journal. "I haven't read that page yet," she said.

"But you know," Wyatt said. "You've read it before."

"The wall was slick, and some fell."

"To their death?"

"The journal doesn't say," Leda said. "But some broke bones."

"It should be dry today," Wyatt said. He peered over her shoulder at the journal. "And there are plenty of hand and footholds."

Leda had been hyper-aware of Wyatt's presence before, and now, feeling his breath on her ear, her thoughts flew back to last night's kiss.

"The woman doesn't write much," Wyatt said.

Leda closed the journal and slid off the rock. Enough of these feelings! She was twenty-four and no longer a teenager. She needed to keep her focus on getting more information from her father. She didn't have time for a silly romance. She leveled a cool look at Wyatt. "It's enough for me," she said. She twitched her braid over her shoulder so it fell down her back.

He reacted to her look with an exaggerated shiver. "I sense a sudden drop in the temperature," he joked. "Are you nervous about something? Perhaps the Barranco Wall?"

Leda took her time sliding the journal into her daypack. She would be lying if she said she wasn't nervous. Heights scared her. Which, when she thought about it, was kind of ironic considering she was climbing the highest mountain in Africa. Plenty of kids fell out of a tree like she did and broke a bone. But they climbed right back up. She never had climbed a tree again. Her father always encouraged her to overcome her fear. If a light bulb needed changing, she got out the ladder and changed the bulb. The two had started hiking mountains when Leda was young, first Mt. Lassen in northern California, then some of the easier mountains in the Cascade Range, graduating to the fourteeners in the Colorado Rockies and finally Mt. Whitney, the highest peak in the contiguous United States. Still, Leda was stubborn about getting back in a tree. It was no secret her pop was stubborn. Maybe her mother was too and she had inherited a double dose of it. Leda sighed.

"Like you said, the wall will be dry." Leda tried for a light-hearted tone as she slipped her arms into the straps of her daypack. "Why should I be nervous?"

"No reason," Wyatt said. He left the rock. Taking his daypack, he strolled over to where the rest of the hiking group, including her pop, gathered near Erik. The dancing was done, and the porters were busy cleaning up the camp, breaking down the tents and loading up their bundles.

Leda did her best to match his carefree saunter, but inside she was tightly strung in nervous anticipation.

Chapter 27

The group followed Erik as the trail dropped into the Great Barranco Valley. More giant senecios and clumps of grass lined the meandering path. Leda could see the wall ahead, but decided to keep her focus on the trail at her feet. A small stream trickled through the marshy valley bottom. Jen stepped onto a stone, and uttered a soft cry as it teetered and sank a little. She laughed at herself when it stopped, shrugged her shoulders and crossed to the other side.

Leda glanced at Wyatt, who was about to cross the stones. He was already looking at her with a slight smile. "Do you want some help?" he said. Leda quickly turned away only to find Gail observing the interaction. Leda returned her own gaze to the marsh, profoundly embarrassed. She remembered how Wyatt had heard Leda yelling at her pop. Gail must have heard her as well. After all, it was Tom who told Leda to shut it. Did Gail know Leda had kissed her son? Not being familiar with mothers, Leda decided to tread more carefully in the future, both as she crossed the stream and with her words and actions. Wyatt waited with his hand out if Leda needed help, but she brushed past with a murmured, "thanks but no thanks." Then, she hurried ahead as if there was nothing between them.

They all regrouped in a shallow cave just beneath a giant boulder. Erik assigned Gail to follow behind him as the group scaled the wall. Leda felt like everyone was staring at her when Erik put her just before Wyatt in the line, but she was on high alert and probably being overly sensitive. At least that's what she told herself, until Jen winked at her and mouthed, "Let's talk later."

Erik started up the wall. Leda swallowed hard, and fell into line behind her father. She could feel Wyatt at her back. Leda's trekking poles were stowed in her backpack. She would need her hands free to grip the rocks as she scrambled from one spot to the next. Her gloves were also safely tucked in her pack.

Her pop paused before beginning the ascent, tilting his head back to take in the full scope of the cliff. "You can do this Leda," he said. "I'll be right in front of you if you need help."

His words didn't surprise Leda. She couldn't remember a time when he hadn't been there for her, but she didn't know why he persisted in refusing to answer questions about her mother. Of course, that was nothing new either. She had to find a way to convince him to tell her everything now she knew more. He would have to realize he couldn't keep her in the dark forever.

The first few steps and handholds were fairly easy, and Leda's confidence grew. One required a bigger step than she thought she could make, but Wyatt gave her a welcome boost. She didn't notice her pop's outstretched hand above her. Porters passed in a continual stream. Leda couldn't believe how they juggled their loads on their heads or shoulders while they seemed to leap up the wall. The group paused often so the porters could go by. Erik finally told them not to worry about the porters. "If you are always stopping," he said. "We will never reach the top." The group continued. Leda tried not to think about how much more dangerous it was for the porters now they had to go around her. She made the mistake of looking down. They were about halfway up the wall, and the Great Barranco Valley seemed to stretch into eternity below her. Leda quickly focused on the section of the wall in front of her.

"What a view," Wyatt said. "Spectacular."

Leda didn't dare look again or even spare a glance at Wyatt behind her. She could only imagine he was relaxed – as always – and enjoying the view like a mountain goat tucked into the crevice at the pinnacle of a cliff. Her pop had moved higher up the wall. Leda couldn't delay any longer. She reached for the next handhold, wedged the toe of her boot in a crack and hauled herself up, muscles straining. She had always known this section of the hike would be one of the most difficult for her, but Leda had imagined her father would talk her through it or even hold her hand if needed. Like he had the time they crossed the boulders in Rocky Mountain National Park, giving her a hand up on the more difficult ones. She could hear Tom encouraging Gail on the rocks just above her, and she was sorry her father wasn't doing the same for her. She wondered why. Did her pop sense her need to keep her distance now? Didn't he know she needed him to help her over this difficult section? Wyatt climbed in silence behind her making no comment on Leda's progress. He probably assumed she could reach the top on her own, except for those places where her legs were just too short to stretch from one foothold to the next. And why wouldn't he assume she could make it? Leda felt more positive just thinking about it, and she worked her way up the wall in bolder moves. Until she reached the kissing rock.

The group had talked about this section at dinner last night. How it got its name because the narrow trail and foot and handholds brought hikers so close to the wall, they could literally kiss it. And now, here it was and Leda was spread across it, hugging it tight, her cheek pressed to the rock. She froze. She didn't mean to, but she didn't think she could move forward. Someone was going to have to hook a cable to her waist, and haul her the rest of the way up the wall. Leda didn't look up. She didn't look down.

"Should I be jealous of that rock?" Wyatt said.

Leda couldn't laugh. She knew if she moved even the tiniest bit, she would lose her balance and plummet into the bottomless valley below.

"You okay?" Wyatt touched her left hand where she clutched the rock in a white-knuckled grip. Leda couldn't nod her head or speak. She was vaguely aware of her pop and the rest of the group somewhere above her. Tiny bits of gravel slid down the rocks and sprinkled her head and shoulders. Dust tickled her nose. Leda was afraid she might sneeze, but instead the clear liquid that had gushed from her nose the other day began a slow slide to her upper lip. Minutes passed, and Leda began to feel overwhelmed by the sheer volume of the wall. She had already climbed for nearly an hour, and had no idea how close she was to the top. Why had she ever thought she could conquer the wall? Tears pooled in her eyes. One drop slipped down her cheek soaking into the rock.

"Leda," Wyatt's voice was gentle. "You're doing great. I know you can make it around this rock."

Wyatt's voice penetrated Leda's consciousness like it was coming from the other side of a dark tunnel. He no longer touched her hand, but his voice steadied her.

"You can do this," he said. "I'm right behind you."

Leda couldn't stay stuck here forever. She didn't know how a rescue party would save her – did the guides carry cables? Maybe they would use a rope. What if the rope got cut on the rock and snapped? Could a helicopter fly in at this altitude? Could a person drop from the helicopter and snatch her from the wall? Leda shuddered. She didn't know which would be worse: the rescue or actually getting around this rock, this damn kissing rock by herself.

"Take your time," Wyatt said. "There's no rush."

The clear liquid ran over her lips and dripped off her chin. Leda's throat ached with dryness.

"Just inch your way around," Wyatt said.

By sheer force of will, Leda shimmied further along the wall. That hadn't been so bad. She scooted a little bit further. Sweat beaded her forehead and armpits.

"Almost there," Wyatt said.

Leda didn't know if Wyatt was telling the truth, but decided she would be better off believing him. She took the tiniest of steps. She hadn't fallen screaming to her death…yet.

A few more shuffling steps and Leda was on the other side of the kissing rock. Safe. Her arms and legs trembled from the tension. She closed her eyes, exhausted for the moment. Leda didn't even think about the grossness of her face until she felt Wyatt dabbing at her cheeks. He had taken his bandana from his head and was using it to dry her nose, wipe her lips and clean off her chin. She smiled at the sight of his flattened hair, dirty and pressed to his head.

"What?" Wyatt said.

Leda shook her head. "Nothing. Thanks for helping me."

"Any time," Wyatt balled up the bandana and stuck it in his jacket pocket. He brushed her lips with a quick kiss. "Now that's why it's called the kissing rock."

"I doubt you're the first to think of that," Leda said.

"Probably not," Wyatt said. "But we can't hang around kissing all day even if you want to."

This time Leda didn't hold back her laughter. It was a laughter birthed in tension, and delivered with relief. Leda grabbed for the next handhold with a sudden surge of energy. The rest of the wall didn't seem as bad although they scrambled up it for another hour. Maybe she could climb the old maple in her front yard. Leda was feeling almost giddy when the ledge of the wall came into sight. Not much further now.

Near the top, Erik sat at the far end of a steep boulder. Leda didn't see any hand or footholds cut into the boulder. She hesitated. She could feel Wyatt behind her, but he waited for her next move without speaking. Another challenge. Could she conquer this one too?

"Trust your boots," Erik called.

Leda swallowed some water from the tube near her mouth. She considered the rock tilting at an alarming angle. Could she trust her boots? They had gotten her up the wall so far. And besides, even the dust couldn't hide the fact they were cute with neon green laces and a cheerful plaid trim around the ankle. Leda smiled.

She stepped onto the boulder, and leaning forward, trusted her boots to take her straight up to the guide. Wyatt clapped below her before tackling the boulder himself. The two slapped a high five when he reached the top. Turning around, Leda blushed to find the rest of the group watching them from a level dirt patch. The snow-covered summit soared behind them. Clouds wreathed the top, obscuring its peak. Her pop stood to the side of the patch, a little bit separate from the rest. She could feel the coolness in his stance, the tilt of his head. But was his attitude directed at Wyatt or her? She didn't know.

"Picture time," Jen said. She gestured to Leda and Wyatt, signaling them to gather with the group on a flat slab. Jen handed her camera to Erik. She stood at the back of the group. Wyatt pulled Leda into a spot near him. Her pop stood on the opposite side of the group from Leda. After Erik had taken pictures with all the cameras, the group ate their snacks and chatted about climbing the wall. Leda's father was silent. She could tell he was brooding. His hat was pushed back enough on his head she could see the crease in his forehead; deeper lines formed a parenthesis around his lips.

"Lose your bandana?" Gail said to Wyatt.

"It was giving me a headache," Wyatt said. "Besides, the breeze feels good."

Leda was grateful Wyatt didn't mention her panic at the kissing rock.

"What took you two so long?" Jen said.

Wyatt exchanged a glance with Leda. "We were enjoying the view," he said.

"I was too scared to look," Jen said. "I'm glad that's over."

"You can say that again." Gail leaned back on her elbows, her face tilted to the sky. "Those clouds look ominous."

Chapter 28

The clouds which had just minutes before encircled only the peak had now spread across the sky. Leda had never seen clouds move so fast before. Erik urged the group to finish up their snacks and get ready to move. Leda made a quick trip behind a nearby boulder. The trail would head downhill for a while, and Leda snapped her trekking poles into the proper position for the downward trek before stepping onto the trail.

"Wait up." Jen appeared from behind the boulder. "Walk with me."

Leda watched as Wyatt's back disappeared down a series of natural stone steps. Her pop hovered nearby. Leda imagined he wanted to talk with her, but Jen had jumped in before him. Now, he had no choice but to fall in behind the two girls.

"Wyatt's hot," Jen said. "No doubt about it. Of course, Chase is hotter."

Leda hoped her father couldn't hear what Jen was saying.

"But don't forget when I warned you yesterday to watch out."

"I won't forget," Leda said. "Tell me about Chase." She was desperate to turn the conversation in another direction with her pop walking silently just behind them. The three negotiated several hairpin turns, stepping down uneven rock ledges, balancing from one rock to the next one just below it. A sudden gust of wind sent shivers down Leda's neck. She zipped her fleece higher, and looked at the sky. The clouds were a dark slate gray. They seemed to have swollen in size, their bellies full of rain, or ice, or possibly even snow. Jen picked up her pace, and soon the three had drawn within sight of the rest of the group.

"I've known Chase forever," Jen said, speaking as if Leda had asked the question moments before. "We went to the same college. We played on the same Ultimate Frisbee team."

"What's that?" Leda said.

Jen launched into a long explanation about Ultimate Frisbee. Leda only paid enough attention to ask questions and keep Jen talking. She could hear her father's heavy footsteps behind her, the occasional rattle of gravel if he slid on the downhill trail.

"Anyway," Jen came to the conclusion of her story, "Chase works for his dad."

"Doing what?"

"Tom's in furniture. He's got some big stores with his name in green cursive. Green because the furniture's environmentally friendly." Jen laughed. "Tom can be a big talker, but maybe he'll do something about those toilets after all. Chase helps on the business side."

"What about you?"

"I'm a software engineer working for one of those dot coms in Silicon Valley. Does that surprise you?"

Leda would never admit it, but she was surprised. Who would have ever thought blond Ultimate Frisbee playing Jen was an engineer? Leda remembered her earlier judgment about Wyatt being a lifeguard.

"I'm not surprised at all," she told Jen.

"I'm not sure I believe you," Jen said, "but it doesn't matter. Let's get back to our original subject...Wyatt."

Leda sucked a big gulp of water from her water tube. It went down the wrong pipe, and she choked and sputtered. She had done all she could to avoid the subject of Wyatt, especially with her pop following so close on their heels, but obviously she had not succeeded in distracting Jen.

"Why isn't he in the family business?" Leda said when she could talk again.

"He went rogue." Jen's statement was matter of fact. "Chase's always been the steadier one. I like that."

Leda's father skidded above them on a new set of hairpin turns. Bits of gravel showered the girls. "You okay Dr. Stanton?" Jen said.

"Sorry," she muttered in a lowered voice to Leda. "I forgot about him."

"It's okay," Leda said.

Jen pursed her lips as if she was thinking about whether she should say more. After a long silence, she said with her voice still low, "I can tell he likes you as more than a friend."

Leda thought about how Wyatt had wiped her face, and then kissed her on the Barranco Wall. So what if he was a good kisser, what else did they have in common? "Look," Leda said. "I'm not here to find a boyfriend."

Jen continued as if Leda hadn't said anything, "I've never seen Wyatt act this way with a girl before especially around his parents. I mean, he's dated and all." She lapsed into silence again. Leda could only guess that Jen was trying to figure out what Wyatt saw in her. She had never attracted his type before; maybe it had something to do with the shared adventure of climbing Mt. Kilimanjaro.

Jen continued, "Just be careful. He doesn't stick around."

"Maybe it's the altitude," Leda said.

"What?"

"The way he's acting."

Jen laughed. "Good point."

"If it makes you feel any better," Leda said. "I'm only here to climb the mountain."

"I hoped I could climb it with my husband," Jen said, her tone mournful. She unwrapped a hard candy with a great rustling of cellophane and popped it into her mouth. "Want one? Jen offered a green piece of candy to Leda.

"No thanks."

"How about you Dr. Stanton?" Jen raised her voice.

"I'm fine," he said.

A tremendous thunderclap seemed to shake the very ground and vibrate through Leda's spinal cord. A sudden icy rain whipped around them. With frantic motions, the three dug in their daypacks for their waterproof gear. Leda pulled on her jacket first, tightening the hood around her face, adjusting the visor to keep the worst of the water out of her eyes. The rain had turned to sleet by the time she got her waterproof pants on. Rivulets of mud seemed to have sprung out of nowhere to dash down the trail. When they were ready, they scrambled to catch up with the others. There was no place to take shelter from the storm, so the three pushed on down the path that had become more treacherous now it was wet.

Leda half ran with her head down, her shoulders hunched against the sleet, doing her best to keep up. Her bare knuckles turned red with the cold, the tips of her fingers grew white. Still, she continued downward, gripping her trekking poles, gritting her teeth. Leda slid on a slick rock, but managed to keep her balance. She knew it was dangerous to be on a high, exposed slope during a thunderstorm. Luckily, they weren't still on the rise where they had taken a picture, but had already hiked about an hour below it. Another clap of thunder sent Leda skittering faster. It must have had the same effect on the others because she was still a ways behind them, her pop at her back. She could see Jen's fleeting form, but the curtain of sleet hid the rest of the hiking group. Leda felt a twinge of fear. She wished Wyatt were nearby. She didn't think to take comfort in her father's close presence.

The wind and sleet plastered Leda's pants and jacket to her body. Her neon green bootlaces were taking a thrashing. Jen disappeared behind a boulder. Leda continued her mad dash down the trail.

A rock underfoot wobbled unexpectedly, her ankle twisted and her leg gave out. Leda tried to recover, but it was too late. She sprawled on the trail, grazing a boulder with her hip. Crap! The expletive was barely out of her mouth, when Leda felt someone behind her. It was her pop kneeling in the gravelly mud. An icy burst of sleet hit her full in her face, wetting her forehead and the top of her head. Raising her hand, Leda realized her hood had been pushed back on her head. She adjusted her hood, calming her thoughts. Her hands were still strapped to her trekking poles, and she took some time pulling them off, and setting them aside. Neither she nor her pop had spoken. The storm howled about them.

Leda probed her ankle with her fingers. It felt a little sore. Hopefully, it was simply bruised. Her pop gestured he would help her stand. Leda hesitated, but realized she had little choice. He supported her elbow, helping her to her feet. Leda leaned against a nearby boulder and gingerly tested her ankle.

"You okay?" her pop shouted above the wind.

"I think so." Leda put her full weight on her banged up ankle. Her boots, although not looking very cute at the moment, the laces a grayish green, the plaid splattered with mud, had not let her down, protecting her ankle from more serious injury. Wyatt appeared on the trail below them. He gathered up her trekking poles and handed them to her.

Chapter 29

Leda smiled up at Wyatt. She felt her father stiffen at her side but didn't acknowledge him.

"Thanks," she said. Leda strapped on her trekking poles, and headed down the trail behind Wyatt this time being more careful of her steps. She was conscious of her pop behind her the whole time. After a while, the sleet let up, and she could see further than just a few feet in front of her. The rest of the group was still not in sight. It seemed to have grown darker, and she wondered how much time had passed. The trekking guide had promised a shorter day today – a little more than three miles – but when they stopped earlier for a snack, Erik said they had taken longer climbing the wall than normal. Leda supposed it didn't matter how much further it was to the camp. She just needed to keep her head down, and gut it out.

As suddenly as it had started, the sleet stopped, and the wind quieted. Even the clouds seemed to disappear in a hurry. The sun glistened on the wet rocks. Leda's breath was a puff of mist. She stopped to pull on her gloves, wiggling her fingers in their dry warmth. Now, with the sun out, it seemed like a whole other day, and Leda felt her spirits rising.

Leda rounded a corner and saw the others ahead. They appeared to be resting. Jen waved and smiled.

"What's up?" Leda said.

"Just hangin'," Jen said.

"I was worried about you," Gail said.

"She's stronger than she looks." Wyatt squeezed Leda's bicep in a playful manner. Leda responded by pumping her fist.

"The storm came up so suddenly," Gail said. "I didn't know how you and your father were managing so I sent Wyatt back" The older woman scrutinized Leda's mud-spattered clothing. "Did you fall?"

"I'm fine," Leda said, distancing herself from Wyatt. So it was his mother's idea to come back up the trail, not his.

"Come sit next to me," Gail said to Leda patting the rock ledge. "And Phillip, how are you?" Leda's father hovered on the outskirts of the group. Not waiting for her father's answer, Leda squeezed onto the ledge next to Gail. For the next few minutes, she listened as the older woman talked about dashing down the trail in the sleet storm. Gail told of Tom practically lifting her off her feet as he rushed her to a less exposed portion of the mountain. Apparently Erik had helped Jen. Leda tried to imagine the guide helping the girl, but looking at him now sitting apart from the group with his face turned away, she couldn't. Now the storm was behind them and everyone had survived in good shape, the family laughed and joked about their adventure.

"And of course, we're happy you two made it as well." Gail patted Leda's knee. She smiled and nodded at Leda's father.

Even if Gail had heard Leda arguing with her pop back at Shira Camp, Leda realized the older woman would never admit it. From what Wyatt had told her, Leda assumed he had argued with his dad a number of times, and yet, because of his mom, Wyatt was here. It was hard not to like the older woman, and Leda felt herself warming towards Gail. She even wondered for a very brief moment what her life would have been like if Gail was her mother. She was pretty in a sensible way. Her nose and cheeks had a smattering of freckles. Leda doubted if Gail's blond hair was natural, but it looked like it could have been when she was younger and blended nicely with her hazel eyes. Very unlike Leda's mother who had an ethereal beauty. Which meant her father never would have been attracted to someone like Gail. Leda allowed her fantasy to slip away.

"We're not used to hiking with a group," her pop said. When no one responded, he added, "we didn't mean to worry you."

Leda studied her father. He had stepped closer when Gail addressed him, but still stood separate from the group. He seemed to have survived the storm well. He hadn't fallen like her, his waterproof outfit was damp, but not muddy or torn. He had pushed his hood from his head, and Leda could see that it must have blown off his hair at some point during the storm because his hair was dark and flattened on his head. In the past, Leda had admired his ability to keep a cool head. He was the stable one she could count on to anchor her. But now, she thought he seemed stand- offish as if the group didn't measure up. Or maybe it was just Wyatt who didn't. Leda accepted a handful of almonds from Gail, and as usual, stowed the stack of energy biscuits handed to her by Erik. The sun warmed the sheltered spot. Before the group resumed hiking, they all put away their damp, waterproof outfits. Wyatt waited for Leda seeming oblivious to her father's presence, and he fell in behind her. Her father walked in front of her. Leda felt like a lone book on the shelf between two bookends. Which one would she lean towards? For the moment, she ignored the tension she sensed in her father's movements, the careful way he placed his feet, the forward thrust of his head, and she looked around. She would probably never return to this trail again. Leda wanted to remember everything she could.

Within fifteen minutes, the group reached the top of a slick wall. Moss and lichen flourished in its cracks. A small trickle of water made its lazy way down the wall, meandering along the path of least resistance. The wall was not as high as the Barranco Wall, but part of the trail's nine hundred foot descent into a ravine. Erik told the group sometimes the water rushed down more like a waterfall. Leda imagined picking her way down during the sleet storm. That would have been a nightmare. She imagined the small trickle a torrent. But the sun was out, and the burst of water was gone and Leda could see the bottom not too far below them.

Erik started down the wall, winding his way between what looked to be descending ledges. The rest followed with some slipping and sliding especially in the mossy parts. Her pop hesitated, but Leda waved him on, saying "right behind you." Instead, she lingered at the top of the cliff. Tom helped Gail over the trickier parts. It wasn't long before the distance between the guide and the hikers increased.

Not psyched up to go just yet, Leda stared off into the distance watching the play of light and shadow as the clouds wandered high above the sand colored plains. She caught sight of a large vulture soaring on the wind currents, its pointed wings spread just below its body. She could see its white head and black mask, and she drew in a breath of surprise.

"The Lammergeier," Wyatt said. "Unbelievable."

The two paused at the top of the wall, Leda hoping to hear the bird's whistling call.

"Remember the lion they saw at Shira Plateau?" Wyatt said in hushed tones, as if the bird was near enough to hear them. "This is almost as good."

Leda wasn't superstitious, but the sight of the rare bird stirred something within her, a feeling of lightness like she had felt the first time she did a perfect glide on her Christmas ice skates. That day had been perfect too except she remembered missing her mother as she slid around the rink in her matching green mittens and hat. She looked at all the moms hanging over the barrier or holding their children's hand on the ice and she wondered whether her mother would have gotten her pink mittens. Maybe pink mittens with a fuzzy white kitten on the back like the ones the little girl in red wore.

The vulture hovered with no apparent effort, balanced on an invisible current. Leda felt drawn to the intimacy the bird shared with the wind, and she didn't realize she sighed when the vulture disappeared into the horizon. "I should have taken a picture," Leda said. "My pop won't believe it."

"It wouldn't be as good as our memories," Wyatt said.

Leda liked the idea of a shared memory with Wyatt.

"Were you very young when your mother died?" Wyatt said.

"What makes you ask that?"

"There was this look on your face while you watched the vulture. I can't explain it."

Wyatt stood at the top of the cliff, his gaze now returned to the spot where the rare bird disappeared. He wore his daypack, but his hands rested in his open jacket's pockets. He seemed to be in no hurry to get started down the wall. But Leda knew he could probably navigate it much like the mountain goat she had compared him to earlier, and easily catch up with the others. She, on the other hand, would need more time.

"It's complicated," Leda said. "We should get started."

Wyatt didn't protest when she took a first tentative step, but simply followed Leda as she worked her way down the slick rock in fits and starts, scooting on her butt when she was too scared to stand. Wyatt made no comment. Still, Leda knew without him telling her that he would catch her before she took a serious fall. Wyatt had proven himself earlier today on the Barranco Wall. But could she trust him with the story of her mother? At least, the little she knew? Leda felt a slight ping in her ankle as she negotiated some of the trickier spots on the wall. Maybe Wyatt had some healing ointment she could borrow.

Leda said a silent hallelujah when she reached the bottom and her boots touched solid ground. She almost felt like falling on her knees and kissing the flat trail in the Karanga Valley. The rest of the group was not too far ahead. Leda could catch up with them as easily as Wyatt could now. She didn't notice while she celebrated her safe arrival, Wyatt moved close enough to speak in her ear.

"That was disappointing," Wyatt said in a low voice.

"Too easy?" Leda said.

"No opportunity to kiss."

Leda tried to laugh as if his comment and his nearness didn't make her feel breathless all over again, like she had felt the entire time she scrambled down the wall. She remembered what she had told Jen earlier: that she and Wyatt were simply friends; that she wasn't here looking for a trail romance; that she had enough on her mind. Leda moved away from him, speeding up her steps to catch the others but Wyatt followed her, his steps mirroring hers.

"Running away?" he said.

"Just catching up with the others." Leda flipped her braid back over her shoulder. Wyatt laughed keeping perfect step with her.

"You don't give up easily," Leda said.

"I wouldn't be here if I did," Wyatt said. "The mountain demands perseverance."

Leda couldn't help but smile, although she hoped Wyatt didn't notice.

"Maybe it'll be another clear night," she said.

"And we can do some star gazing?" Wyatt grinned and held his hands together as if he was praying. "I can only hope," he said just before the two caught up with the rest of the group.

Chapter 30

Leda had no idea of the time. Her stomach rumbled. Usually, she would take that as a sign it must be lunchtime, but her stomach had behaved oddly with off and on bouts of nausea since yesterday, so she didn't think it was a very good gauge of the time. Erik had mentioned another hot lunch today, this time at camp. They weren't there yet. The trail remained relatively flat as it wound through the valley. Earlier hikers stayed in this valley, and Leda imagined drank the water and washed in the stream, but toilets built too close to the stream threatened to foul it and the camp had to be moved onto the plateau overlooking the valley; the stream was one of the last sources of clean water close to the summit.

A porter waited by some boulders at the base of the day's last uphill, a thin track that climbed at a scary angle. The porter held two lunch boxes, one for Gail and the other for Tom. Last night, Tom asked for an earlier lunch. He said he had a hard time waiting so long for lunch when they climbed to the Lava Tower. The older couple settled on one of the boulders, and opened their lunch boxes. Both had big pieces of roasted chicken, a hardboiled egg, an orange and *sambosas*.

Leda looked at the lunches with longing. She dug into her pocket for her flavored lip balm and smeared some on her lips.

"That looks good," Wyatt said. He leaned in jostling the lunch box on Gail's knees.

"Settle down," Tom said. "You made your choice this morning. You'll get your hot lunch on top." He bit into the chicken and made a show of smacking his lips.

"You're terrible," Gail said. She took a dainty bite of chicken.

"How about sharing?" Wyatt said.

Gail took a bigger bite. "You just go ahead. Don't worry about us."

Jen had already started up the steep trail on the other side of the ravine. Leda couldn't wait to sink her own teeth into a piece of juicy roasted chicken and she followed the other girl up the zigzags. Before she was too far up, Leda felt out of breath. Jen slowed in front of her. Leda could hear her pop and Wyatt talking behind her. She was too tired and hungry to worry about their conversation, and was dragging by the time they reached the sloping plateau.

Their tents were set up further down the slope than others, and were more scattered than before because of the rocky terrain. Leda and the rest headed straight to the dining tent only to find out their hot lunch wasn't ready. Wyatt handed around one of the energy biscuit packs he had saved. Even Leda was desperate enough to take one.

Munching on a biscuit, Leda trudged to the tents. The porters had dumped her stuff in the same pup tent with her father's. Leda looked around the campsite for her pop. He wasn't around. Should she move to Jen's tent? Her father had given no sign during the morning hike he would reconsider and tell her more about her mother. But if she stayed with Jen would she miss out on another opportunity to persuade him? Leda was still trying to decide when Jen called to her from a pup tent staked just up the slope. "Stay with me again." Leda hesitated. Experience told her that her pop would not change his mind. That she would give in before he did. But hope kept her lingering at the door of the pup tent. She saw her father walking up the hill from the toilet, head down, watching, she assumed for stray lava rocks that could trip him. Before this trip, Leda thought she had her pop figured out. The photo of her mother and his admission it was her mother had stunned Leda. Her old assumptions about her parents were like the tiny clouds of dust puffing from the soles of his boots as he came closer. And that's where her pop had been quite clear he wanted to leave her questions about her mother: behind in the dust. Leda grabbed her duffel and her sleeping mat. She tucked her sleeping bag under her arm and moved to Jen's tent. The girls had just finished setting up when lunch was announced.

Leda ducked into the dining tent with Jen. A large metal pot steamed on the table, spewing the familiar scents of ginger and garlic. Leda knew ginger was supposed to settle your stomach, but she was beginning to loath the smell; maybe because she had come to associate it with the nausea rising in her stomach. Another serving bowl was filled with what looked like cooked cabbage. Platters of pineapple slices and white bread rounded out the meal.

"There's no chicken." Wyatt said. "We've been robbed." He picked at the food heaped on his plate.

Leda thought of Tom and Gail enjoying their cold chicken lunches, and from the disgruntled looks of the others, she imagined they were thinking the same. Her pop took a chair about halfway down the table. He spooned a heaping lump of cabbage onto his plate, balancing two pieces of bread on top. There was no choice but to eat what was before them, and soon Leda joined the others in spooning the now familiar broth, chewing on the disappointing cabbage, and breaking off pieces of the tasteless white bread. Leda thought of roast chicken and hardboiled eggs. Yes, she was hungry, but her stomach was too tender to imagine anything richer. She sipped her cup of hot water.

After lunch, Leda wound her way down to the nearest outhouse, her thighs aching with the tension of navigating the steep, gravelly slope. Her tender ankle protested. She would have to remember to ask Wyatt about some ointment, and maybe she would need to wrap her ankle to give it more support. The outhouse perched at the lowest edge of camp. Like the others, it consisted of wooden planks nailed together to make the narrowest possible room. Leda knocked and called out before reaching for the door. The latches didn't always keep the door secure. Leda didn't want to surprise anyone already using the toilet hole. She would be humiliated if someone opened the door on her. No one answered, so Leda pulled the door open and halted in surprise. The small building had only three walls, the back one was missing and opened to a spectacular view of the Karanga Valley. She supposed that was one way of keeping the horrible smell down. She, however, would not be lingering to enjoy the view!

Leda headed back up the hill to her tent. She couldn't imagine negotiating the rock-strewn slope at night. Still, the camp was completely devoid of bushes, so it would take a brave soul and a very dark night to pee just outside the tent. Leda sighed. If she were a man, Leda could pee in one of her water bottles: if she had brought an extra one. Leda knew she shouldn't complain. She had chosen to make this climb. She had looked forward to this climb. She was in Africa. Somehow, the same excitement just wasn't there. Her pop stood outside his tent. Waiting for her? Leda stopped by him.

"Staying with Jen tonight?" he said.

"She asked." Leda scuffed the toe of her boot in the dirt.

"It's different hiking with a group." Her father seemed to choose his words carefully. Leda said nothing. "You seem to be making new friends," he said. Again, Leda kept quiet. "This type of experience tends to heighten emotions."

Leda looked at her pop, "what are you saying?"

"Just a word of caution," he said. "Intense adventures can lead to intense bonds that often don't hold up later." He fiddled with the ends of his kerchief.

"Like us? Is that what's happened to us?" Leda said. "All those hiking trips together, and now you refuse to answer my questions about my mother." She kicked a rock loose from the dirt. "I trusted you." She thrust her clenched fists into her jacket pocket.

Her father took a step back towards the tent. "I was talking about Wyatt."

"Seriously?" A bubble of laughter shot from her. She couldn't help it.

"Does he know about Henry?"

"There's nothing to know about Henry," Leda said, her voice rising. "We went on one date."

"You're not talking marriage?" His eyebrows drew together, his forehead wrinkled.

"It was a joke," she said. "And yes, Wyatt knows I don't have a boyfriend."

Her father's forehead cleared. "All the more reason for you to exercise caution," he said, speaking as if Leda were both his daughter and his employee. "Trail romances don't often work out in real life."

"Pop this isn't a reality show," Leda said. "Or are you talking from your own experience? Did your college romance go south?"

"I've never stopped loving your mother." Her father's words were quiet.

"Why did you separate then? Did she stop loving you?"

A sigh shook her father, surprising Leda. "I don't believe so," he said. He turned, crawled into his tent and zipped the flap before Leda could say anything more.

Chapter 31

David pulled out the chair at the end of the table and sat with his back to the tent flap and the night outside. He was glad to be back with his group. They looked rested and happy in the flickering candlelight, eating good helpings of beef stew on rice. David and two porters carried the fresh meat up the mountain from the Mweka Gate late this afternoon. Getting used to the altitude was not a problem for him or the two young men. They could climb up and down this mountain all day long. Peter Mgubo ran up the mountain and back last year setting a new record. Too bad his Chagga ancestors did not have the same abilities. A doctor in one of David's hiking groups explained why. The doctor said once the Chagga began climbing the mountain, it took many generations before the boys (or girls) were born with lungs made for the thin air. Whatever the reason, David thanked God for his special lungs. They helped him earn more money than others. His family lived in a house with a separate bedroom just for him and Grace.

His hikers needed protein if they were to be successful. Not all of the trekking groups got fresh meat. When the ice melted, food poisoning sickened many hikers. His group had been lucky yesterday with the sleet storm. The drop in temperature made it possible for the older Americans to still enjoy the last of the chicken.

Tonight, David only had one worry. He couldn't find Erik Ngala. None of the porters knew where the assistant guide was. Erik led the group to the Karanga Valley, and then vanished. It was hard for a man to hide on the barren slopes. But still, Erik was doing it. David remembered his talk with Erik at Barafu Camp. The older man was understandably bitter about the death of his nephew.

But that was the nature of life.

Death was not uncommon in their country from AIDS/HIV. It was a less frequent visitor to the mountain, but still a visitor. Maybe Erik's nephew would have lived if he owned a warmer coat. Maybe he wouldn't have. It was a risk all the porters and guides took each trip. Who knew what could happen? The mountain might get stirred up and snatch someone who looked healthy. David remembered passing one white man who looked to be about 40-years-old lying dead by the trail less than one kilometer from the final camp on his way to the summit. Luckily, night covered most of the mountain and no one in his hiking group noticed the man was dead. They were too busy with their own struggles to the summit. Later, people said the man fell over with a heart attack. They pressed their hands to their own chests and talked about the surprise of it.

David accepted a big serving of stew from Gail.

"How's Chase?" The young American woman leaned across the table asking her question before David could eat a single bite of the stew. She seemed worried; her voice shook around the edges. David remembered her smile the first day on the trail.

"He is well," David said. "Almost as soon as we got to the rain forest he was much improved."

"Good." The young woman still leaned on the table.

"He will greet you at the Mweka Gate." At the young woman's puzzled look, David explained, "At the finish."

"Three more days!" Jen said. "I don't know."

Gail rubbed the young woman's back. She spoke to Jen in a soothing voice. "It's not forever."

Jen slumped in her chair. "I guess." She spooned some stew into her mouth.

"I'm glad you're back," Gail said to David. "I missed you."

"I'll second that," Tom said.

"Erik is a fine guide," David said. "He brought you to Karanga Valley."

No one spoke. The silence got David to thinking about Erik again. Why would the older man leave when he knew David and the others would be coming today? Had Erik left because David was returning? If the other guide didn't appear soon, David would ask the porters to help look for him. Erik couldn't survive the night outdoors. It would be suicide to try such a thing. If it came to that, all David could do was pray. But for now, David simply hoped the man would reappear. It would be best for all of them.

Distant shouts drew David from his chair and to the flap of the dining tent. Many lights waved and scurried further down the slope. Someone ran by, shouting in Swahili that a *wazungu* had fallen.

"What's going on?" It was the older son, speaking behind David's shoulder.

"Someone is hurt," David said. "I'll be back." David stepped outside.

"I'm coming." The older son was already clicking on his light and zipping his coat. David hurried to the spot where the lights seemed to have stopped. He heard Wyatt zigzagging behind him, surefooted in his steps.

A loose group of people gathered near the three-walled toilet. A white woman with a red cap and a pink snow coat rocked back and forth on the ground her leg bent at an odd angle. She groaned and cursed. A man, maybe her husband, patted her shoulder. Wyatt pushed his way to the front of the group. He knelt next to the woman. David saw the young American's lips moving, but couldn't hear his words over the woman's curses.

Someone, it must be the woman's guide, appeared with a stick that looked like a tent pole. Together, the second man and Wyatt worked to straighten the woman's leg and tie it to the pole. When they were about done, two porters showed up with a stretcher. David hoped the woman's guide had enough pain medicine to help her down the mountain. It would be a long bumpy ride on the stretcher. It had taken David most of the day to climb up. Downhill was shorter, and the porters would run. Still it would be four to six hours before they reached the bottom of the mountain. The husband gripped the woman's hand as the porters lifted her, but he was forced to stay behind as the porters disappeared into the night jogging with the injured woman.

"Will her husband follow?" Jen's voice came from behind David. He turned and saw his group gathered near him.

"Most likely," David said. "There is his guide."

"I want to go with them," Jen stepped forward.

"The summit is very soon," David said.

"I don't care," Jen said. "I want to be with Chase. I never should have let him go back down the mountain alone."

"Are you sure?" Gail touched Jen's arm. "David told us Chase is fine."

"He's resting at the hotel," David said.

"Then that's where I want to be." Jen's voice was firm.

"Let her go," Tom said. "Love conquers all, but apparently not the summit."

No one laughed at Tom's joke. Wyatt snorted.

Jen walked over to the man with the injured wife, and David was forced to follow.

"That one is helpful." Erik spoke from the dark. David looked out of the corner of his eye. He was embarrassed he had not noticed Erik's approach.

"Who?" David said.

"The young American," Erik said.

David watched Wyatt speaking to the upset husband. "Where have you been?"

"The elephant graveyard."

David turned to stare at Erik. "No one knows where that is."

"Our Chagga ancestors did. They told of dying elephants throwing themselves into an ash pit." Erik spoke with authority.

David persisted even though he knew it might be thought of as rude to question an elder. "Where is the pit?"

Erik stared at the ground, kicking the toe of his boot against a rock. When he looked up, he kept his lips pressed shut. David wouldn't get any answers about the graveyard from the older guide. It was useless to keep asking. Erik appeared well, and that was all that mattered. His presence would be important to the success of the group.

Wyatt joined the two guides. "Poor woman," he said, shaking his head.

David was already thinking about how he should warn his group about the dangers of moving around the camp at night. His group was growing smaller and he couldn't afford to lose any more.

Chapter 32

Leda shivered on a boulder outside Wyatt's tent waiting for his return. This was the last full night the group would spend on the ascent trail. Tomorrow, they would start for the summit at midnight. While she had been shocked by Jen's abrupt departure, Leda understood Jen's motives. What she didn't get was her father. He said he never stopped loving Leda's mother. He said Leda's mother loved him. Then, why did they separate? Why didn't her father cross the ocean to be with his love? Why did his love cross the ocean to get away from her pop? Was the separation somehow Leda's fault?

Tents glowed here and there from within, hikers getting settled for the night. Leda figured between one and two hundred must be camped on this plateau. Some groups didn't bother to make this stop, but continued on to Barafu Camp at 15,200 feet. She had read pros and cons about sleeping at the higher altitude camp. Both she and her father decided it would be best to spend the extra day on the trail. Sleeping at higher altitude could be a problem. Some groups hiked all the way to the crater and spent the night at 18,500 feet before climbing to the summit. Staying a little more than 800 feet from the summit seemed good in theory, only a one mile hike required in the morning. But, Leda learned some in those groups suffered severely from altitude sickness and had to abort their summit attempt altogether. Better to be safe than sorry.

Leda hunched into her down coat. Wyatt and his parents had helped Jen pack up her things and get on her way back down the mountain to Chase. A porter would follow Jen with her duffel and sleeping bag, but the tent still stood with Leda's stuff inside.

The clear night sky Wyatt had wished for arched overhead, bursting with stars. Leda could even see the lights of the city of Moshi twinkling in the distance. She could no longer feel the tip of her nose. She wriggled her toes in her boots to keep them warm. A few more minutes, and then she would give up and return to the tent. But which one? Should she stay by herself in Jen's abandoned tent or rejoin her father? Leda touched the photo of her mother in her coat pocket. She brought it to show to Wyatt. After seeing the way he helped the injured woman, his patience and care with her, Leda was ready to tell Wyatt her story. He was a guy; maybe he could give her some ideas on how to get the information she wanted from her pop.

Leda stood and stamped her feet to keep them warm. Wyatt seemed to materialize out of the dark beside her. "Hey," he brushed against her, bumping his shoulder against hers. Leda pressed her hand against her mouth muffling her startled scream.

"You scared me." Leda tapped Wyatt's upper arm with a light fist. "Where's your light?"

"No need for it," Wyatt said. "Look how bright the stars are."

Leda shivered and jammed her hands further down into her coat pockets. "What took so long?"

"You've been waiting for me?" Wyatt said.

Leda took a deep breath. Her exhale was a ghostly fog. "You asked me today how old I was when my mother died." Leda paused.

Wyatt stayed silent as if he sensed her need for some space, relaxed in his stance: his gloved hands held loosely by his side, his head tipped back so he could view the stars. Leda studied his shadowed face. He was different from anyone she had ever known. Wyatt lived comfortably in his own skin. He didn't seem to care what others thought. Leda wished she knew his secret. She didn't realize until now, this moment, how limited her world had been. She couldn't blame her pop. She was an adult. She had chosen the ease of familiarity. But now her worldview was skewed, and she could use Wyatt's help.

"I'd like to tell you," Leda said. "It's kind of a complicated story."

"Your tent or mine?" Wyatt said.

Leda hesitated.

"Be practical," Wyatt said. "It's freezing out." Wyatt blew into his gloved hands.

Leda was silent.

"It's strange to see those city lights," Wyatt said turning to face Moshi. "We think we're so far back in the wilderness. Dirty. Struggling to survive. I remember hiking in the Desolation Wilderness one time near Lake Tahoe. Climbed a mountain expecting to see more wilderness, but the South Lake Tahoe Casinos were right below me. Lined up on the shore. I could even see cars driving on the road." Wyatt shook his head. Leda shivered again. "Your tent or mine?" Wyatt said.

Leda clicked on her light and headed to Wyatt's tent, paused for him to unzip the flap then crawled in. Wyatt followed her, first taking the time to remove his boots. Leda had never thought of him as large, but his presence filled the tent.

"Want to take off your boots?" Wyatt said.

"That's okay," Leda said. She sat with her boots towards the door, her sweeping gaze taking in Wyatt's tent. Clothes exploded out of his duffel, and if Leda didn't know better, she would have said a child had gotten into his daypack, crumbs, half-eaten bars and wrappers littered the small area. His rumpled sleeping bag was the only clear space.

"I'm the bane of my mother's existence," Wyatt said without apology. He began cleaning the tent, stuffing his clothes back into his duffel, shoving the wrappers and food into his daypack. "Didn't expect company." He finally settled on his sleeping bag, stretched out with his feet still encased in his wool socks near Leda, his head propped on his open palm. "I'm not sure you want to spend much time near these." Wyatt wiggled his toes.

By this time, Leda figured something would have to smell really bad – like the African toilets - to bother her. She didn't even think she stunk, which probably wasn't true, but given what she had to compare her body odor with she knew she couldn't trust her own judgment. She remembered returning to civilization from other backpack trips with her father. The two thought they looked and smelled pretty good in the clean t-shirts they had saved for just this purpose. That is until they slid into a restaurant booth and noticed the other customers didn't have stains on their shirts or dirt lining their fingernails or greasy hair stuffed in their ball caps. Still, Leda scooted closer to the end of the tent where Wyatt had set up his pillow, straightening her legs but keeping her boots near the tent flap.

Leda began to feel nervous about showing Wyatt the photo. She chose a safer topic, "Jen all set?"

"Think so," Wyatt said. "How's your ankle?" He offered to massage some ointment into her ankle earlier, but Leda simply accepted the tube he held in his hand.

"Better," Leda said. "Thanks for the loan." She dug in her pocket and held out the tube. Wyatt pointed to his duffel, and she tucked it inside.

The tent grew silent. Leda played with the tip of her braid, and then turned to look at Wyatt. He watched her beneath lowered lids. Leda felt warm, the persistent nausea she had felt since dinner nearly forgotten.

"I remember asking you about your mother" he said.

Leda didn't know where to begin. For one thing, looking at Wyatt stretched out on his sleeping bag made her want nothing more than to lie down next to him and feel his arms wrapped around her, comforting her, keeping her safe. And afterwards, who knew? Leda's cheeks flamed.

"I'm a good listener," Wyatt said. "I'll just lie here until you're ready." Wyatt unzipped his down coat, and rested his head on his pillow. He closed his eyes. Leda studied his face. The constant mountain wind had burned color into his skin, peeling spots on his cheeks and his nose. After four days growth, his beard looked soft. Leda imagined if she kissed him now, her chin wouldn't be scratched like it had been at the Barranco Valley camp. She unzipped her jacket. Wyatt opened his eyes at the sound. "It's getting warm in here," he said. He took off his wool cap and tossed it aside. Leda smothered a smile at the sight of his shaggy hair, sticking together in clumps like messy, greasy French fries.

"Hey," Wyatt said, "my hair's too short for a braid."

"I don't know." Leda leaned close and grabbed a fistful of his hair. She tried to braid a section of it, but Wyatt playfully slapped her hands away and reached for the rubber band holding her braid in place. Somehow in the ensuing scuffle, Leda lost her headlamp. The light beam shot uselessly towards the side of the tent. But Leda didn't notice as, tossing all her usual caution aside, she lowered her face to kiss Wyatt. He tasted like garlic and ginger, and she imagined she did too. Leda still wore her down coat and her boots, and her skin flushed red, her forehead beaded with sweat. Her heart raced. Overheated, she broke off the kiss. Wyatt touched her back. He didn't press for an explanation. Leda burst into tears.

One part of her observed the girl sobbing in Wyatt's tent as if she were an alien creature. Leda didn't allow emotions to rule her. She had learned that lesson well from her father. Overwhelming emotion meant weakness. And Leda was not weak. But now, here she was: a sodden mess. She felt exposed, raw, broken and ashamed. She didn't know at what point Wyatt sat up and drew her into his arms. She didn't know when she relaxed and pressed her cheek to his chest, her tears soaking his down jacket. All she knew was she wasn't alone.

Leda's headlamp still shot its light at the side of the tent, a round circle doing nothing when she stopped crying. She kept her eyes closed. She stayed with her cheek nestled in the damp softness of Wyatt's down jacket.

Leda's leg muscles were beyond sore. Her skin felt dirty, her hair greasy, her stomach sick. She was exhausted from climbing the mountain and trying to figure out why her mother left her, why her father wouldn't talk to her about it. For now, just for now, she wanted to stay in this moment, in Wyatt's arms.

"Do you want to spend the night?" Wyatt's voice was low. Leda felt his warm breath on her hair.

"I never do this."

"Do what?"

"Spend the night on a first date."

"I thought our first date was at Shira Camp," Wyatt said. "We didn't even kiss until our second date last night."

Leda's laugh was small and shaky.

"You're going to have to take off your boots."

Leda laughed again and withdrew from the circle of Wyatt's arms. Pushing her hair out of her face, she swiped at her eyes with the back of her hands. She considered Wyatt's mummy bag. "Can we both fit in that?"

"If we take off our jackets," Wyatt said. He unzipped his and threw it towards his duffel.

Leda unlaced her boots and set them side- by- side near the tent flap. Her back was turned, but she heard Wyatt unzip his sleeping bag. His pants flew by her face and landed on his clothes explosion. When she looked around, he already was in the sleeping bag and holding it open for her. He wore his complete set of long underwear, and Leda imagined his socks. The underwear wasn't tight. Still, Leda could see the outline of Wyatt's muscles. He didn't appear to have an ounce of fat.

Leda stripped off her jacket and pants and tossed them by Wyatt's. She slid into Wyatt's sleeping bag, definitely a tight fit. With a quick tap of her finger she clicked off her headlamp and plunged the tent into darkness.

Chapter 33

"Shit" Wyatt pulled away. "I've got a neck cramp."

"Bad?" Leda said.

"Hurts like hell." Wyatt rubbed his neck, nearly poking Leda in the eye with his elbow.

"Watch it," she said, swiveling her head just in time.

"Sorry. I must have strained a muscle when I helped lift that lady onto the stretcher. Just my luck."

Leda pushed the sleeping bag down past her waist to get some air.

"You're leaving?" Wyatt said. He still massaged his neck and the top of his shoulder.

Leda sat up. She pressed her palm against her mouth. "I feel sick"

At Leda's words, the two started laughing. Leda struggled to keep her laughter quiet; she didn't want to wake the others. Soon, tears streamed down her face and she felt on the verge of another crying jag.

"We're a pair," Wyatt said. He settled on his back.

Leda's laughter died down to hiccups, "Which shoulder?"

Wyatt pointed to the one furthest from her. "Come back," he said. "You won't hurt me."

Leda returned her head to his chest "Guess hiking four days at high altitude isn't the best foreplay," she said.

Wyatt wrapped his fingers around her shoulder. "And not mentioned in the guide books."

The two started laughing again. Leda felt the rise and fall of Wyatt's chest, his heartbeat in her ear.

He pulled the sleeping bag back up so she wasn't exposed to the freezing temperatures. "So what did you want to tell me about your mother?"

Leda couldn't help the laughter that bubbled out of her. "Seriously?"

"Of course."

"A dark tent is perfect for...talking."

Wyatt expelled an exaggerated sigh, and pressed a soft kiss on her hair.

Leda snuggled into Wyatt, the top of her head in the crook of his neck. She did find it easier to talk about things that truly mattered in the dark. She didn't know how the habit had developed. She knew she hated the shadow of disappointment or the fleeting grimace that would cross her father's face at certain topics, especially those involving her mother. He always said Leda could tell him anything. But as a child and then as a teenager, she tuned into his expressions like an alert cat ready to dart out of harm's way. In the dark, she could relax in the feel of someone nearby, someone she could hear breathing but not have to look at. Her mind was always clearer, freer somehow.

"You asked earlier how old I was when my mother died," Leda said. She took Wyatt's grunt as acknowledgement and she plunged into the heart of her recent discovery.

"My father let me think she died when I was really young, maybe two. But I found out on my London stopover that she died in a car accident when I was twelve."

"That's crazy."

"My father lied to me."

"What about your mom?" Wyatt said.

Leda felt the tears threaten again. "I have a photo of her in my jacket." She sat up to retrieve it, the sleeping bag falling from her shoulders again. Leda lay back down, holding the photo above her, staring at it as if she could see her mother's face in the dark. "When I got it, I wasn't sure it was her. I guess I was in shock. I didn't ask too many questions."

"Has your dad seen it?"

"At Shira Camp," Leda said. "He said it was her."

"That's the night you were yelling at him?"

Leda nodded even though she knew Wyatt couldn't see. Maybe he felt her head move against his chest.

"I'm sorry," Wyatt said. "That's tough."

The tears spilled at Wyatt's words, running unchecked down Leda's cheeks. Neither spoke. The tent and campsite hushed as if holding its collective breath.

Wyatt's next words were barely above a whisper Leda strained to hear.

"Maybe your dad thought he was protecting you," Wyatt said.

Leda sniffed. "I haven't been a child for a long time."

"What about your mom?" Wyatt said. "Did she call or email?"

Leda mumbled, "No."

"But your dad, he's always been there for you? Taken care of you?"

"I could have written my mom, called, maybe visited."

"You were just a kid," Wyatt said.

The truth of Wyatt's words hurt. She had just been a kid. A kid her mother didn't want. It felt like a heavy hand squeezed her heart. Leda peeled the sleeping bag from her shoulders.

"You don't understand," she said through gritted teeth. She clutched the photo in her hand, bending the edge.

Leda struggled to sit up, but Wyatt's grip tightened on her shoulder. "I know it hurts," Wyatt said. Leda ignored him, continuing with her struggles. Wyatt let her go. "If you're thinking of running to your tent you'll freeze your butt off in that underwear."

Leda freed herself from the mummy bag, the warm cocoon slipping to her waist. What did Wyatt know about hurt? He hadn't been abandoned like a deformed puppy left by its mother. In fact, Gail begged him to come on this trip.

"Now we're both cold," Wyatt snatched at the bag and arranged it to cover his chest.

"I can't believe you're a lifeguard," Leda said. "You have zero empathy."

"I get that you were shocked," Wyatt said. "And your dad shouldn't have lied to you. But maybe, in the end, he did you a favor."

Leda stuck the photo back in her jacket pocket. She crossed her arms over her chest to control her shivers.

"You turned out okay," Wyatt said.

Leda wasn't sure about that – there must be something wrong with her if her mother threw her away without even giving Leda a chance to prove herself.

Wyatt spoke in measured tones, "People make choices."

"Choices to abandon their child?" Leda wanted to shake her fist against the injustice, preferably in Wyatt's face, he was being so aggravating, but necessity kept her hands busy rubbing her arms. Her teeth began to chatter.

"Sometimes, yes," Wyatt said. "But your dad stayed."

Leda remembered her father saying much the same thing at Shira Camp. Would her life have been better with a mother? A mother who lived overseas and exchanged occasional emails? Maybe not, but Leda would never know. And that was the crux of the matter. Leda hadn't been given the opportunity to make that decision. She forgot all about Wyatt's point that she had been a child during that time.

Biting cold seeped into her bones. Leda could pull on her pants, slide her arms into her down jacket and thrust her feet into her chilled boots. She could dash to her tent, the tent she was supposed to share with Jen. She could take off her boots, jacket and pants and slither into her freezing sleeping bag. How long would it take for her body heat to warm it? And even then, how warm would she be through the rest of the night without another person in the tent? She thought about fighting the gravity of the slope. Waking up to find her body huddled against her duffel bag at the bottom of her tent. Straightening back up, only to repeat the same motions over and over again throughout the night. Or, she could lie back down and be instantly cozy next to Wyatt: his body fighting the pull of gravity with her.

Wyatt didn't speak. But Leda knew he would welcome her back into his arms. Leda sighed. Her tent seemed miles away in the frigid dark. She might stumble over a rock. Break her leg and even suffer a concussion like that woman. Wyatt held the sleeping bag open for her.

"Come back," he said. "I won't leave you."

His words sounded sincere, and somehow Leda knew she could trust Wyatt. He had stuck with her on the trail, encouraged her to conquer the Barranco Wall. There was no reason she shouldn't believe him when he promised to stay with her. She thought of Jen's warning, at least he couldn't leave until the end of the trail.

Leda lay down. Wyatt rearranged the sleeping bag. He rubbed her arm with his warm hand. Leda settled herself against him more than glad she had chosen him over her cold tent. Wyatt's shirt was damp from her tears and she smelled a faint hint of pine in the wet fabric she imagined came from his laundry soap. The worn material was a soft cushion, and Leda relaxed into Wyatt's embrace. Her stomach was heavy with a feeling like seasickness, her heart swollen with a black grief for the mother she never knew. The nausea would go away as soon as they got to a lower altitude. But her heart felt like it would be damaged forever. Leda snuggled closer to Wyatt – it was a good fit and she felt safe. Soon, Wyatt's hand dropped away. Leda wondered if the cramp in his neck had worked itself out, if he had fallen asleep. Her eyelids fluttered closed.

"Sometimes I look at Chase and Jen and I wonder if I've fallen behind," Wyatt said.

Leda's eyes snapped open. "Fallen behind?"

"My younger brother, married. Pulling in the big bucks. Talking about buying a house."

"You love your job."

Wyatt chuckled. "Look who's talking."

"I asked you to forgive me."

Wyatt's arm tightened around Leda. "Maybe it's not the job, maybe it's the relationship."

Leda stilled. Wyatt couldn't be talking about her. Could he? She had never pictured herself with someone like Wyatt. He was attractive in an earthy sort of way. So different from the academic types she usually dated.

"You're young," Leda said.

"I'm twenty nine. Most of my childhood friends are like Chase."

Leda didn't know what to say. Maybe Wyatt was simply making a general observation. Maybe he wasn't suggesting anything personal. Maybe she imagined he drew her closer. Her heart raced anyway.

"But then I think about your parents and mine," Wyatt said.

Leda's heart slowed. "What about your parents?" she said.

"My dad cheated on my mom." Wyatt spoke like he was reporting the news, but it wasn't hard to pick up on the hurt underlying his words. "I don't know if it's possible to be happy with one person for the rest of your life."

"You can't mean that," Leda said.

"I'll risk my life all day to save others," Wyatt said. "But love… I don't know."

"Just because your dad hurt your mom? Or is it because he hurt you?" Wyatt liked to give the impression he was a go with the flow kind of guy – and he was very good at it – but now she was getting a glimpse of a deeper layer.

"So you're a romantic?" he said, changing the subject.

"I always thought my parents' story was romantic," Leda said. "They got married after a short time together, and then my mother died tragically. My father never remarried. I thought he could never find anyone like my mother."

"Maybe he couldn't."

Leda shrugged.

"You don't know the whole story," Wyatt said. "Maybe something kept them apart. Something out of their control."

"Now you sound like a romantic," Leda said. "Besides, my pop won't tell me anything so I'll never know the truth."

"The truth isn't always what it's cracked up to be." Wyatt was silent for a moment. Leda listened to thud of his heart, her ear pressed to his chest. "I was happier in my ignorance."

"Why did your mother take you dad back?" Leda wondered why the two reconciled when her parents didn't. "Was she afraid of being alone?"

"Tom asked for her forgiveness."

"And she gave it?"

"She didn't take him back for a long time," Wyatt said. "They had to go to counseling. She had to see he meant it when he said he was sorry."

"What happened then?"

"My mother's big on forgiveness," Wyatt said. "She hasn't stopped dropping hints to me this whole trip. She'd like me to forgive Tom."

"Will you?"

"About two months after my mom kicked Tom out, he got in a car accident, rear-ended on the freeway, his car pushed into another," Wyatt said. "The front end collapsed and crushed his leg. They had to cut him out. I figured he got what he deserved. That God was punishing him for what he did to my mom."

"And you don't think he's suffered enough?" Leda lifted her head and tilted her chin back to look at Wyatt.

"What about your dad?" Wyatt said.

"My mother was the one killed in the car accident," she said, settling her head back on Wyatt's chest. "Not my father."

Chapter 34

A dim light filled the tent. Someone walked by, boots scraping against a rock. Leda surveyed the small space between her lashes, disoriented for a moment, not sure why she couldn't move her arm.

"Hey sleepyhead." Wyatt's voice sounded scratchy.

Leda tilted her chin up to look at him. He kissed her. So that's why she felt so warm, she still pressed against Wyatt in his mummy bag. Her arm, fallen asleep, trapped against his body. As much as she enjoyed the kiss, Leda was distressed it was morning. She had meant to sneak back to her tent just before dawn to avoid being seen emerging from Wyatt's tent. Wyatt's kiss deepened, and Leda forgot all about her worries. Her father's and Jen's warning couldn't be further from her mind. She really liked Wyatt

"Habari za asubuhi." A porter spoke on the other side of the tent flap.

"Dammit," Wyatt flung back the sleeping bag. "Guess we'll have to finish this another time." He reached for the tent flap.

Leda slid deeper into the sleeping bag, pulling it over her head. Her arm and fingers tingled as the blood rushed back. Maybe she could somehow get to her tent unnoticed.

"Nzuri," Wyatt said to the porter outside the tent. "Asante sana."

Leda waited until she heard the zipper close before she emerged from the bag. Wyatt held two steaming cups. He grinned and held one out to her. "We're not fooling the porters."

Leda groaned. "How will I face your mother? Not to mention my father?"

"They're old, but they're not dead," Wyatt said. He took leisurely sips of his coffee as if he didn't care what their parents thought. Somehow his hair looked the same as it had last night. The dirt and grease apparently holding it in place better than any expensive hair gel. Leda raised her free hand to her own hair. One side was flat, the rest felt hopelessly tangled.

Wyatt leaned over to kiss her. His breath tasted like coffee. "You're a mess," he said, his tone cheerful.

"You're no help." Leda tried to mimic his uncaring attitude. She stopped patting her hair and lifted her coffee to her lips. The hot liquid scalded the back of her throat. She swore she could feel it shoot all the way down to her stomach. She gave up on her pretense. "I should go. Maybe no one else is out of their tents yet."

"What if someone sees you like this?"

"Quit joking around." Leda put her cup down.

"Don't rush off." Wyatt held her hand and dropped a light kiss on the palm. Leda couldn't help but shiver.

"I'm great with knots," Wyatt said. Leda raised her eyebrows. "It's a lifeguard thing."

Wyatt set aside his cup. "Turn around."

A few more minutes wouldn't matter. And truthfully, Leda wasn't in a rush to leave Wyatt's tent and possibly run into his mother or his father, and especially not her own father. Leda wasn't sure she believed the lifeguard and knots bit. Wyatt probably learned to braid hair by practicing on other women. She found she didn't care as Wyatt worked at her tangles with gentle care. He took his time picking at the knots, and when he was done freeing them all, he ran his fingers like a comb through her hair. Leda enjoyed every bit of the attention. She felt disappointed when he divided her hair into three sections and efficiently threaded them into a braid. Leda brushed the finished product with the tips of her fingers.

"You are good," she said.

Wyatt leaned in for another kiss, but Leda turned her face so his lips landed on her cheek. "Breakfast will be ready soon," she said. "I need to get out of here." She started to scoot to the end of the tent for her clothes and boots, but Wyatt's hand on her arm stopped her.

"Maybe I've been wrong about love," he said.

Leda looked at him. "Meaning?"

"Maybe you'd like San Diego."

Someone walked too close to the tent, boots scuffling before Leda could reply. She reached for her clothes and boots, nervous about discovery and nervous about what Wyatt was suggesting. She heard Wyatt rustling around, but concentrated on her own efforts. She laced her boots, her fingers faltering over the loops, running one explanation after another through her mind as to why she spent the night in Wyatt's tent, why Wyatt mentioned San Diego to her. Wyatt crawled up next to her. He had pulled his wool cap low over his forehead, his down coat was zipped; he held his thick gloves in his hand.

"I'll see if the coast is clear," he said unzipping the tent flap. His breath fogged in the blast of early morning air. He winked at her, mouthed the word "later" and zipped the flap behind him. Leda waited. She heard his boots crunch on the dirt – it must be frozen. Seconds passed. Impatient, Leda raised her hand to unzip the flap.

"Hey Mom." Wyatt's voice sounded not five feet away. Leda held her breath.

"Habari za asubuhi," Gail said. She sounded as cheerful as her son.

Leda listened as the two headed away from Wyatt's tent, their voices dwindling. After a few more moments of silence, Leda pulled the zipper. She felt like a thief, and she grimaced when she pulled too fast and the zipper's teeth came apart with a *zwooop*. Leda poked her head out of the tent, and just as quickly ducked back inside. Wyatt's father rumbled after Wyatt and Gail, his voice raised in greeting. Her father was unaccounted for. Should she wait in the tent or risk stepping out? Leda huddled behind the nylon flap for a few more anxious moments. Her pop must already be in the dining tent, and Leda really had to pee. She nearly jumped out of the tent, stumbled and righted herself. Leda hurried down the slope, her chin tucked into the zipped neck of her down jacket.

Today was an earlier start than usual so the group could reach the final camp before the summit in time for a hot lunch. The rising sun tinged the edges of some clouds suspended over the valley with soft pinks and oranges. But with the summit at Leda's back, most of the clouds reflected the mountain's looming purple shadow.

Leda dug her hands deeper into her pockets. She had forgotten her gloves in Wyatt's tent. She didn't remember where she tossed them last night. Leda took her time picking her way down the slope to the outhouse, worried about further injury to her ankle. It felt fine this morning, Wyatt's ointment apparently doing wonders, but it wouldn't hurt to be careful especially with the summit attempt just around the corner.

A bitter wind whipped through the missing wall of the outhouse, and Leda gritted her teeth before lowering her pants. She didn't think her butt had ever been this cold before. Steam rose from the pit when she was done. Leda didn't linger, stepping out of the outhouse before her pants were fully zipped. Her pace up the hill was quicker. The dining tent would not be significantly warmer, but maybe hot food would heat her from the inside. Her hands would feel better wrapped around a mug of just boiled water.

The hiking group huddled around the dining table wearing down jackets, hoods or wool caps. Now that the group was down by two, it seemed small, and a little bit weird that Wyatt and Leda were left to hike with their parents. Leda dropped into the seat next to Wyatt.

"The usual?" Wyatt held out a cup of hot water to her. Leda accepted the cup, gripping it in her chilled hands, enjoying the warmth it spread to her fingers. For a brief moment, she imagined sitting at a small table with Wyatt in San Diego. Would it be awkward or feel as natural as it did now?

"No gloves?" Tom said. "You're brave this morning."

"Forgot them in the tent," Leda said. She risked a glance at Wyatt who grinned like an idiot at her. A warm flush crept up her cheeks. Her father cleared his throat. He seemed to be frowning at her red knuckles. When he opened his mouth, Leda cringed at what he might say, but he simply asked for the platter of watermelon. Just then David entered and sat down. Leda couldn't have been more grateful for his arrival than if he had wheeled in a blazing log fireplace.

Talk turned to the day's hike ahead. The group would climb steadily uphill for about two and a half miles to Barafu Hut at 15,200 feet. Today the hikers would find out if the hike and lunch to the Lava Tower paid off as Barafu Camp was at about the same elevation as the Lava Tower.

Ignoring her ever-present nausea, Leda ate a bowl of ginger-flavored porridge. She choked down some fried eggs, a piece of dried toast and a little bit of watermelon. She refused the sausage. The breakfast passed like any of the other meals, the conversation less lively than before. People were wearing down.

After breakfast, David urged the group to gather their daypacks and be ready to start immediately after the goodbye song. Wyatt slipped Leda her gloves while the others danced, somehow managing to hold her fingers a little longer than necessary. Even though she knew this was one of the last goodbye songs, Leda still didn't feel like joining in. Dancing had never really been her thing. Turning away from the dancers, Leda bent to check her snacks and water supply for the day.

"All set?" her father said.

Leda closed her daypack and straightened. She pulled on her gloves

"I see you found them," he added, nodding at her gloves. After the first couple of days of sickness, her pop looked fully recovered. His pants were dirty, his beard a mottled swirl of brown and white. After their last mountain climbing trip, he hadn't shaved for another two weeks just to see how he would look with a beard. That was all it took for them both to agree he looked like a skinny Santa Claus right after a serious hot chocolate spill. Leda smiled at the memory.

"I went by your tent this morning," her father said, "tried to rouse you, but no luck. You warm enough last night?"

Leda felt the heat rising up her neck. "Plenty warm."

"Leda!" Gail called from the middle of the dance. "Come on." The older woman waved her over.

"Leda shook her head. "Maybe next time," she said.

"Only one more time," Gail said. "That'll be your last chance."

It felt like she had been on the mountain forever, but Gail was right. The group would only spend one more night on the trail. And that would be when they were headed downhill and close to exiting out the Mweka Gate.

"I've missed you." Her father's words drew Leda's attention back to him. "Hike with me today?"

Leda nodded. Her father busied himself with getting his daypack organized, taking out his snacks and other supplies, checking his water. Leda was surprised he wasn't ready. He was usually the first and stood around waiting for the others with his daypack already on. When David started up the trail, the other three followed, and still her pop lingered. Now, Leda was suspicious her pop hoped for a bigger gap between the hikers, with the two of them lagging behind. She steeled herself for a lecture about Wyatt, not daring to hope her father planned to tell her more about her mother.

Her father finally slung his daypack on his back. Leda followed behind him without talking. The two continued in silence for some time. The climb seemed easier than previous days, the trail a path worn down by the many boots passing over the mostly bare gravel slope. Leda hoped the feeling of ease meant she was getting used to physical exertion at a high altitude. The glacier capped summit towered in front of them. Massive barren slopes of scree could be seen on the nearer shoulders of the mountain. Leda knew glaciers had covered those shoulders before, hugging them in a frozen embrace. Past explorers to the region were certain the white they saw on the mountaintop were clouds. It never occurred to them there could be snow in Africa. It only showed how preconceived notions could fool you.

"It's too bad about those ice fields," her pop said. "I'm glad we get to see the glaciers that are still here."

"Yeah," Leda said. "They're something." She watched Wyatt walking with his parents. Her thoughts wandered again to the possibility of visiting him in San Diego. Had his invitation been serious?

"I've thought about what you said," her father said, getting her attention. "About how you're an adult now. In fact, I spent a lot of the night thinking. It was too cold to sleep."

Leda felt a twinge of guilt that she had left him alone, and she prepared herself for her pop's lecture. She was certain he was going to warn her again about Wyatt. She wished she didn't have to listen, but there was no escaping, no bushes to disappear behind on a pretend bathroom break - the mountain was completely barren except for some scattered, low-growing Everlastings clinging to the slopes. The altitude kept her from speeding up. She cursed the nausea clinging to her like a leech.

"I've never loved anyone like your mother," he said, his words punctuated by his heavy breathing.

Leda nearly stopped hiking she was so surprised, but she kept putting one foot in front of the other, hardly daring to do more than breathe and keep moving.

"Of course I love you," he said. He stopped and Leda nearly ran into him. "I hope you know that."

Leda looked at her father, standing slightly above her on the trail. The summit's massive bulk was directly behind him. "I do," she said. She wanted to wriggle her hands out of her trekking pole straps and hug her father – he was talking to her about her mother - but he nodded and turned away. They resumed hiking *pole pole.*

His voice floated over his shoulder. It was easy to hear him. The wind wasn't blowing. No birds flew overhead. No giant senecios existed to provide shelter to animal life.

"There was a wildness about her," he said, in between breaths. "A passion for life I found irresistible."

Leda was shocked. She couldn't picture her staid father attracted to wildness in her mother or anyone. She looked at her father's back: the daypack he had purchased for this trip with its myriad of pockets sized for optimum organization. She could see the worn khaki material of his hat, the same hat he had worn on more hiking trips than she could remember. She considered his plodding steps, the deliberate placing of his trekking poles. Leda shook her head.

"We needed each other." Her father's voice sounded sad. "Like you used to need me. But apparently, I've never been enough."

Leda lifted her hand still attached to her trekking pole. She started to reassure her pop. This was her role. But she caught sight of Wyatt not too far ahead; she remembered his air of confidence, his refusal to cater to his father and her hand dropped. She stayed silent. Waiting. Listening. Hoping more was to come.

"You needed a mother," her pop said, "but I was afraid. After your mother left, I couldn't let myself get hurt like that again. What if I fell in love with someone just like her?"

Leda heard footsteps behind her. She expected other hikers to pass like they had done so often on the trail, and she was impatient for them to go by. Her father wouldn't say more until they did. When no one walked past her, Leda looked behind. Erik followed them. She had completely forgotten about the guide. Leda turned back to her father. She had slowed while she looked back, and her pop was ahead now: too far ahead. Leda sped up.

"What do you mean?" Leda's breath was short by the time she caught up to her pop. "Someone like her? What's wrong with that?"

"I've watched you since you were a little girl," her father said. "Every time you got excited or sad, I held my breath, hoping that your emotions wouldn't go too far."

"Why?" Leda grabbed her pop's arm. "Stop. Let's take a break. I can't think."

Her father stepped off the narrow trail onto the graveled slope. "You feel sick?"

"A little." Leda sipped water from the tube near her mouth. Last night's camp appeared like a miniature below them, the orange, yellow and blue tents small colorful triangles in the rocky gray landscape. Was it only a few hours ago she had felt safe slumbering in Wyatt's arms? The mountain's lower slopes and valleys blurred into a bluish, purple haze that hid the city of Moshi. Nearby, hardy grasses and clumps of everlastings – these with larger white flowers than those at the lower altitudes – clung to life amongst the rocks. The sick feeling Leda now counted as part of her daily routine settled in her stomach. Now, she remembered Wyatt's defense of her father, Wyatt's statement he had been happier ignorant of his father's affair. Leda hoped she was ready to hear what her father had to say.

He stood near her. She watched as he opened a bag of trail mix and shook some into his mouth. It was another of their special mixes, this one a jumble of dried cranberries, yogurt covered raisins, almonds and carob chips. He held the bag out to her. Leda shook her head. She drank more water.

"What were you looking for?" Leda said. She curled her toes in her boots as if she needed a better grip on the mountain.

"Natalie, your mother, suffered from bipolar disorder," her pop said. He drew the back of his hand across his lips, rubbed his palm across his beard knocking off the almond crumbs. "I hoped you didn't. As far as I can tell, you don't."

Leda sucked in her breath at the news. She forgot she held the water tube in her mouth, and she coughed and gasped at the surge of water into her windpipe. Her father attempted to pat her back, but she waved him away. Seconds passed while she struggled to regain control.

"Would it be so terrible if I did?" Leda finally gasped. She didn't know much about bipolar disorder, but she assumed medication could help it. "Would you have stopped loving me?"

"I suppose I deserve that." Her father shook his head. He crumpled the empty plastic bag in his hand and stuffed it in a random pocket of his daypack. He looked at Leda and the corners of his mouth turned down. His voice softened, his words broken by his labored breathing. "Natalie stopped taking her medication when she found out she was pregnant with you. I didn't know. She told me later she didn't want to harm the baby. After you were born, she fell into a deep depression. I begged her to get help. I was afraid. I threatened to commit her – at least for a seventy-two hour hold, but she pleaded and begged me not to separate her from you. She got better, and for a long period of time, she was energetic and happy. The two of you seemed to be thriving."

Leda's father took off his sunglasses and wiped the back of his hand across his eyes. He stared into the valley before sliding the glasses back on his face. Leda's toes began to cramp and she was forced to wiggle them in her boots.

"Then, I came home from work one day and you were both gone." This time, he didn't stop the tears. "I didn't think anything of it. It had been a long time since one of her dark periods. Sometimes Natalie lost track of time. It's common enough for mothers of young children. But then the doorbell rang. It was one of our neighbors bringing you home. She said Natalie left you with her earlier that day."

"Where was my mother?" Leda's voice shook. Not only was her father crying, but her toe cramp wouldn't stop. A needle-like pain shot up her arch.

"She went back to her parents, to England." Her father untied the red kerchief and pulled it from his neck. He wiped his cheeks.

"Did you go after her?"

"I flew to England, but Natalie refused to see me. She told her father not to let me in. She told him to tell me she couldn't be trusted with a child. She said I should think of her as dead. After a few days I left. I needed to think of you. But I never could bring myself to divorce her."

"Why didn't you force her to come back?" Leda said, her voice a breathless cry.

Her father was silent, holding his wadded kerchief to his mouth. Finally, he said in a low voice she could barely hear behind his kerchief, "It was for the best." His shoulders dropped. He turned to look at Leda. "She was an adult," he said. His voice had a finality to it as he shook out his kerchief. "Like you. I couldn't force her to do anything."

"And now she really *is* dead." The foot cramp released leaving Leda's sole tender.

"In a car accident," her pop shook his head. "I wonder."

"What?"

"If it was an accident."

"You think she wanted to die?" Leda couldn't believe what her father was suggesting. Why would her mother take her own life?

"She lived with a lot of pain," her father said simply "At least now she's at peace."

Chapter 35

Erik urged them to move on sooner than Leda was ready. But her pop knotted his kerchief around his neck again and gave her a sad smile. "Your mother loved you," he said, and then he returned to the trail and started hiking up the mountain. Leda had no choice but to follow. The others were much further ahead now. Her father quickened his steps. Leda didn't know what he was thinking, but she welcomed the punishing pace. It matched the speed of her thoughts.

The picture of her mother's bewildered face flashed in Leda's mind. Her mother's startling blue eyes. Her cloud of swirling golden hair. Did she share more than wild hair with her mother? Did she carry the seed of mental illness? Her father didn't think so. Leda had never thought she had a mental illness, until this climb she felt in control of her emotions and had never acted impulsively. In fact, her friends would say she was the polar opposite of impulsive.

Leda knew virtually nothing about bipolar disorder except that some of those who suffered from it could experience turbulent mood swings – they could be extremely energetic and happy, they could be very depressed and have low energy. She supposed medication took the edge off those swings. Surely her mother's doctor didn't recommend she stop taking her medication while she was pregnant. As for the emotions churning insider her now, Leda was sure she could blame them on the blow of finding out her mother didn't die in Oregon after all.

Leda thought of her father's words. "She didn't want to harm the baby." "She loved you." Could she believe it? All she had was her father's say so.

And then there were her father's tears on the trail. Her pop never cried. Her pop hated emotional displays. And yet, he'd chosen her mother. He married her and swore to stay by her mother's side in good times and bad. But, he left her in England. Leda had never known her father to give up on anything. How many times had he urged her not to quit? How many times had he said quitters were weak? How many times had he plotted a rigorous course up a mountain just to prove what persistence could conquer? And now, here they were on Mt. Kilimanjaro attempting to summit a mountain taller than any they had ever climbed before. Leda didn't get it. The story was so unlike her father she almost didn't believe it could be true. Leda thought of the photo she carried in her daypack. Eleanor and Russell said nothing about mental illness. Maybe they thought it wasn't polite to talk about. Why did her pop keep it a secret all these years? It wasn't like her mother was a raving lunatic. Leda began to suspect her father hadn't told her the whole truth.

The two caught up with the rest of the group stopped by the side of the trail, shedding their wool hats and down coats. Leda swung off her daypack to do the same. She was determined to ask her father more questions after the break. She pulled out a granola bar and un-wrapped it.

"Aren't you tired of those?" Wyatt said.

"It's all I have left." Leda took a bite. She grimaced and swallowed.

"Try this." Wyatt poured a mix of almonds and Jelly Beans into her open palm.

"No more chocolate?"

"That was gone the second day."

Leda crunched on a few of the almonds. They didn't taste horrible. She washed the bits down with a swig of water. She selected a Jelly Bean and popped it into her mouth. "Not bad." She finished the ones Wyatt gave her, and held her hand out for more. Wyatt was shaking some into her palm when Leda noticed her father's frown. Leda instinctively started to pull her hand back as if she had been caught doing something naughty by the teacher, but Wyatt steadied her hand with his so the snack wouldn't spill to the ground. Leda curled her fingers over the almonds and Jelly Beans. Ignoring her father, she smiled at Wyatt.

"How's your day going so far?" Wyatt said.

Leda shifted so her back was turned towards her pop. "Tell you later," she said.

"That bad?"

Leda nodded.

"This afternoon?" Wyatt leaned his head close to hers.

The group would spend the afternoon resting at Barafu Camp for the night's summit attempt. Leda imagined most of the afternoon would be passed in the pup tents. It would be too cold to be outside. Leda squeezed Wyatt's wrist. She tucked her half-eaten granola bar back into her daypack. Her father appeared absorbed in a conversation between Tom, Gail and David. Soon, David signaled they should start up the trail again. Leda hoped to talk with her father, but he fell in behind David. Tom followed quickly on his heels.

For the next hour, Leda trailed behind the group thinking about the holes in her father's story. Maybe her mother had left because she didn't want to be a mother. Maybe her father had made up the bipolar part, but why would he? She thought about what Wyatt had said last night about her father's lie and her mother. Leda wasn't a parent. What did she know about raising a little girl? Sure, her father had made mistakes, but, as Wyatt said, she turned out okay.

Sometimes it sucked to be an adult, to realize you might have to live in a gray area making your way forward without answers. Someone once said the color of truth is gray but Leda couldn't remember who. She sighed.

"That sounds serious," Gail said.

The older woman hiked just steps in front. Leda had been so lost in her thoughts she didn't notice Gail's presence.

"I didn't know you were there," Leda said.

"I figured as much," Gail said in a staccato breath voice. "I've been trying to talk with you off and on for a while."

"Sorry," Leda said. "I've got a lot on my mind." She realized she was thirsty, and she turned her head, grabbing the tube of her water pack with her teeth.

"Anything I can help with?" Gail said.

Leda looked further up the trail. It had turned and the Southern Ice Fields now flanked the group on the left. The rest of the group had moved ahead of the two women, and the gap appeared to be widening. Leda studied Gail in her wide-brimmed hat and loose hiking pants. The older woman was probably in her mother's age range – if Leda's mother still lived.

"You're a mother," Leda said.

Gail chuckled.

"Sorry, that sounded dumb," Leda said. "Can I ask you something?"

"Ask away," Gail said. "I'll do my best to answer."

"Have you ever been depressed?"

"That's an odd question."

Leda apologized. "It's too personal. I understand."

"I'm not offended," Gail said. "But why do you ask?"

Leda took as deep of a breath as she could given the high altitude. The two walked side by side now. Leda thought about how to best form her question.

"Do you think it's possible, as a mother, to be so depressed you don't want to be with your baby because you might hurt her?

"Are you talking about mothers in general? Or did you have a specific person in mind?"

Leda cleared her throat. "In general, of course." She felt Gail look at her, but Leda kept her focus on the trail.

Gail said. "That's tough." She chewed her lower lip. She said, "I know depression can be debilitating, and some moms suffer from depression after their baby is born."

"Did you?"

"A little,' Gail said. "My hormones were raging." She chuckled. "Tom would probably say I was more than a little off my rocker for a while there what with no sleep. Wyatt was an active little guy. I don't remember him ever wanting to take a nap. But to not want to be with my baby or to hurt my baby? I was never that depressed."

The two hiked in silence. Leda digested the little bit of information Gail had offered.

"There was that woman who drowned her children," Gail said. "Said she was depressed and didn't know what she was doing."

Was that what her pop had meant when he said Natalie told him it wasn't safe for her to be with her baby? Had she really heard him mumble that Natalie's departure was for the best? And, thinking back, she remembered her pop saying he was afraid. What had he been afraid of? Natalie harming herself or hurting her baby? Leda felt more nauseous than she had all day.

"You and Wyatt seem to be getting along well," Gail said.

Leda snuck a look at Gail. The older woman's expression seemed unchanged. She wore sunglasses so it was hard to see her eyes. Her lips, like everyone's, were chapped. At the moment, Gail wasn't smiling or frowning. Leda said. "He's easy to talk to."

"He's a friendly guy." Gail pulled a pack of energy biscuits from one of the many pockets on her hiking pants. She peeled a corner of the cellophane and bit off a piece. "I wish he spent more time with us." Gail seemed pensive nibbling on the energy biscuit. "I miss him, but I guess that's the way with mothers and their sons. They grow up and become adults with their own interests."

"I wish I could have known my mother."

"You're very close with your father."

"Maybe too close," Leda muttered.

"He seems to have gotten used to hiking with our group."

Leda looked ahead on the trail where the three men hiked behind David. Wyatt was first behind the guide, followed by her father and then Tom. They didn't appear to be talking. Leda wasn't surprised. Her father never talked much to her when they were on the trail, this morning was a huge exception. While she watched, the four stopped for what appeared to be a snack break.

"I hoped with Chase gone, Tom and Wyatt would spend more time together," Gail said. The two women ambled side by side in silence, their scuffling steps and those of Erik behind them the only sound on the otherwise still mountain until Gail finished the pack of biscuits and crumpled the cellophane. Gail said, "Mothers don't have favorites, but Tom can be hard on Wyatt. I feel I have to make up the difference." She stuffed the bit of trash in her pants pocket, and then stopped. "Hold on," she said. She pressed her free hand to her forehead. "I feel lightheaded."

Leda paused next to her. She put her hand at Gail's elbow in case the older woman needed to be steadied.

"You're a nice girl," Gail said. She squeezed Leda's hand, before continuing her *pole pole* pace up the trail leaving Leda wondering if the older woman had just issued a very nicely put warning with her talk about Tom and Wyatt spending more time together.

Chapter 36

The young woman stood next to David. When she strode past the three men, she offered the older son a simple smile and nod. David knew the two shared a tent last night, but that wasn't his business. His business was making sure the group got to the top of Mt. Kilimanjaro. What they did along the way didn't matter, unless it interfered with a successful summit, of course. Others had met and shared tents along the trail. David noticed those often did better. Two in a tent were warmer and slept better. David handed the young woman a pack of energy biscuits and some chocolate.

So far the weather stayed calm. David thanked God for the clear skies. The Americans had described in much detail the sleet storm of yesterday. None mentioned Erik. Had the older guide been nothing more than a shadow leading them along the trail? David studied Erik. The guide slouched alone, his face towards the ice field. David thought of one of his father's favorite proverbs: "Solitude leads to much harm and an early death." David hoped it hadn't been a mistake for Erik to return to the mountain so soon after his nephew's death.

David needed to be mindful of another useful proverb: "No fly catches for another." He was going to ask Elihud to help with the summit attempt, and he decided to ask another porter too. Many groups brought extra hands for summit day. He couldn't worry about Erik's thoughts. So far, the group seemed strong. They had done well on the trail. But the summit day could break any one of them. It was best to be prepared. David thought about the order he would put the hikers in on summit day, the slower ones in front, the faster ones behind to push them up.

David felt someone touch his arm, the young woman. He had been lost in the puzzle of the summit climb and he shook his head to clear it. He held out another pack of energy biscuits, but Leda didn't take them.

"Do you have children?" she said.

David tucked away the biscuits. "A son and a daughter," he said.

"And a wife?"

David nodded.

"Do you climb the mountain often?"

"I'm a guide."

"Your family must miss you."

Chaggas were known as hard workers and good providers. If that meant David must climb the mountain many times a year, he would. He didn't expect Grace to do all the work while he drank *mbege* like men from other tribes.

"Seven days is not too long," David said. "Eight if I guide on Lemosho."

"I guess it depends on what you're used to," Leda said.

The young woman looked at the ice fields. David wondered if she saw something there, her eyes lingered, but just when David was tempted to look there as well, her eyes moved to Wyatt. Now David studied the American. Wyatt wasn't like the others who shifted on their feet or bothered their daypacks. He appeared as much in tune with the mountain as if he had grown up in its shadow. Many hikers thought their fancy equipment or mountain clothes would connect them somehow to the mountain. But it took something more. David didn't often see it in a *wazungu*.

The young woman spoke. "Pop and I talked about climbing Mt. Kilimanjaro for many years," she said. "I never imagined it would be like this." Her eyes flickered to where her father stood with the others and then returned to David.

David could tell she was sad from the way her voice dropped. Her body seemed to sway. Was she losing hold of her spirit? Her will to summit? She would need both to succeed. He was wondering how he could help her, when the son left his parents and walked towards them. Wyatt didn't seem to be in a hurry. His attitude reminded David of how he used to act around Grace before they were married. Like he didn't care. Women could be as skittish as gazelles with their quivering bodies and legs poised to bolt if they sensed danger. And standing next to Leda, David felt the energy course through her again at Wyatt's approach. He doubted she would bolt. The air was too thin for running.

He had seen this many times before. The strangest couplings on the summit trail. Hikers drawn together by the challenge of conquering the mountain. Love on the Mt. Kilimanjaro slopes. The *wazungu* seemed to thrive on it. The descent was a different story. Everyone worn to a daze, wanting only two things: a hot shower and a beer. Love forgotten.

Wyatt stopped. David stood between the two.

"Feeling okay?" Wyatt said.

The son looked at Leda. David knew the question wasn't for him. He kept silent, as did the young woman. But her smile said everything. In his head, David changed the order he would put the hikers in on summit day. These two needed to be together.

Chapter 37

Leda couldn't stop thinking about what her father told her earlier, and the later conversation she had with Gail. Had Leda's mother been a danger to her baby's life? Wyatt sauntered over. Leda couldn't help her smile or ignore the lift in her mood. But then she remembered his mother's wish that Wyatt spend more time with his father, and Leda stood a little bit straighter. Had she been the catalyst that drove her own parent's apart? If she had never been born, her parents might still be together. Leda didn't want to be the reason Wyatt and his father didn't have the time to reconcile on this trip.

Leda turned towards David. "How far to camp?"

"Not far, but the air is thin and we must walk pole pole."

Leda pulled on her daypack and looped the straps of her trekking poles over her wrists as if David had said they were leaving right that moment.

"I guess you're good then," Wyatt said.

Was he laughing? He looked as relaxed and unruffled as usual, a slight smile on his lips. "See you at camp," he said.

Leda's voice was calm; she could be cool too. "Til then," she said.

The rest of the morning was spent hiking over the desolate landscape on a well-worn path. Leda gave up trying to corral her father. She could talk to him at camp. Instead, she did her best to study the landscape, hoping for a distraction from her thoughts. She really couldn't compare the surroundings to anything she'd ever seen before. Very little could survive at this altitude and with so little water. Rainfall was barely measurable here. The last water supply was at the Karanga Valley, and Leda had seen the porters filling up the water jugs there for camp at Barafu Hut. They would have to make another trip back to the valley for more water while the hikers attempted the summit. Her guidebook described this section of the mountain as experiencing summer every day and winter every night. Leda caught occasional glimpses of low-growing lichen clinging to the lava and every once in a while a meager cluster of everlastings hugging the ground. She was amazed at the plant's hardiness, the smaller shape of the plant's flowers and its leathery leaves. It had obviously adapted to life in this harsh environment. Leda knelt to finger the fine hairs on one nearby plant.

"The thick skin keeps the plants moist," David said. "The tiny hairs gather the sun and trap air to keep the plants at a good temperature."

"Amazing." Leda stood. "I can't believe anything can survive up here."

"If we have time, we can visit the everlastings in the crater," David said.

Leda shook her head. How could a plant adapt to the hostile conditions at more than 18,000 feet?

A steep climb led to the Barafu Camp. Leda remembered Barafu meant ice in Swahili, and one glance at the exposed campsites told her how it had earned the name. The group picked its way through the jagged lava to a pair of circular metal sheds riddled with rust. A scarred wooden bunk bed and a low wooden table nearly filled the space. Leda signed the logbook open on the table, registering her presence at the camp as she had at every other camp. She watched Wyatt sign his name. His signature reminded her of his tent – messy.

After everyone had signed, the group turned as one and headed to the spot where their porters had set up camp. The trail was treacherous, lumps of jagged lava protruding through the gravel at the most unexpected spots. At the back of the group, Leda tripped and caught herself before she sprawled. Tom wasn't so lucky. He was near the front of the single line walking just behind David. His fall seemed to happen in seconds and yet, at the same time to take long minutes, Gail, who walked behind him reaching out her hands in a vain attempt to stop her husband's fall. And David. Was he so focused on the trail and getting his group to camp he didn't hear Tom stumble? He turned too late, Tom's fingertips already having traced an invisible line down David's daypack. The guide grabbed air. He called out a warning that came too late. And then he was on his knee at Tom's shoulder. Gail dropped to the trail as well. She seemed to somehow crawl towards Tom. Leda distracted by Gail and David, didn't fully look at Tom at first. But when she did, it was a startling tableau.

Gail kneeled in the dirt, her hand on Tom's hip. David spoke to the fallen hiker in a low tone. Wyatt was the only one in the family still standing, unmoving, looking as if he were hypnotized by the blinding sun glinting and winking along the black metal of Tom's exposed calf.

Leda and her father stood apart. She didn't mean to stare at Tom's inhuman left leg, but she couldn't help it. She remembered Wyatt telling her Tom's leg was crushed in a car crash. But she had never thought it was ruined beyond repair. Gail helped Tom sit up, and now Leda could see the robotic looking piece, what appeared to be two thick bands of some type of dark metal - only extended as far as his knee.

"I'm fine," Tom said, "no bumps or scrapes on me." He laughed as if the fall was all part of a normal hike, as if everyone had metal calves instead of two made of flesh and bone. He lowered his pant leg, hiding its difference. Tom accepted David's outstretched hand and levered himself back to a standing position. Wyatt still hadn't moved. Gail's forehead wrinkled with worry.

"Can you walk?" Gail said.

"Nothing hurts," Tom said. "Wasn't paying attention. Tripped. Not a BIG DEAL." As if to prove his point, Tom took a few steps, but even Leda could tell he walked gingerly.

Gail linked her arm with his. "In that case, let's get to camp."

Tom didn't protest, but moved forward, pretending he didn't need his wife's support. Wyatt shook himself as if waking from a trance before falling in behind.

"Did you know about that?" Leda's father said. The two remained still, watching the others.

"Wyatt said his father was in a car accident, but I had no idea." Leda shook her head.

"Wyatt didn't seem in a hurry to help."

Leda felt a rush of anger at her father's observation, even if it was true. She hurried to catch up with the others. Wyatt's reaction had bothered her. He had told her he felt God punished his father in the car accident for cheating on Gail. But still, Wyatt wouldn't forgive his father, even though Tom had suffered the loss of his lower leg. Leda heard her father's footsteps behind her. She slowed, not wanting to fall and get hurt. The two picked their way down a slight slope into the camp.

The porters had set up their camp in a tight but prime spot, nestled in a crook of lava rock ledges curled in a semi-circle. The dining tent staked about fifteen feet away and two rudimentary outhouses completed the circle: the three sharing the edge of a sheer drop with sweeping views of the rugged slopes and creeping fingers of mist below. It would be close quarters this afternoon.

As soon as the group arrived, the porters welcomed them with a song. This was a first, and Leda supposed it was fitting, as the group would be attempting the summit later tonight. The area was small, the number of porters large – three for every hiker, and not even Leda or Wyatt could avoid getting swept up in their enthusiastic greeting. Even Tom appeared game, shuffling his feet in a way Leda had always recognized as having no rhythm but now she knew why. The left one must be some sort of metal. Leda could hardly keep her eyes from straying to Tom and his feet.

Just as the song finished, a strong gust of wind swept through the camp. Leda shivered and for the first time noticed only three tents in the small clearing. The porters had not set up Jen and Chase's old tent. So, now Leda had to decide. Would she stay with her pop or Wyatt? Gail unzipped the flap of the tent just off to the side of the other two and crawled inside. The remaining two tents were staked not more than a foot apart. Leda's duffel and sleeping bag were piled by a nearby rock. She could only assume the porters had left her pop's stuff in one tent and Wyatt's in another. Leda remembered her resolve to get more information from her pop. She thought about Wyatt's refusal to forgive Tom despite his fake leg. She retrieved her down jacket and wool cap from her daypack before tossing the pack with the rest of her stuff. Lunch was the first order of business. Maybe Gail would talk about Tom's metal leg, and then Leda could decide where she would set up her gear.

Leda felt better than she had at Lava Tower, but when she ducked into the dining tent the food did not look good to her. She settled into a chair next to Tom. Leda filled her mug with hot water and waited. No one mentioned Tom's fall, even David ate quietly. Wyatt focused on his plate, not speaking. Leda followed suit.

Leda didn't feel hungry at all, but everyone else ate and she knew she should as well. She downed two bowls of broth. When the platter of thin, crepe-like pancakes came around, she selected two. She rounded out her meal with three pineapple slices and a chicken leg, more of the fresh meat brought up by David. A second mug of hot water washed it all down. In the end, she didn't feel any more or less sick to her stomach. She supposed that was a good thing. Empty platters and plates littered the table, and still nothing had been said about Tom. Gail seemed to sit closer to Tom than usual, watching her husband eat his lunch. When the meal was over and Tom's plate empty, the older woman leaned back appearing satisfied her husband was, as he said, fine. The two left the tent with David, leaving Leda alone with her father and Wyatt. The three sat in silence. Leda shifted in her chair.

Chapter 38

Leda looked across the table at Wyatt. Although it was sunny, the dark green walls of the dining tent kept the interior dim. Wyatt didn't appear to notice his parents had left. Leda could hear the wind shrieking along the ledge below them. Every so often it would sneak over the rocks and rattle the flap of the tent or a stronger gust would shake the very foundation of the tent pulling at the ropes holding it taut.

"Tom does well with that metal leg," Leda's father said. His voice appeared to startle Wyatt who looked up from his intense study of the checkered tablecloth. Wyatt nodded.

"I've seen stories on the news about wounded soldiers with those legs," her father said, "but never seen one in person."

Leda and Wyatt remained silent.

Her father cleared his throat. "Amazing stuff," he said. "And Tom's climbed all this way with it." Leda's father shook his head as if he couldn't believe Tom's perseverance. Leda wished her father would stop talking. She wished he would leave the tent so she could talk to Wyatt alone. But her father leaned back against his chair like he never planned to leave. Wyatt dropped his gaze to the tablecloth again.

"Wind's kicking up," her father said.

Leda got up and left. She still didn't know where she should set up her gear. Instead she made a quick trip to the outhouse. Luckily, these ones had four walls. She was glad, as her quads were sore and she had to prop her hands against the walls to help her squat. She would not miss this part of the hike at all. And, she would never complain again about having to go in the bushes on future hiking trips. She wondered if Tom really would do something about these toilets when he got home.

She peeked into the dining tent when she was done. Wyatt sat alone, his shoulders slumped now, his head between his hands. Leda sank into the chair next to his. She rested her hand on his shoulder. Wyatt leaned back in his chair.

"Want to talk?" Leda said.

"About what?" Wyatt crossed his arms over his chest and leaned further back, tilting his chair up on the back two legs. "I told you about the accident."

"You didn't say anything about your father's fake leg."

"I told you his leg was crushed. It's not my fault you didn't figure it out."

Leda let her hand drop from Wyatt's shoulder. His sharp tone stung her.

"Your father lost his leg, and you still can't forgive him?" Leda said. "Does he need to be paralyzed to earn your forgiveness?"

"You of all people have no right to lecture me." Wyatt said. He leaned forward dropping his chair back to all four legs. "Your dad has done nothing wrong."

Leda stood, her hands shaking. "You don't know what he told me today." She almost said, "My mother could have killed me. My father knew she was dangerous." but she didn't because she didn't know if it was true. She still needed to ask her pop more questions. Leda stared at Wyatt. He seemed like a total stranger with his lips thinned and his wool cap pulled low over his eyebrows. His hands were unfamiliar clenched fists on the table. She thought of her father saying that her mother had a wildness about her, an innate passion he found hard to resist. She remembered her earlier thoughts about Wyatt, how he appeared to belong in the rugged landscape, how he could track down lions and how he climbed walls like a mountain goat. Leda pushed her chair back against the table with careful motions. Then, she turned and left the dining tent. The wind snatched loose strands of her hair sticking from her wool cap. It snuck up inside the waist of her down jacket where it bunched from her trip to the outhouse. Leda hurried to her pile of stuff leaning against the rock. She knew which tent Tom and Gail shared. She stepped close to the other two and listened for sounds of movement. Leda grabbed her duffel. She brought it to the tent she would share with her pop. "Can I come in?" she said. She unzipped the flap at her father's mumbled yes.

Her pop had already set up his mat and sleeping bag. He knelt by his duffel, some of the extra clothes he would wear tonight in his hands. After a brief glance, he turned back to his work.

Leda took off her down jacket. She quickly set up her mat and sleeping bag. Her mother's locket hung from her neck, swinging as she smoothed her sleeping bag. Next, she made a neat pile of the clothes she would wear on the summit attempt not counting the long underwear and clothes she already had on – basically all the clothes she had brought. Tonight she would add another set of long underwear under her hiking pants. Her waterproof pants would go on top of those. For her top half, two pairs of long underwear – one thin, one thick – her fleece, a down jacket, and her waterproof jacket, also a knit hat with an opening for her face, a wool scarf and her wool hat for her head. Her hands would be tucked into two pairs of gloves with hand warmers slipped in between, for her feet, two pairs of wool socks and toe warmers. Leda loaded her daypack with snacks, toilet paper, antibacterial lotion and four liters of water divided between her water bottles and her camel back.

When she was done, Leda rocked back on her heels. She slid the locket back and forth on its chain mentally checking off what she would need. Satisfied, she crawled into her sleeping bag to rest. Her father was already stretched out on his bag, his wool hat resting on his face. Leda assumed he was using it to block the afternoon sunlight, but maybe he didn't want to talk. He had done everything he could to avoid her on the trail after his initial revelations about her mother.

The tent was warm in the afternoon sun. Leda drowsily studied the pile of clothes she had prepared. The headlamp she would use. What on earth had the earliest climbers worn to keep warm on their summit attempt? What had Emily used to light her path in the dark? Maybe groups had climbed to the summit during the day, the high altitude sun beating on their backs, the gravel slipping under their feet. The thoughts passed quickly through Leda's mind, like a fine vapor not meant to linger for more than a moment.

Nowadays most made the summit attempt at night when the gravel was frozen in place. Many wanted to reach the peak just before sunrise. David said it was too difficult to time a sunrise summit. You never knew how long it would take, he said. Some got to the top too early, and couldn't wait in the cold for the sunrise.

"Our group is slow," David said at lunch. "Very pole pole."

Leda didn't care how long it took them to get to the peak. In fact, at this point, she was wondering why she and her father ever had the crazy idea to climb Mt. Kilimanjaro. She was tired of feeling sick. She was tired of her leg muscles being tender to the touch. She was tired of the never-ending uphill. Why did people climb mountains? Why was Tom climbing this mountain with his metal leg? Why couldn't Wyatt forgive him? It had been crazy to think she knew Wyatt well after only a few days.

The wind slapped the tent carrying the guttural cry of a white-naped raven – the only bird Leda had read could fly in the strong winds at this altitude. She tugged her sleeping bag over her head. She was too tired to think about anything. She gave into the exhaustion that nagged her, falling into a deep slumber.

Chapter 39

The temperature was lower when Leda woke up. She could tell it was colder by the tip of her nose. She had stuck her face out of her sleeping bag sometime during her nap to get some air, and now her nose felt chilled. Temperatures at this altitude could drop as much as twenty degrees in the same number of minutes depending on the wind and clouds. The light in the tent was dim. Leda assumed the sun had sunk lower. Dinner must be soon, and although Leda still didn't feel hungry she would eat because food would propel her up the mountain. Her father was still asleep, his wool cap in the same position. He didn't appear to have moved at all. There was no point in getting up. Not until dinner. Leda stayed in her sleeping bag and waited for her father to wake up. The wind had stopped. An almost eerie stillness seemed to have settled over the camp. Leda was curious about the change, but not enough to leave the warmth of her sleeping bag.

Soon, her father stirred. The wool cap slid from his face and his eyes opened. Leda gave him a minute to yawn, rub his eyes, and sit up.

"Good nap?" she said. She had pulled the sleeping bag up over her ears so she imagined she looked like a mummy, just her face peeking out.

Her father rubbed his arms. "It's freezing," he said. He reached for his down jacket and pulled it on.

"Pop?"

"Hmm?" Leda's father settled the wool cap on his head.

"Can I ask you something about my mother?"

"I've told you everything." Her father scooted to the end of the tent. He reached for his boots.

"Did you think my mother was dangerous?" Leda sat up, still clutching the sleeping bag around her.

"What do you mean?" Her father's hand paused in mid-air, and then dropped, his fingers never touching his boots.

"You said she told her father to tell you she couldn't be trusted with a child. And you left. So, you must have believed it."

"That was a long time ago."

"But you believed it, didn't you?" Leda decided she wouldn't let her father leave the tent. She would grab his boots; she would tackle him if she had to.

"Leda, some things are better left alone." Her father turned his back and reached for his boots again.

"Why did you tell me anything then!" Leda said. Her cry sounded similar to the ravens.

Her father turned back towards her, one boot in his hand. The skin on his face seemed to sag below his cap. He blinked his eyes as if caught in a dust storm. After a few seconds, he dropped the boot and covered his face with his hands. It appeared the altitude had worn down her father as well.

Removing his hands, he said, "Truthfully?

Leda nodded. Was her father tearing up again?

"I told you about your mother because I didn't want to see you make the same mistake I did." He paused, and then said, "I was worried after you spent the night with Wyatt."

Leda pulled the sleeping bag tighter around her. "You wanted to break us apart?" She couldn't believe it. "Otherwise you never would have told me?"

"Love can make you do crazy things," her father said. "Things you never thought you would do."

"Pop," Leda leaned forward, "what did my mother do to me?"

"She never meant to harm you."

"What did she do?"

"I've spent my life protecting you." Her father picked up his boot again. "I'm not going to stop now, or cast aspersions on your mother's memory."

Leda lunged from her sleeping bag and grabbed at her father's other boot, but he got to it first. He unzipped the tent flap. Freezing air blew inside.

"Maybe she didn't do anything," Leda shouted. "Maybe she was fine, and she just didn't want anything more to do with you or me."

A pained expression crossed her father's face. "I'm putting these on outside," he said, scooting out of the tent on his butt, the boots in a tight grip. He looked back into the tent. "The altitude has gotten to us both. I'll be glad when this trip is over." He zipped the flap closed.

Leda felt like throwing her father's careful pile of clothes set up for the summit attempt tonight. But that would be childish. She wasn't going to act like the child her father thought she was, doling out information about her mother to keep her from Wyatt. Leda snorted and swatted the side of the tent. Part of the roof suddenly let in more light. Leda huddled in her sleeping bag. Her father hadn't said so, and probably would never admit it, but despite her final accusation, Leda was certain her mother had tried to do something to harm Leda. Her father said he threatened to commit Natalie to a seventy-two-hour hold. Someone could only be committed if they were a danger to themselves or others. He said he was afraid. Leda shivered. Her pop said love made you do crazy things. Had he been blinded by love to the danger her mother posed? Had he left a young Leda alone with Natalie even though he knew his wife might do something? And if she had, he still traveled to England to try and get Natalie back. Even now he talked about protecting Leda, but refused to tell Leda the whole truth. It seemed like the person he really was protecting was Natalie. Leda remembered her pop saying he had never stopped loving Natalie. Leda grabbed the locket and yanked it. The thin chain broke. Leda flung the necklace into the corner not caring if she ever saw it again. She felt desperate for air, even the thin, bitter air of base camp. She wanted nothing more than to get out of the confines of the tent.

Dressing quickly, Leda ducked outside. Snow had fallen in the afternoon. The tents were dusted with a powder like fine sand, the cracks of the lava rocks outlined in white. The ground smelled wet, more like after a rainfall than snow. Leda jammed her hands into her pockets. She lifted her face to the gray sky. Her cheeks stung from the cold. Thin lines of faded blue appeared every once a while between the moving clouds. Leda stood by her tent, watching the clouds. Earlier, she had seen the summit soaring above her tent, but now clouds hid it. She wondered vaguely if the group would still attempt the summit tonight. It just didn't seem that important to her anymore. Leda turned and surveyed the small camp. She couldn't see her father anywhere. Her legs, her arms, her entire body felt heavy.

Wyatt and his parents stood near the ledge, as far from the outhouses as possible. The three appeared to be having an animated conversation. Leda watched Gail as she clutched both Tom's arm and Wyatt's acting like a bridge between the two. She seemed to be doing her best to broker a peace between the men. Leda wondered why the sudden urgency. Maybe Gail simply realized the trip was almost over, and if Tom and Wyatt were going to reconcile it might as well be now. Neither man looked inclined to agree with Gail's argument, Tom stiff as an icicle in the dead of winter and Wyatt shoulders up to his ears, both hands in his coat pockets. But that didn't stop Gail, she continued to talk and hold their arms. She might be more stubborn than the two of them. Leda headed to the outhouses, acting like she didn't notice the three even though they were less than six feet away. As she walked, she felt as if she were fighting her way through huge snowdrifts even though the ground was more muddy than snowy. Leda caught snatches of Gail's words before she stepped into the outhouse, the door banging behind her before she could stop it. She held her breath, like always.

The three still stood together when she emerged. Now, Wyatt rubbed his hands together and stamped his feet. Tom looked at the ground. Leda didn't hear anything when she passed. Maybe Gail was making some progress.

Leda was the first in the dining tent. She squeezed her way past the chairs crowded against one side of the table to the end furthest from the open flap. The plastic plates, silverware and cups were stacked on the red-checked cloth, but no food or hot water. The group wouldn't share too many more meals at this table that had become so familiar. She remembered her first impression, how taken aback she was to be sitting on a chair at a table on a mountain hike. Now, it seemed as if the group had always eaten together, but maybe that's because the shared meals were the only "normal" thing about this whole experience. The outfitter had done a good job at providing all the necessary food groups for the climb. Leda and her father had read about other, less reputable companies that ran out of meat or didn't serve fruits or vegetables. Still, at this point, the last thing Leda wanted to think about was food. Maybe some other hikers dreamt about a juicy steak or their favorite fries, but all food seemed gross and disgusting to her right now. At least her nausea was manageable and she could keep her food down. She could hear the porters shouting to each other. The familiar smell of garlic and ginger punctuated their words.

Wyatt entered the tent next. He smiled at Leda, and tipped the chairs against the table so he could pass by them and get to the chair next to hers. He leaned closer as if he wanted to say something, but kept quiet when his father held the flap of the tent open for his mother. Gail pushed her way past the chairs, Tom close behind. The two settled side by side, Gail taking the chair by Wyatt. Everyone kept coats and hats on. It was as cold in the tent as it was outside since the wind had stopped blowing. The cook started to pass the food in, and still Leda's father hadn't shown up. Probably wandering around grieving his dead wife, Leda thought bitterly, sad that Leda came along and ruined everything.

David came through the open flap, helping the cook carry the numerous platters of food. Dinner wasn't much different from lunch except the pineapple had been replaced by watermelon. It didn't matter to Leda: none of it was appealing. The others seemed to select the food by rote, forking the chicken, pancakes or watermelon onto their plates in small movements. Once all the food was on the table, David took the seat by the lowered flap. He filled his plate with heaping portions, and dug in. After a few forkfuls, David looked around the table. "Where's your father?" he said to Leda.

Leda shrugged. "I haven't seen him since he left our tent."

"I'll look for him." David was half out of his chair when Leda's father entered the dining tent, lifting the flap with a gust of air, making the candles sputter. He pulled out a chair on the opposite side of the table from everyone and sat down. The candles provided a meager light. The tent was more shadowed than illuminated.

Tom spoke, "I might stay in camp tonight." He chewed a piece of chicken.

"You've come all this way to stop now?" Leda's father said. His plate seemed to have the same amount of food as when he started. Leda wondered if he had just pushed the chicken and watermelon around. An untouched pancake hung over the plate's edge.

Tom swallowed. "I don't need to summit," he said. "This is already higher than I've ever hiked before."

"You don't strike me as a quitter," Leda's father said. "I'm impressed by your fortitude so far. And with a metal leg." Leda cringed, but her father merely speared a small piece of chicken with his fork and put it in his mouth.

Tom said, "I don't need to prove anything."

"I wasn't suggesting you did," her father said, his tone mild. "Once I've set my mind to a goal, I like to accomplish it." The group was silent. "Of course, everyone's different," he said.

"It's Tom's decision," Gail said. "I'm going ahead."

Leda let a small piece of watermelon slide down her throat. "I'm thinking I might not attempt the summit either," she said. She focused on the tines of her fork, picking at the pancake left on her plate.

"Why?" Wyatt said.

Leda shook her head. "I'm not sure I have the stomach for it." She didn't have to look up to know her father stared at her. She could feel his eyes burning holes in her wool cap.

"It's common to feel nervous," David said. The guide had worked his way through most of his food. "Tom and Leda, you have come this far. Don't allow bad thoughts to take over your mind."

The group stayed silent.

"You must sleep more," David said. "Sleep is important. I'm positive you will all feel better. A porter will wake you up at your tent."

"What time?" Gail said.

"Tea here at 11:30. We will be on the trail at midnight."

Leda couldn't imagine sleeping more than she had this afternoon. But somehow her eyelids drooped.

"Wear your warmest clothes and coats," David said. "Now the skies are clearing, and, God willing, they will stay without clouds. The higher up we go the air will become more cold. Maybe more cold than minus twelve degrees. A strong wind could make it more cold even."

Icy fingers seem to tremble along Leda's spine as she thought of the hike ahead, and she burrowed deeper into the collar of her down coat. David's words were not motivating her to try for the summit.

Conversation was sparse considering it was one of the last dinners together. But everyone was suffering from the lack of oxygen one way or another. That's why they wouldn't spend a night here after the summit attempt. Sleeping at this altitude could be tricky and dangerous. David left after urging Tom and Leda again to attempt the summit, and asking if anyone had questions. He answered the few that came – how long would it take? How much water should they bring? How long would they stay at the top? He appeared disappointed when Tom announced he definitely wouldn't be making the summit attempt. He tried to talk Tom into changing his mind, but when Tom held firm, David gave up with a shake of his head. Leda kept silent. David left presumably to organize Erik and the porters going with the rest.

Gail pushed back from the table, her chair falling towards the tent wall. Tom caught it and restored it to an upright position. Gail squeezed Wyatt's shoulder, and then left the tent with Tom. The tent flap settled, Leda could hear the couple's boots on the gravel, when her father spoke, "You're going to be a quitter as well?"

Leda looked at her father studying him as if he were a stranger. And she thought he might be given what she had learned this afternoon. The candles had burned low; a sputtering light lit her father's face. His shadow was monstrous on the tent behind him. Against all odds, the ends of his red handkerchief stood valiant against his neck even now but maybe they were starched with a mix of sweat and dirt. In the past, his challenging words would be a clarion call to her. Leda wasn't a quitter. She never had been. But tonight she felt defeated, betrayed and let down by the two men who sat in the dining tent with her. Her words were soft, "What if I am?"

Her father leaned back in his chair. His shadow grew until it seemed to tower over him, bending and touching the very peak of the tent.

"What if I'm just like my mother?" Leda said, drawing the words out, emphasizing each one. "She quit on both of us."

The front legs of her father's chair landed in the dirt with a soft thud. He stood and stalked from the tent. The flap fell behind him. Leda listened to her father's receding footsteps. She didn't really think her father would make up her mother's mental illness. Her words were meant to hurt him, to ease some of her pain. But they hadn't. She could hear the snatches of conversations outside, whether it was the porters, David and Erik or Tom and Gail, she couldn't tell. Wyatt covered her hand with his. She stared at his wind roughened knuckles. Then, she slipped her hand away. Wyatt captured her hand with both of his.

"I'm not a quitter," he said.

"Why should I care?" Leda stopped struggling. It was easier to just let Wyatt hold her hand. It wasn't as if she couldn't break free if she wanted to. His fingers were warm.

"I'm sorry," he said. One of the candles burned out. Half the tent was dark. "I shouldn't have snapped at you earlier."

Tears beaded on her lashes, dribbled just below her eyes. Leda dabbed at them with the forefinger of her free hand.

"Life's too short," he said. "I forgave my dad this afternoon."

"Why?" Leda's voice was rough.

"When he fell, I don't know, it's like something snapped in me," he said. "Tom tried to brush it off, but I could tell he was shaken from his fall. I'm not surprised he doesn't want to summit. Besides, I couldn't stand the way you looked at me. I saw how bitter I'd become."

"Probably no more bitter than I feel now."

Wyatt squeezed her hand. "That bad huh?"

Leda nodded. She couldn't see his face in the dim tent. The one weak flame fluttered behind him. He leaned close. She could smell the garlic on his breath. He touched his lips to hers in a kiss as gentle as the touch of the lightest feather. Leda leaned her head against his shoulder.

"What are you thinking about?" he said.

"Nothing," she said. "Life."

She could hear the wind rippling along the tent. It played with the tent flap, lifting the edges on brief gusts. She breathed in the scent of Wyatt's coat, a blend of trail dust and smoke from past hikes. She pressed her cheek against the coat's downy softness. The cook and his helper bustled into the tent. They stacked the plates and platters, grabbing silverware into bunches they tossed into the empty soup pot. Leda and Wyatt ducked out of the tent. Leda hesitated. She dreaded crawling into the pup tent with her father. She wouldn't be able to sleep. Her summit attempt was basically over. She crossed her arms against the bitter cold. She didn't know she still blocked the door, until Wyatt pulled her out of the way so the cook and his helper could get out without knocking her over. The two ambled the few feet towards the pup tents.

"No stars tonight," Wyatt said.

Leda tipped her head back. She thought she could see clouds wreathing the summit but they were a close color to the gathering dark. With her gloved hands tucked firmly in her armpits for warmth, she studied the sky. "Could be some there," she said, "where those clouds just parted."

"Can't see them," Wyatt said.

They had arrived at the pup tents. The camping area was so small, there was no space to linger, nowhere to stroll without hazarding a fall from the ledge. Leda clenched her jaw. Might as well get in the tent with her father. The shelter was dark and quiet. Maybe he was asleep or at least pretending to be. "Goodnight," she said. She reached for the zipper.

"Leda?" Wyatt spoke in a low voice behind her.

She waited.

"Are you attempting the summit?"

Leda turned back towards Wyatt. "I don't know."

"What happened?"

Leda shook her head. She could feel more tears and she blinked her eyes and looked away.

"Don't let your father ruin this for you," he said. "You're so close."

"There's no guarantee I'll make it to the top."

"At least try."

Leda brushed a brief kiss on Wyatt's cheek. "Maybe," she said. She reached again for the zipper to open the pup tent.

"One more question," Wyatt said. "Will you stay with me until we leave tonight?"

Wyatt's voice sounded hesitant as if he feared rejection. Was it only last night he had glibly asked her whether she wanted to talk in her tent or his? Now she no longer had a tent of her own to go to. And why should the porters set up one more tent in this limited space? It was foolish to spend the night hours alone when two bodies were more efficient at keeping the pup tent warm. Leda could get in the tent with her father – who had been ready to sacrifice her on the altar of his love for Natalie - or she could be with Wyatt.

Leda unzipped the pup tent she shared with her father. "Can you help me move my stuff?" she said to Wyatt.

Chapter 40

David stepped out of the dining tent into the windy dusk – the sun had set, but complete darkness hadn't yet settled over the camp. Barafu Camp had the most hostile environment of all the camps. Its Swahili name fitting – Barafu meant ice. He hoped all the hikers would go to their tents and get in bed. Rest and a good mental attitude were both key to a successful summit experience. David had watched closely to see what the hikers ate at dinner. None seemed too hungry, but all had eaten. It was a good sign of strong wills and determination. David was sorry the older American, Tom, wasn't going tonight. But it would be better if he stayed behind if he did not have the will.

Now, David needed to find Erik. The light was fading, but the area of the camp was small and the older guide shouldn't be too hard to find. Since Tom dropped out of the summit attempt, the extra porter would not be needed. Erik and Elihud would be enough. David thought he saw Erik standing by the ledge, but when he reached the man, it was only one of the porters. He didn't know where Erik was.

David circled the camp again. The pink was gone from the clouds, the tents were dim shapes; night shadows were growing. He was ready to ask the extra porter to come along even though the young man spoke little English. Erik appeared out of the shadows dressed in what appeared to be a loose gray robe. At first David thought the guide was his ancestor's ghost and he stopped dead in his tracks wondering what the visitation meant. But Erik didn't smell like an ancestor, he smelled like an African guide who hadn't bathed in weeks. The robe turned out to be nothing more than a dusty blanket stained with grease.

David was mindful of giving his elder the proper greeting, *"Shikamoo"* but then asked, "Where have you been old man?"

"In the toilet," Erik said. "My stomach is bad."

David knew the guide lied. He had checked both toilets in his search of the camp. "Are you too ill for the summit?" David said.

"Don't think you are cutting me out," Erik said. "You know the Americans are generous with those who help on summit day."

"I didn't think anything old man," David said. He remembered the story of the snail hidden behind the banana leaf, waiting for the quenching rain, the lesson to be both humble and observant. Now, he would be humble. "Of course you are on the summit climb."

Erik smiled, his teeth gleaming in the dark. "What time?"

"We leave at midnight."

The older man grunted and turned away.

Tonight, David would be observant. He would put Erik with Wyatt and Leda. The two were strong and wouldn't need much help. The pace would be pole pole, the hikers bunched together, no further apart than a boot length. David would lead the group, Gail, right behind him, followed by Phillip, then Erik, Leda and Wyatt. Elihud could be at the back. They would take breaks together at times David determined. Nothing would happen without him knowing.

Chapter 41

Leda and Wyatt worked quickly shifting Leda's summit clothes, daypack, sleeping bag and mat the two feet to Wyatt's tent. The light from Leda's headlamp dashed over her father's sleeping bag many times. He never moved, but kept still with his back towards them, his body a series of hills and dips.

They left Leda's stuff piled in the opening of Wyatt's tent. He crawled inside and shoved his sleeping bag, mat and duffel to one side. Leda was careful unrolling her mat, smoothing her sleeping bag and restoring order to her pile of clothes. She checked to make sure she had her water supply and snacks. She wasn't sure if she would attempt the summit, but it wouldn't hurt to be ready just in case she decided to go for it. When she was done, she laid on her side on top of her sleeping bag and watched Wyatt rifle through his gear.

His pile of clothing reached higher than hers, but Leda figured that was because his clothes and jackets were guy sized. There didn't seemed to be any order to the disarray of his belongings, one boot peeked out from under his waterproof jacket, the other was stationed by the tent flap, his gloves appeared to be rolled with his socks. But Leda had never seen Wyatt less than prepared, so she figured he must have a system all his own.

While he sorted through his things, Leda took off her top layer and slid into her sleeping bag. She tucked her miniature pillow behind her head. She longed for her own pillow and bed. The rain forest of the first day seemed so long ago. They had hiked through several different microclimates since then, but she had been caught up in her own turmoil and hadn't really paid attention. She did remember the butterflies in her stomach on the first day, the feeling like she was stepping onto an unfamiliar roller coaster. Leda couldn't tell if the butterflies were there. If they were they were masked by the nausea that nagged her the past two days. She would be glad to be rid of it. She would be glad to move, and think and feel at a lower altitude where she could gulp a great lungful of oxygen, where her brain wouldn't feel so sluggish. Leda was tired, so tired now. She couldn't muster up the energy to think about what her father or mother had done. She felt like the time she had her appendix out, just before the nurses pushed her bed through the doors to surgery, her limbs heavy from the pill they gave her, her brain cottony. She did know she was happy to be with Wyatt instead of her pop.

Wyatt had strung up his headlamp so it shone a spotlight on the area where he worked. He moved with an economy of motion in the small space. He removed his down jacket and added it to his pile of summit clothes. Was she in his tent because her father opposed it? Leda didn't think so. She liked Wyatt. She sensed a kindred spirit in him. She would be sad to say goodbye at the end of the trail. Leda didn't think he had been serious this morning when he mentioned San Diego.

Wyatt finished his preparations. Like Leda, he removed his top layer of clothes and slithered into his sleeping bag. Stretching out his arm, he snapped off his headlamp. The tent was the dark gray just before night. Wyatt gathered Leda's hand in his as if it was the most natural thing in the world. His kiss felt familiar and easy, but no less moving. Still, Leda felt no pressure to go further. It didn't need to be said that if their physical condition was bad last night, it was worse now at 15,000 plus feet. Making love for the first time – dirty, smelly and sick – was not something Leda wanted to do: especially with the tents so close together. She imagined she could hear Tom and Gail breathing in their tent nearby, her father's sleeping bag rustling as he turned over. Besides, the point of the climb – achieving the summit – happened tonight. She assumed Wyatt didn't want to jeopardize the attempt by unnecessary physical activity. They pulled apart, their noses separated by inches, their fingers intertwined.

"How's your neck?" Leda said, her voice low.

"Better, but sore," Wyatt said. "Your stomach?"

"Same, unfortunately."

"Come to San Diego when this is over?"

Wyatt's repeated invitation surprised Leda enough that she angled her head back the slightest bit to study his features. "I thought you didn't believe in long-term relationships," she said.

"Five days is hardly long-term," Wyatt said. He kissed her hand. "Would you think about it?"

"I suppose I should try to straighten things out with my father first," Leda said.

Wyatt smoothed a loose piece of hair from Leda's forehead. "Seriously?"

"Maybe we can have a rational discussion at sea level." Leda sighed. Would anything be different at home? "But I'm not promising anything. Besides, you might not recognize me if I come to San Diego. No braid, clean fingernails, fresh clothes."

"Sounds nice," Wyatt said.

Leda flicked his head with her index finger.

"Ow. What I meant was I would recognize you anywhere," Wyatt said.

"That's better."

A comfortable silence filled the tent. The wind seemed to have picked up outside, it shook the tent's nylon walls and rushed around the lava rocks. Leda thought of the ranger hut where they had signed the ledger in the early afternoon. She supposed the metal walls provided a barrier of sorts against the elements, but she imagined the wind moaning against the tin roof, pressing to get inside where there was a small modicum of warmth. The hut had two beds. It would be a lonely life for one, stationed at this forbidding outpost.

"Why are you asking me?" Leda said. "To San Diego? I'm dirty, I've worn the same clothes for days and my hair's a mess."

"Watch it," Wyatt said. "I made that braid this morning."

"I'm serious."

"I like you," Wyatt said.

Leda squeezed his hand. She looked at the blank tent wall behind him. For the briefest of moments, the awards and framed degrees in her bedroom flashed in her thoughts, accomplishments Wyatt knew nothing about. Her hip ached against the hard ground, the thin sleeping pad a poor mattress. She shifted. "I've never met anyone like you," she said.

"Does that mean you like me?"

Leda smiled. "Yes," she said. "Yes, I do."

After a while, Leda spoke again. "About the summit," she said.

"Nervous?"

"No more than I was back at Shira Camp."

"That seems a lifetime ago."

"Mt. Kilimanjaro - an exotic challenge and romantic." Leda paraphrased Wyatt's words from the night they had stood looking at the summit.

"Is that what I said?"

Leda's laugh was soft. She didn't want to waken the others.

"I sounded like an ass."

"I remember earlier on the trail when you quoted Hemingway about the leopard."

"How about this part, at the end of the story," Wyatt said. "And there, ahead, all he could see, as wide as all the world, great, high and unbelievably white in the sun, was the square top of Kilimanjaro. And then he knew that there was where he was going."

Leda spoke the last words with him.

"So you're going to do it?" Wyatt said.

"Attempt the summit?" This time Leda's smile felt sad. "Maybe."

Wyatt yawned. "Let's sleep, we have a long night ahead." He closed his eyes. Leda lowered her lids, staring at Wyatt through her lashes. She wasn't done talking, but when his eyes stayed closed, she realized he was done. She snuggled deeper into her sleeping bag giving into the lethargy that sapped her limbs.

"San Diego."

Leda's eyes snapped open. Wyatt didn't move. His eyes were shut, his breathing steady. Would she recognize him in San Diego? She remembered bumping against him in the Land Cruiser on the ride from the hotel to the Machame Gate. How he smelled fresh and clean. Leda closed her eyes. She would know him anywhere.

Chapter 42

The quiet voice outside the tent startled Leda awake. Wyatt stretched in his sleeping bag. Leda didn't remember falling asleep but she must have, the tent was pitch black.

"You coming?" Wyatt's voice sounded scratchy from sleep.

Leda felt a nervous excitement, a buzzing inside her. How could she have doubted whether she wanted to reach the summit? Wyatt was right. She wouldn't let her father take this from her. This was probably the last time she would ever get the chance to climb the highest freestanding mountain in the world. In eight hours, she could be standing at the roof of Africa.

Leda sprang into action. Clicking on her headlamp, she began to methodically dress in all the clothes she had laid out earlier. She double -checked her daypack for her snacks and water. Her granola bars were harder than usual – frozen. The water tube she used to draw water from her camelback, also a block of ice. Ice shards sloshed in her two water bottles. Wyatt was just emerging from his sleeping bag when Leda left the tent.

The sky had cleared while they slept. Now, she could see pinpricks of light bobbing along the trail up the mountain – other hikers already on the move. Leda crossed the small campsite and ducked into the dining tent. She was the first to arrive. The cook was setting the table and shooed her out.

"Come back," he said. "Five minutes."

Somewhat deflated, Leda returned to the tent where Wyatt was just sitting up, his sleeping bag draped around his shoulders.

"Who lit a fire under you?" he said.

"Say what you want." Leda crawled out of his way. "I'm excited."

Wyatt yawned, "me too."

Leda sat as quietly as she could in the back corner of the tent, while Wyatt took up the rest of the space pulling on all his layers. She felt like biting her fingernails while he carefully checked his daypack and water supply, but her hands were encased in her gloves, so she couldn't. She knew the group wouldn't leave without them, but logic wasn't doing a good job of convincing her nerves. His headlight adjusted, Wyatt turned towards Leda.

"Finally!" Leda scooted towards Wyatt. "Let's go to the dining tent."

Wyatt crawled out of the pup tent, Leda pushing out behind him. She could see a longer line of lights strung along the summit trail like a string of Christmas bulbs. More hikers headed to the peak. It was surreal to see the lights. She had known all along many attempted the summit – at least 60,000 a year. Some of the campsites had housed hundreds. But now, many of the various trails had converged on this single summit route, and she was stunned to see how many lights there were.

Somehow, the two were the last to enter the dining tent. Leda's gaze went straight to her father. He didn't look over or greet her, but sat ramrod straight at the table. Like everyone else, he wore his many layers of clothes. He looked bulky, bumpy, bigger somehow. Leda felt a passing sorrow. The two had planned to summit Mt. Kilimanjaro together. It was to be their grand achievement; the crown of all the mountains they had climbed together. Tonight, they would be climbing in the same group, but it wouldn't be the same. It would never be the same. Leda suppressed a sigh. She didn't know how to talk with her pop anymore. Wyatt pulled out a chair for her, and she sat down next to Tom. He had come to the table apparently to wish the others good luck. It looked like he had pulled on his clothes haphazardly; his face was puffy with sleep. Gail and David rounded out the group.

Leda ate the porridge and tea set before her even though she wasn't hungry. The hot food warmed her. David told the group the order they would climb. They would move even more *pole pole* than before up the steep three- mile distance. If a person felt tired, he should give his daypack to one of the guides or porters. There would be no shame in making the burden lighter. David guessed they would reach the summit that towered a little more than 4,000 feet above them in about eight hours. They would stop once each hour, everyone taking care of eating and personal matters at the same time.

"Empty your minds," he said. "Focus on Uhuru Peak and you will reach your goal."

Tom shuffled back to his pup tent and bed. Leda and Gail inserted foot warmers into their boots, and hand warmers into their gloves. David organized the hikers into a line with Gail first, Leda's father second, then Erik, Leda, Wyatt and Elihud, the one porter. The hikers took their places in silence. Leda thought her father nodded at her, but maybe he was bending his head, making sure his scarf was wound tight around his neck so no air could sneak through. David led them off into the dark, winding through Barafu camp and towards the summit trail. Leda did her best to empty her mind while she skirted the rough lava rocks in the camp, scrambling over those too big to get around. She wouldn't worry about whether her father nodded. She thought of the comforting glow her foot warmers spread to her toes, the toasty ends of her fingers thanks to her hand warmers.

Just as they reached the outskirts of the camp, Gail balked at a steep boulder the hikers would have to climb. Since she was in the front, just behind David, the line came to a halt. Leda nearly stepped on Erik's heels. She felt Wyatt brace himself against her daypack.

"I can't do this," Gail said, her body melting to the ground like she had no bones.

Leda felt an answering panic rising in her. Could she do this? She began to doubt her own abilities and will power. The boulder slanted up and away and into the dark. What if the entire climb was like this? Leda had read the trail was mostly gravel. Where had this boulder come from? Her father stood silent. Leda felt Wyatt lean past her, as if he planned to go to his mother's aid. But then David spoke, his voice firm and commanding.

"Yes you can," David said. He gripped Gail's elbow and pulled her to a standing position. Her knees wavered. But David's tone made it clear he would not accept defeat this early. "I know you can do this. No more stopping until I say." Gail obeyed, shuffling forward. The hikers clambered up the boulder behind her, Leda surging up the steep angle suppressing her own doubts, working at emptying her mind of all but the summit. The group climbed up a series of rock steps and boulders, the trail weaving and snaking its way up the mountain in tight turns. Leda felt, more than saw, the dim shapes of other hikers resting by the side of the trail. She could hear even more on the switchbacks just above her – the scrape of boots like sandpaper on frozen gravel and the heavy breathing of many struggling climbers – weirdly loud in the absolute silence.

The first break came earlier than Leda imagined it would. She wasn't hungry, but ate. She wasn't thirsty, but drank. She didn't have to pee, but went anyway. David warned her not to stray too far from the trail in the dark. Were there cliffs nearby? Leda couldn't see a thing beyond the scanty circle of her headlamp. She followed Gail to a clump of boulders. Other hikers passed less than three feet away. None lifted their heads or gave any indication they noticed the women.

Leda's group got back into line and onto the trail. As the group continued shuffling uphill, all Leda could see was the bottom of Erik's boots, the toes and heels worn smooth. Leda began to feel like one of those horses she and her father used to ride at campgrounds when she was young. Plodding along the trail, the nose of each horse pressed to the tail of the one in front. Those had been fun, carefree days – when she was the rider and could see where she was going. They had never ridden horses any other time, just those few years before she was old enough to backpack. Now, the days of car camping seemed enveloped in a golden haze. The crackling flames of the campfire, the smoky smell of her hair on the bed pillow her father let her bring, the cool water of a rippling mountain stream, her pop helping her as she navigated the sharp river bed stones on tender feet, the melt in her mouth goodness of the fresh trout her pop helped her catch, gut and sear in a splash of oil.

Leda thought even further back to the first mountain she had climbed with her father. The trail was a dusty fire road and she was four-years-old. She didn't remember getting to the top, but her pop said she did. What she did remember was the red and purple flowers blooming in the wild grass alongside the road and the wide- open sky bigger than anything she had ever seen. She remembered her pop carrying her piggyback. She remembered bouncing on his back like she did on those trail horses, especially at the end when he ran through the rain to the car.

Other memories of hikes with her father rotated through her mind, until she reached the beginning of this climb. She wondered how he was doing, whether he was struggling. He would never tell her. He never had. Were her earlier memories an illusion? A wishful dream she had created to foster a false sense of closeness with her pop? Her love for him was real. She could have sworn his love for her was real too.

Leda began to think of her father and her mother, her thoughts going over and over what she knew and didn't know her father's lie her mother's depression her father's choice her mother's choice grateful her mother didn't harm her sad her mother had to leave to keep Leda safe happy her mother loved her enough to leave angry her father would have put her at risk in order to get her mother back churning and churning with each sluggish step until she finally remembered David's advice to empty her mind. Leda concentrated on her breathing, the hard pull of what little oxygen the air offered into her lungs. It felt like trying to sip pudding through a narrow straw. She thought about wiping her nose – it was dripping again – but that would mean taking off her heavy outer glove so she could reach into her pocket and get a tissue. Instead, she dabbed at her nose with her scarf. She lifted each leg in turn and slowly, slowly gained ground.

Leda thought of the song she listened to repetitively whenever she missed her mother. The song would give her hope – she always imagined her English mother was a huge Beatles fan - maybe the song would work now on this dark mountain. *Here comes the sun, Here comes the sun, and I say, it's all right. Little darling it's been a long cold lonely winter feels like years since it's been here. Here comes the sun, Here comes the sun and I say it's all right*. The lyrics ran through her brain on an endless loop. She forgot about everyone else in the line. All she knew was the boots in front of her. Somehow she made it to their fourth break, and then their fifth. The same song circled through her mind, but no matter how many times she thought it, the sun never came.

She didn't know the time. All Leda knew was it was still dark, dark, dark, and she had been on this trail longer than forever staring at the boring gravel in the fragile circle of her headlamp. They had passed other groups. Other groups had passed them. She had pulled off her outer glove to eat her snack at each stop – how she despised her granola bars, she would never eat granola again. Ever. She didn't care if it came in a bar or a bowl. If she ate it in a box or with a fox. Now, three of her fingers on her right hand were numb. Leda felt certain they were frostbitten black, withered dead and in need of amputation. Her heart beat like a hummingbird's wings in her chest. Each step felt as if she were lifting twenty pound buckets of sand. She fought the constant thought of stopping. How easy it would be to give up. The last lines of the poem *"Invictus"* popped into her head. *"I am the master of my fate. I am the captain of my soul."* It was a favorite of both her and her father's, and it powered her further. But suddenly, she could not lift her leg. She could not take another step. She stopped. Erik, mere steps ahead of her, kept walking. The thought of calling out to him for help didn't cross her mind. Instead, she watched his back move away in a kind of daze.

"Give Elihud your pack," Wyatt said. He spoke through his muffler, his voice sounded hoarse.

And somehow, Elihud was next to her, reaching for her daypack, helping her slide her arms out of the straps. He slung the pack across his chest like it weighed nothing. Leda felt wonderfully lighter. She was certain she could keep going now.

Time passed. Or at least Leda thought it did. She had no way of telling. She felt the granola bar she had eaten earlier gurgle in her stomach. Then her intestines cramped.

"I'm going to be sick," she moaned. She stumbled to the side of the trail, pulled down her pants and squatted. Other hikers passed within two feet of her. None spared her a glance. When she was done, she readjusted her pants and returned to the trail. Elihud waited for her. The others were gone. The two continued up the trail, Elihud in the lead. He seemed to walk at a more punishing pace, and Leda fought to keep up. Maybe he was trying to catch the others. She felt weak. Finally, she grabbed his jacket.

"I need fuel," she said, sinking to the ground. Elihud handed her a packet of energy biscuits from the store in her daypack. They still tasted like paper. But she would have eaten anything – besides a granola bar. She swallowed some of the ice water in her water bottle, wishing it was hot water from a thermos. Elihud pulled her to her feet when she was done, and the two set off again without exchanging any words.

Was she truly the captain of her soul? Was this what it was like to be in hell? Struggling climbing boots inching along never ending gravel no sense of place in the stygian dark head down nauseated freezing the knowledge of others nearby but no strength to talk or reach out?

Chapter 43

The group chose not to stop. It was too cold. They had paused to talk about it. Long enough for Phillip to push his outer glove off his wrist and aim his headlamp at his watch. It was one of those fancy temperature gauges many of the hikers now had, the numbers flashing an unnatural green. David wished the American wouldn't announce the temperature but he did.

David never understood why the climbers wanted to know the exact temperature. He didn't think it helped them get to the summit. How could they empty their minds if they thought about how cold they were? It was never a good thing to focus on something they couldn't control. Already, he could see how Gail and Leda slumped a little more when they heard the temperature.

"Gail?" David said. "You are feeling fine?"

The woman lifted her face. David studied it for signs of severe altitude sickness. Her eyes were red, but not puffy. Her lips and cheeks were covered with her hat and scarf. Gail nodded.

A light wind worried the edges of Gail's scarf. It was probably colder than Phillip's gauge said. The group had been lucky so far, but David knew the wind would most likely blow harder just before dawn. And no one knew what it would bring with it. The mountain was fickle and would do what it wanted.

"I think my fingers are frostbitten." The young American woman held out her hand to David. He grasped it between his hands. Elihud had done a good job bringing her back to the group. David would make sure the porter got a large share of the tips.

"My hands are cold too," David said, loud enough for everyone to hear. "Every time I go to the summit, I can no longer feel the fingers on my left hand. I think they will fall off. Every time they are fine." David hoped the young woman believed him.

Erik said nothing. But David saw he carried someone's daypack on top of his own. David considered the little group huddled around him, bundled against the cold. Their eyes appeared sunken in the shadows of their headlamps. He could tell from their slack expressions this was the hardest they had ever worked, and he couldn't help himself, at this point, he never could. He wondered why. Why did the *wazungu* pay good money to suffer like this?

Grace said he shouldn't worry about it. If the *wazungu* wanted to throw their money away, why should he care? He should concentrate on getting the *wazungu* to the top. He should think about taking special care of them and the good salary and tips he was earning.

It wasn't just the *wazungu* though who suffered pain, who risked their lives to climb this mountain. David thought about his Chagga ancestors: the ones who sought the treasure at the top of the shining mountain. And now, here he was, a Chagga climbing the mountain for treasure. He wasn't the only one. He only needed to look ahead and behind, and he would see Chagga and Masai leading the *wazungu*, all streaming towards the summit across this infertile land like a herd of gnu stumbling after the scent of water.

David looked at Erik. The older guide nodded as if he understood.

Grace was right. These thoughts wouldn't get his *wazungu* to the summit. They wouldn't put dollar bills in his hands or pay his children's school fees. These thoughts would only keep him from success. He always reached the same conclusion at this point. It was as if the mountain was playing a trick on him. Trying to keep him from getting to the top by sneaking into his mind and filling it with all sorts of useless thinking. That was why he loved this mountain so much. That's why he led groups up this trail so often. The mountain was a worthy opponent and deserving of his respect. David wasn't like the foolish king at all. He wasn't like Erik.

David couldn't stop the wind. He couldn't stop the American from telling the temperature. He could follow his own counsel and empty his mind of worthless thinking. He could hearten the hikers to keep going. He liked the *wazungu*. He wished he could count some as his friends, but none lived in his village. Most were only passing through.

The temperature announcement had not been good. David sensed it weakened the climbers' will. Standing around would just make the hikers colder and encourage more bad thinking. He continued up the trail, but now, he sang.

He sang in Swahili, his voice carrying over the lifeless mountain. The tune was a hymn they sang in church. He hoped it would distract the hikers from the temperature and the dark. Chagga and Masai leading other groups up the trail began to sing the hymn. They would all sing their clients safely to the summit. David imagined the song soaring on the wind like a bird. They would trick the wind and use it for their own success.

Chapter 44

The color of the sky shifted from oppressive black to a gray black while Leda wasn't paying attention. Her focus was still on the gravel at her feet; her mind was as numb as her fingers. A sharp wind snapped the loose material on her waterproof jacket. She barely noticed Wyatt nudging her arm.

"Sun's coming up," he said. "You can turn off your light."

His words caught Leda's attention. She lifted her eyes and squinted in the direction he pointed. A thin line of sunlight spread along the eastern horizon. She could make out the faint jagged outline of Mwenzi. Nearby, small, bluish purple mountains and hills looked like an art project made of torn construction paper. Now, the sky was a gray pearl as shafts of sunlight poured over the edge of the world. Leda shaded her eyes. She had forgotten more existed, and she soaked in the expanding view, the vista of unending mountains hazy in the morning mist. She imagined people going about their business in the unseen villages and cities below, and elephants, gazelles and lions moving about the brown plains.

"There's Kenya," Wyatt said.

"What time is it?"

"Sunrise is about 6:30."

After climbing in the dark for six hours, her world reduced to the tiny circle of her headlamp, Leda felt like a blind person seeing for the first time. She closed her eyes and imagined the rays of the morning sun warmed her skin even though she knew it wasn't logically possible. She opened her eyes and looked down the mountain at the trail they had followed, a bare path worn into the gravel by thousands. While they were climbing, she had felt as if they were headed straight up from the camp. But she couldn't see the camp now: a thick layer of clouds hid it. She swiveled her head and looked up towards the crater rim. They would rest briefly at the crater rim before continuing on to the summit. Someone in a red coat that stood out like a paint splotch on the gray slope approached what Leda thought must be Stella Point. She could see huge rocks outlined by the early morning sky, the bulk of the summit off to her left. The red spot looked tantalizingly close.

"We should be at Stella Point in another hour," Wyatt said.

Leda studied the trail that seemed to slope up and away at a nearly vertical angle. She hated to admit it, but Wyatt was probably right. At least the sun was up. It was amazing how much better the light made her feel even though now she could see what she was climbing. She strained to see further, tilting her head back more than she should have given the altitude, and nearly lost her balance as a wave of dizziness swept over her. Wyatt caught her, holding her steady.

"Drink some water," Wyatt said. "You'll feel better."

Her water was in the pack carried by Elihud, and she signaled to him that she would like a drink. Wyatt massaged his neck.

"Should we rest?" Leda said.

"If you want to."

"What about you?"

"I'm fine."

Leda studied Wyatt. He dropped his hand at her regard. He still carried his daypack. Her own dizziness had passed. Wyatt looked okay. A little ragged around the edges, but she probably looked worse. He reached into a pocket of his daypack and pulled out his sunglasses. It almost looked as if he had tiny bruises underneath his eyes, but now the sun shone in Leda's face and she couldn't really tell. Wyatt put on his sunglasses.

"Not sure I'll need these for long." Wyatt gestured towards the clouds below them. They seemed to have boiled up since she last looked, swallowing more of the trail. "We'd better get going if we want to beat that."

Erik seemed to agree. He started up the trail without comment, leading them to the summit. Wyatt fell in behind him, Leda and Elihud following.

Although the sun rose higher, the air seemed to get colder, the wind seeking out the tiniest cracks and crevices in Leda's many layers. She felt a freezing touch on her neck, and then at her lower back where her pants didn't quite meet her coat, and then along her wrists in the spot where her gloves gaped away from her sleeves. Dried snot crusted the back of her outer gloves, and she raised her scarf just the tiniest bit higher so her nose could drip directly onto it. She thought about retrieving her sunglasses but decided it would be too much effort to get them from Elihud. Leda still wore her headlamp although she had switched it off. The glimpse of the crater rim spurred her forward, as well as the threat of the clouds at her back.

A fine mist eventually enveloped them and spit tiny pellets of snow. Leda could no longer see Stella Point, but knew it wasn't too far ahead. She could hear the muffled shouts of those who reached the rim. She had read in the guidebook most hikers reveled upon reaching the crater rim, and she imagined that's what they were doing. As for reveling, she would wait and see. Now, she concentrated on the trail in front of her. She was somewhat discouraged the mist hid the trail, and she could see only a little more than she had during the long hours of the night.

This wasn't the first time she had climbed a mountain in a snowstorm. It wasn't her favorite thing to do. The snow made the climb more miserable, but not unachievable.

"Take my hand." Wyatt's voice seemed to float in the air, and looking up, Leda realized how thick the mist had become. Erik was nothing more than a shadowy shape in front of Wyatt. Leda linked hands with Wyatt, and the two arrived at the crater rim together. Leda could tell they were at the rim because the trail leveled out, a noticeable difference after seven hours of uphill. She couldn't see into the crater. But walking on level ground was enough for her to celebrate. She exhaled a short "whoot!" Wyatt's laughter in response sounded giddy.

"Is that the best you can do?" he said.

"'Fraid so."

The two followed Erik about a hundred yards to a rocky outcropping where her father, Gail, and David rested in a sheltered spot. Stepping behind the rocks and out of the storm, felt like entering a whole other world. Leda hadn't realized how loud the constant wind had been until she entered the quiet. The little nook where the giant boulders almost touched at the top seemed warm. Gail and her father had unzipped their jackets, and wore their scarves loosely about their necks. They sat on rocks near each other eating their snacks with languid movements. David leaned against the rock wall. Erik and Elihud joined David while Leda and Wyatt settled on rocks near the others. Wyatt pushed back his wool cap. Leda unwound her scarf. She felt so good to be at the crater rim, she smiled at her father. She didn't think the altitude was making her giddy, but maybe it was. He seemed to smile back, his lips pursing as he chewed his snack.

"How you doing mom?" Wyatt said.

"Better than expected," Gail said. "Thanks to David, I'm nearly there." She smiled at the guide. "Besides," she said. "I figure I can do anything now."

Watching the two smiling at each other, Leda guessed Gail was talking about her success in getting Wyatt to forgive his father.

"I never doubted you could," Wyatt said.

Gail reached across Wyatt and patted Leda's arm. "How about you? Glad you came?"

"Now that we're so close, yes," Leda said. "If you asked me a couple of hours ago, I would have answered differently."

"That bad?"

Tears pooled in Leda's eyes. She swiped them away and nodded. "I didn't know it would be this hard."

Wyatt covered her gloved hand with his. Her father watched but said nothing. "You okay Dr. Stanton?" Wyatt said.

Now, her father looked stony and discomfited as he shifted on his rock. She wasn't surprised Wyatt called him Dr. Stanton even though he had called her father Phillip in the dining tent not more than seven hours ago.

"I'm fine," her father said. He finished chewing and brushed the crumbs from his snack off his gloves.

"David," Gail said. "The hymn you all sang was beautiful. It kept me going." Gail hummed a few bars of the song. "Can you sing another one on top?"

"Will you sing with us?" David said.

"Of course!"

"I wonder what the temperature is here?" Her father started to pull his glove back from his wrist, but before he could announce the temperature. David stood. The snow outside the nook blew in short bursts: some flakes whirling into the sheltered spot on random blasts of wind.

"We must go now to reach the summit," David said. He helped Gail to her feet. "The rest of the climb is gentle steep."

Leda didn't know what gentle steep meant. But she hoped it meant the final push to the summit wouldn't be as hard as this morning's climb. She hated to leave the shelter, this small desolate oasis on the mountain. Still, she was excited to reach the summit and she and the others gathered their scattered trash and water bottles, stuffing them into their daypacks along with their headlamps. Coats were zipped. Scarves resettled. Hats pulled low over eyebrows. The four remaining hikers and their guides stepped out into the swirling snow.

Chapter 45

David remembered surveying the crowd of hikers at the Machame Gate. He remembered the young American woman being careless with her snack, the monkey stealing her granola bar. Who would have guessed that she would be one of the hikers so close to the summit? Numbers favored the older American woman. For some reason, women her age got to the summit more often than younger men and that had proven true with this group: one son was about to reach the tip of Uhuru Peak on the Kibo summit while the other had to descend from Shira Camp. You never could tell who the mountain would favor. Even Erik seemed to be in a better mood, surprising David by joining the others in the rock's elbow.

David had climbed the mountain many times in mild snowstorms like this one. The snowflakes felt like Grace's gentle kisses – but colder of course – on his cheeks. It was a bother, clear weather was always better, but he wouldn't complain. The hard part was over, the Uhuru summit sign was just ahead. After pictures at the top and singing one hymn, the group could turn around and go down into the crater. It was a little side trip many liked. The journey back to Barafu Camp from there would take a little less than two hours. The hikers were always surprised at how quickly they could descend, skiing down the gravel on their boots using their trekking poles for balance.

Lunch and a short rest at camp, and then a further hike down the mountain to Millennium Camp. The last day would see them through the jungle and emerging at Mweka Gate in the afternoon.

For the first time, other hikers passed on the way down. This was the only place on the mountain where hikers were going in both directions. David smiled at the encouraging words spoken by those who had reached the summit and were on the way back down. *Not far now. Congratulations. Almost there. You're gonna make it.* He didn't have to look behind to feel the new energy flowing through his group. He could hear it in the quickening of their steps: the eager strike of their boots against the gravel.

The group gained the top of a small rise. David led them across a short level spot, and then onto a large snowfield. Many boots had worn a deep gray groove into the snow. New snowflakes softened the icy field, but the ones that fell into the groove melted quickly.

A change in the wind, and the mist lifted enough so David could see the new green summit sign, he could see the colorful bulky blobs of yellow, red, orange and black – the coats of others gathered in front of it. He heard the squeak of his group's boots behind him in the snow. Glaciers were dimly visible to the left. Many people said the glaciers were taller than buildings, but the tallest building David had seen was in Arusha, so he didn't think he could make a fair comparison. Maybe they would get lucky and the cloud would completely disappear and they could see the glaciers in the crater.

Another guide approached, leading his client by the hand. The young woman looked dazed and she stumbled, like she had drunk too much *mbege*. The guide was gentle with her encouraging her with soft words. David exchanged a quick nod with the other guide and prepared to step aside so the two could pass on the narrow trail. Everything changed in that moment.

Chapter 46

The guide's mouth fell open and he dropped the young woman's hand. David heard a guttural scream behind him. It sounded like the cry of the Colobus monkey – the pre-dawn call many tourists mistook for a crying child. The unfamiliar guide had only taken a few steps away from the young woman – she was still sinking to the snow, like a leaf fluttering to the ground, when David whirled to see what had happened.

Leda's head was down, her concentration on the trail, but not so much she didn't notice the wind drop or the snowflakes dwindle. She looked up, hoping the cloud had lifted, hoping they were close enough so she could see the famous sign. She had forgotten for the moment that a new green sign had been installed. Other hikers stood in front of it, but she could see the sign behind them. It looked like they were posing for pictures. Leda was too far away to read the writing on the new sign, but she knew from pictures the old sign of two wooden poles and three cross boards offered congratulations on the top board, the second board announced Uhuru Peak 5,985 meters and the lowest board added Africa's Highest Point, the World's Highest Freestanding Mountain. She was almost to the Roof of Africa, the top of the Kibo summit. It seemed so close, and yet, there was a snowfield to cross and another small brown rise before they reached it.

Still, Leda's spirit lifted, and she felt like she could skip along the trail. She searched for the right word to describe her feeling and her sluggish brain settled on the word elated. She rolled the word around in her mind deciding that, in this instance, when she was about to reach the highest summit of Mt. Kilimanjaro, elated was more than a feeling but an actual noun, a thing like a big helium balloon and a foolish grin splitting her cheeks. The group continued at a pole pole pace. Just because she felt like skipping, didn't mean she could. Each step was labored. Each breath strained. Each heartbeat seemed faster than before. She remembered Wyatt joking that he would jump at the top and reach a height higher than the Roof of Africa, and she turned to remind him.

She didn't see Gail crumple.

Leda only had time to register the startled look on Wyatt's face, before he pushed past her. She fell sideways against the snow bank, Wyatt's heel hammering hard on the toe of her right boot. She couldn't help her surprised scream.

David dropped to his knees beside the fallen woman. He yanked Gail's scarf, felt for her pulse under her jaw. Gail's open eyes stared at nothing; a small snowflake landed on her lower lip. He was about to begin CPR when Wyatt bowled into him, knocking David aside. The young man grabbed his mother's shoulders and shook her. "Mom," he said with a desperate urgency. "Mom. Can you hear me?" Of course, Gail could not answer. Wyatt stuck his finger down Gail's throat probing for any object that might be stopping her breath. "Get her chest." David pressed Gail's chest, his prayers rising up to God, pleading for her life. This couldn't be happening. Wyatt blew air into his mother's mouth. David prayed the young man would restore life to his mother. After all, she had given life to him.

Leda hovered behind her father. What had happened? Had Gail had a heart attack? Wyatt and David seemed to think so. Leda felt someone's presence on the other side of her: Erik. His eyes were unfocused, and yet he seemed to stare at the glacier off to the left. Leda's father turned and drew her close to him. He murmured in her ear, urging her to keep calm. His voice was white noise to Leda like the whirring of a fan. She stared over his shoulder at the scene before her. She felt as if she were both present and outside what was happening: hyper aware of Gail sprawled on the trail and yet somehow able to take in what everyone was doing. She could even see Elihud slouched to the side, her daypack slung across his chest.

Sweat beaded on David's forehead so that his wool hat itched. He could feel the dampness under his arms. His bare hands turned red in the cold. He didn't even remember tossing his gloves aside. Still, he continued to work. He continued to pound on Gail's chest, pressing it with the rhythmic motion he had been trained to do. His mind empty of everything except the count and his constant prayers. He sang snatches of the hymn he planned to share with Gail at the top: How Great Thou Art.

O Lord my God, when I in awesome wonder, consider all the worlds thy hands have made. I see the stars. I hear the rolling thunder, thy power throughout the universe displayed. When I look down from lofty mountain grandeur. Then sings my soul. How great thou art.

The song would have been perfect for the top of the mountain and maybe God would answer David's song and prayer now, even though they were not at the top. Long minutes passed but Wyatt did not stop breathing into his mother's mouth, so David did not stop his labors either even though both God and Gail did not respond.

The wind seemed to have stopped. Or maybe it just felt like it had while they stood in this deep groove. That's how Leda knew the low, keening moan was not the wind. She realized the eerie noise came from her right: Erik. The guide rocked on his heels, not seeming aware of those around him. A guide Leda had never seen before clambered up onto the snow bank, pulling a girl behind him. The girl looked confused. The two headed downhill, the girl faltered only staying upright because of the guide's steady hand. Now, Erik levered himself up out of the groove and onto the other side of the snow bank. He floundered, tripping and sprawling in the snow before pushing himself up again. Then, he wandered off heading perpendicular to the group towards what Leda could see was the crater. His boots left vague prints in the new snow.

Leda could hear David, the hollow-sounding thumps on Gail's chest, Wyatt's gasps in between blowing. The squish of Erik's boots as he vanished. If she concentrated, she could tease out her father's words, his urgent pleas to let him lead her away. The smell of damp muddy snow was strong. She watched the weird dance of David and Wyatt, their shoulders moving up and down, and for some reason she thought of the porters dancing in the morning, Gail in their midst, her hands lifted high, her feet lost among the crowd surrounding her. Now, Leda could see the bottom of Gail's boots, the legs of her gray waterproof giving no resistance but slipping with each push – the edge of her matching jacket scrunched so the pale skin of her stomach showed. Other hikers passed at the edges of Leda's vision. Ascending. Descending. Noticed like she would register flitting shadows. Slow tears stung her wind- chapped cheeks; she tasted the salty mix of snot and tears on her lips and tongue.

And even in the second before Wyatt stopped, his shoulders slumped, his head bowed, Leda knew.

Gail was dead.

Leda vomited onto the trail, a thin tan stream of energy biscuits splattering the edges of her boots.

Chapter 47

Leda felt her father's strong grip on her arms, holding her tight as she bent over the trail. When nothing more would come out of her stomach, she crumpled against her father's chest, her face pressed against his shoulder. He patted her back in silence. Her pop had never been good at offering comforting words. Leda heard some noises behind her, and she opened her eyes and looked around.

David no longer kneeled over Gail, but used the snow bank as a support. He wiped his wet forehead and cheeks with the bottom edge of his sweatshirt that stuck out below his jacket. He looked exhausted and beaten, two words Leda never would have thought to use to describe him. She could see the summit sign behind him. A group of hikers posed in front of it for pictures. Leda's stomach turned and she stepped away from her father thinking she might vomit again.

Wyatt bent over his mother, his mouth close to her ear. His lips appeared to be moving, and Leda wondered what Wyatt said to Gail. When he was done speaking, Wyatt kissed his mother's cheek. Then Wyatt did the most surprising thing, he covered his face with his hands and sobbed. Leda could hear his great sucking gasps for air. His body swayed as he grieved. Watching him, Leda stepped backwards so that she was standing shoulder to shoulder with her father. She didn't know what to make of Wyatt's reaction. His raw emotion scared her.

After a while when Wyatt's body stilled and his sobs slowed, David touched Wyatt's back. "I'm sorry," he said.

Wyatt's hand lingered over his mother's face; he closed her eyes with gentle fingers. "Me too," he said.

"She was fine," David said. "She showed no symptoms…"

Wyatt stood. "I didn't see any signs either," he said. "What did I miss?"

David studied Gail's face. He shook his head. "I've never seen something like this before," he said. David covered his eyes for a moment with his hand, cupping his forehead. "I'm sorry."

Wyatt nodded. Tears streamed down his short beard, got lost in the folds of his scarf. He looked towards the sign, his gaze caught as if he needed to study the words and get them right. He sniffed and turned back towards David. "Now what?" he said.

"I must wait with your mother," David said. "The ranger will need to investigate." Wyatt settled back onto the trail next to Gail.

"You cannot stay," David said. "The altitude is too much for you. You will get sick. All of you must leave and return to Barafu Camp."

Leda shuddered. Her pop rubbed her arms, and then let her go to gather up her dropped trekking poles. He adjusted their length for the descent twisting the poles and locking them in place at shoulder height. Elihud did the same for Wyatt's trekking poles.

"Wyatt," David said, his voice urgent, "you must go."

"I'd rather stay." Wyatt's voice was matter of fact.

"I understand," David said. "But who will tell your father?"

Wyatt frowned. Leda didn't want to, but she felt herself shrinking back when Wyatt swiveled his head and leveled his gaze on her and her father. He couldn't expect either one of them to tell Tom the tragic news. Leda wouldn't know where to begin. She pictured Tom's large frame, his metal calf. What if he broke down like Wyatt had? Leda trembled. Her father would probably tell Tom in a few clipped sentences, slap Tom on the back and then bolt to his tent. Wyatt's brows drew down.

"She would want me to tell him," Wyatt said. "She wouldn't want me to stay here." Wyatt shook his head and stood. He grabbed his trekking poles, yanking them from Elihud with a swift gesture. "This is a fucked up way for you to get me to talk to Tom," he said to his mom. "Take good care of her," he said to David, and with that, he plunged back down the trail, shouldering past Leda and her father, ignoring Leda's outstretched hand.

Leda didn't understand how Wyatt could leave his mother lying on the trail. How he could think telling his father, a man who Wyatt said thought of his son with contempt, was more important than staying with his mother. Wyatt may have forgiven his father, but would Tom ever forgive him for what just happened?

Leda watched the top of Wyatt's wool cap recede down the groove in the snow bank. A cold fog seemed to have settled in her brain after the adrenaline of the past thirty minutes. She felt lethargic. How easy it would be to lie down and take a little nap. She could hike back down the mountain when she woke up.

"Leda." Her pop's voice penetrated the fog, and she twisted her head to look at him. "Here." Her father worked the straps of her trekking poles over her limp wrists. He curled her gloved fingers over the handles. "Let's go," he said. "We can't do anything more here." He held her elbow in a firm grip and guided her stumbling steps down the trail,

Elihud following close behind. A large group squeezed past on their way up to the summit. Leda thought she heard gasps when they saw Gail's body, but Leda couldn't be sure, maybe she imagined them, maybe she was dreaming, maybe she had curled up in the snow and fallen asleep.

They stepped off the snow pack in what seemed like a few minutes. Now, here they were in the sheltered alcove. Elihud handed Leda her water bottle. It was no longer frozen solid. The ice had cracked and splintered into large pieces. She supposed the bottle had warmed while it rested on Elihud's chest. Her head hurt and felt like it too was splintering. Her thoughts floated here and there. It was difficult to get hold of them, to pin them down. She realized something or someone was missing, but she didn't know what or who. Her father was silent. Elihud allowed them a few minutes rest in between the boulders, and then he urged them on down the mountain. They didn't follow a trail, but slid straight down the gravel in great lunging steps, sliding and kicking up clouds of dust.

After an hour, Leda's thighs began to ache from the new motion of going downhill after six days of mostly going up. They were below the snow cloud shrouding the summit, and she wasn't much of a skier but Leda imagined the slope was steeper than a quadruple black diamond if such a label even existed. Elihud stopped, and the three drank some water. Leda's head didn't hurt as much. She realized now that Wyatt was not with them. Leda scanned the mountain below them but didn't see his distinctive orange cap.

"Where's Wyatt?" she said.

Elihud shook his head. He shrugged his shoulders in a signal that he didn't understand her question. Leda held her hand above her head to indicate Wyatt's height. She pointed to herself and her father. "Three," she said, holding up three fingers. "Now two." She put down one of her fingers.

"Okay?" Elihud said. "Food?" He dug in his pants pocket and pulled out a crushed pack of energy biscuits.

"Don't worry about Wyatt," her father said. "He won't get lost."

"He's never been on this trail."

"We're not on a trail."

Leda opened her mouth to argue, but her father spoke, "It's a straight shot. You could roll down the mountain and land in Barafu Camp."

"But his mother just died," she said.

"He's probably hurrying to tell Tom. They're family, they need each other now."

Her father didn't say it, but Leda knew how to read the underlying message. It was written all over her father's face, in his raised eyebrows, the slight purse of his lips and the tilt of his head. Family should and would trump a trail romance.

Leda thought of Wyatt sobbing at his mother's side, how his cries had frightened her so she backed away. She thought of her father being attracted to Natalie, and how that experience had taught him to keep his emotions in check, so he wouldn't be hurt again – an example Leda had followed without questioning. Leda thought of Wyatt pushing past her on his way down the trail, bumping her outstretched hand. She regretted her actions on the summit. She didn't want to be like her father, shying away from emotions she didn't understand or couldn't control.

Now, Leda didn't respond to her father's comment. She simply started sliding back down the mountain again toward Barafu Camp, which always seemed to be just below the angle of the slope.

Chapter 48

David radioed the ranger. He waited by Gail's body, now leaning against the snow, now stamping his feet and blowing on his gloved hands. Others passed, going up, going down. Most fell silent and pretended not to stare at the crumpled body. But David could feel their looks. He never raised his face. Not even when the other guides and porters passed. He didn't want to see their thoughts. He knew how they would look. He had looked the same in the past. He had kept the same thoughts. He had thought his prudent behavior would keep his hikers safe. He had pretended to respect the mountain, but the mountain knew he was lying. He didn't know what to think about God's silence.

After a long while, no more hikers or guides passed. David was alone on the mountain with Gail: the dead woman who gave no sign she was sick. David thought about the start of tonight's hike. He thought about how he grabbed Gail's elbow. How he demanded she not give up. At the crater rim, she thanked him, and then, not much later, she was dead. Now, David didn't know what to think.

Erik was gone.

David hadn't seen him leave, but the young woman pointed to his tracks in the snow. David would tell the ranger about the guide. Others could search for Erik. Maybe he had returned to the elephant graveyard. Wherever that was. He couldn't worry about the older man; his job was to stay with the body.

David thought of the three he had sent down the mountain with Elihud. A good porter. Someone who could be trusted. David didn't know why but he prayed God would guide the three safely to Barafu Camp. His prayers couldn't hurt. Maybe they would help. David didn't want more sickness. He didn't want more death.

He turned his face towards the summit sign. No one stood in front of it now. All the hikers had gone down the mountain. The fresh green paint seemed to mock him even from this distance. His group had been so close. It was too hard to think about what had happened. David emptied his mind and waited for the ranger, keeping a silent vigil by the dead woman.

Gail's cap fell into the snow when David helped load her body onto the stretcher made of aluminum. David forgot about the cap as he and several others skied, then carried the stretcher back down the mountain. He was glad the ranger hadn't come right away. He didn't know what would happen if they passed the others on the way down.

*****

The camp looked deserted when Leda, her father and Elihud picked their way down the boulder-strewn path to the small site. Wyatt's tent was gone. His floppy duffel and two rolled up mats and stuffed sleeping bags were piled against a pointed lava rock. Leda heard the harsh cry of a white-naped raven, but couldn't see it below the rocky ledge. She peeked into the dining tent; it was empty, the table set for lunch. Just behind the tent, hidden from first view, the cook stirred a pot of ginger soup over his kerosene stove. Only two pup tents still stood. One was her father's, where Leda saw the soles of his boots disappear as he crawled inside, and the other belonged to Tom and Gail. The flap was zipped shut. Leda tiptoed past Tom's tent. She strained to hear any sounds of conversation or crying, but the tent was quiet. Maybe Tom and Wyatt had gone for a walk.

The plan was to pack up, eat lunch and hike further down the mountain (6,500 feet) to Millennium Camp for the night. Leda assumed her father was getting a start on his packing. There would be no room in the snug tent for her to pack up at the same time. She headed to the toilet. When she came out, Wyatt stared down into the valley near the rock ledge where she was sure she saw him just yesterday with Gail and Tom. Wyatt gave no sign he saw her, but kept his focus in the distance. Leda joined him at the rock ledge. She moved close so her shoulder rubbed against his arm. Minutes passed in silence except for the occasional cries of the raven. Leda could see the bird now swooping in and out of the mist below them, it's black wings spread: a fleeting shadow. She dug her hands into the pockets of her coat, shrugged her shoulders so that the zipped collar of her down coat would cover her chin. A slight shiver made her tremble, but still Wyatt kept silent.

"I'm so very sorry," Leda finally said, her voice cracking.

"Me too." Wyatt said. He turned away from the valley and looked at her.

He wasn't wearing his sunglasses; his eyes were red, the skin underneath puffy. Leda touched his shoulder, and Wyatt pulled her towards him. He hugged her tightly, his head lowered so that his chin rested on her shoulder. He smelled like dust and sweat. Leda squeezed her arms around his waist, leaned her head against his. The camp was quiet. Leda could hear the clank of the cook's spoon as he stirred the ginger soup. They stood together, the wind nipping at the exposed flesh of Leda's cheeks and nose.

"I don't know how you could leave her," Leda spoke into Wyatt's coat, her voice a croak, not knowing how the words bubbled up from where she had held them since Gail's death. "She's your mother." Leda had struggled with this thought since Wyatt bolted down the mountain. Given the choice, she was certain she would have stayed with her mother. The mother-sized hole inside her, which she thought had shrunk into a hard knot the last time she was in this camp, had ripped open when Gail died.

Wyatt dropped his arms and stepped away. A gust of wind rushed between them. Leda shivered and crossed her arms over her chest.

"My mom's dead," Wyatt said. "God, it hurts to say that." He covered his mouth with the palm of his hand and looked down the valley again. He let his arm fall to his side. "She's in a better place now, he said. "I know she believed that I have to believe it too. I also know she would want me to tell Tom. She wouldn't want him to hear the news from a stranger."

"You're practically strangers," Leda said. "Before this trip you barely talked to him."

Wyatt turned back towards her. Tears sparkled on his lashes. "He's my dad," Wyatt said. "I forgave him, remember? What happened in the past doesn't matter."

"How did he take the news?" Leda said. "I bet he blamed you for not saving her."

Wyatt shook his head. "He's upset," he said. "His wife died." His eyes narrowed. The muscles in his jaw twitched. Leda opened her mouth to speak, but Wyatt cut her off. "My mother was a good person. I'm going to do my best to live up to what she saw in me," he said. He pointed towards her father's pup tent. Leda turned her head and saw her pop emerging with his stuffed sleeping bag. "Life's short. Didn't we both just experience how short? My mom died three hours ago! You should forgive your father. Stop blaming him for what happened. You're not helpless. You can choose the life you want to live. I did. I know you're hurt by what he did, but you're beginning to sound like Tom. Bitter and angry. Is that what you want? I've already told you I don't."

Leda closed her mouth. She hugged her arms more tightly around her body. Still, the flood of words battered her. The corners of her eyes felt wet. She bit her lip, and held still. If she blinked or returned her gaze to Wyatt, the tears would leak. His words hurt. She thought she could trust Wyatt to see things her way. Had he already forgotten how her father had left her, a young child still in diapers, to chase after his wife? How her mother had fled the country and left her behind: unwanted; unloved.

"Well?" Wyatt said. Leda didn't move. Wyatt shook his head and strode to the dining tent. Leda stared out over the valley. Now that Wyatt was gone, she blinked her eyes. Slow tears trickled down the sides of her cheeks and dripped off the point of her jaw near her ears, dribbling onto the collar of her coat. Leda heard Wyatt greet her father, the rumble of her father's voice in return; she heard the emphatic *zweep* of a zipper being opened, and the crunch of Tom's slow, heavy footsteps diminishing in the direction of the dining tent. More tears worked their way down her face. Leda's nose dripped. She swiped at her nose and the tears with the back of her glove. She inhaled a deep, ragged breath.

The mist below looked like tattered shreds of dirty chiffon. The raven had vanished somewhere into the thin vapor. Leda swiveled. A thick cloud cover hung low over the summit. She still couldn't believe Gail had died up there. It all seemed so surreal now that she was standing back in Barafu Camp. And what had just happened with Wyatt? Leda had offered him sympathy, asked him a question, and simply repeated his words back to him. And he accused her of sounding bitter and angry. Now, the men were in the dining tent eating lunch. Leda knew she should eat, but refused to go near the tent.

Leda hurried towards her pop's pup tent for her duffel. She would pack it up, and eat whatever granola bars still lingered at the bottom of the duffel. She didn't care if she had vowed earlier never to eat another granola bar. Leda crawled part way into the tent so she wouldn't have to remove her boots. Her unzipped duffel appeared to be the lone occupant of the otherwise empty tent. She pulled the duffel towards her, and rooted around in it with her hands. She couldn't find any granola bars, so she removed her gloves for a more thorough search. Pawing over the few neatly folded items left in the duffel, Leda didn't care that she rooted the clear plastic bags with her soap and toothpaste from their usual spot or that her dwindling roll of toilet paper got mixed in with her dirty socks. The interior of the duffel was dark. Leda had to drag the bag outside to peer into its many crevices. The tips of her fingers brushed against a granola bar, and Leda seized on it as if she had discovered gold.

The bar tasted dry and was difficult to chew; Leda needed a large swig of water to get it down. She discovered another bar. Sitting with her legs straight out in front of her, Leda bit off tiny pieces of the bar, chewing and swallowing until the last bar was gone. Leda brushed the crumbs from her coat. She stuffed the crumpled wrappers into her duffel. She zipped the bag closed and rubbed her hands together with a satisfied feeling. Grabbing the two handles, Leda lugged the duffel over to the pile with her stuffed sleeping bag and rolled up mat. The men had not come out of the dining tent yet. She hoped the two granola bars she ate would be enough fuel to power her the remaining six miles to Millennium Camp. There was no way she was eating ginger soup with Wyatt, her father and Tom. Gail's empty seat would be too painful of a reminder in the small space shared by the three men.

Chapter 49

The hikers were silent, Elihud led the way over a gentle slope of scree. Leda trailed at the back. She had forgotten to take off her extra layer of long underwear, and she paused to peel off her down jacket and wool cap, inserting them into her daypack before scurrying to catch up with the men. Her father looked around to check on her every so often.

Gail's absence dogged Leda's steps along with Wyatt's accusation. Each time Elihud vanished around a bend or over a small knoll, Leda could imagine Gail was walking ahead with him. But when the whole group came into sight again, Gail was never there. Leda couldn't believe Gail wouldn't be at the last camp, sitting in the dining tent, joking about their final bowl of ginger soup. She tried to focus her thoughts on Gail in the protected knoll just above the crater, remembering the loving exchange between mother and son, but always the shocking sight of Gail sprawled dead on the trail intruded. Leda's mother had died in a car accident. Did it really matter that her father let her grow up with a mother fantasy? Maybe her father did make the wrong choice by keeping her mother's condition secret. The truth was out now. Leda could continue blaming her father for his silence or she could admit her hurt and move on. Although Wyatt and Tom hiked closed behind Elihud, Leda watched as her father dropped behind, the gap growing between him and the rest so he could stay close to her.

The easy slope came to an end, and Elihud stopped. The others halted close behind him. Leda kept walking until she reached them, sneaking a peek at Wyatt's face. It was difficult to tell what he was thinking behind his sunglasses. He had tied his bandana over his hair again. She wondered if he had somehow washed out the tears he had wiped from her face on the Barranco Wall. He didn't smile at her.

"No *pole pole*," Elihud said looking at Leda. He pointed at the sky. "Night."

Although it wasn't dark, Leda knew what Elihud meant. He was worried her slow pace would keep them from reaching camp until after nightfall. Leda bit her lip, and nodded. She pushed to walk more quickly.

Soon the group plunged down a series of deep steps, dropping from stone after stone to the trail. Leda's thighs trembled; her knees ached. But still, she, and the others, remained silent. There were no rest stops. Elihud was moving at a rapid pace, using hand gestures to urge the group along. Leda was debating the wisdom of skipping lunch when she saw the conical blue rooftop of the ranger station at what she hoped was Millennium Camp. The relief she felt wasn't enough to get her moving faster, but at least she knew now she was going to make it. It wouldn't be long before she could rest in the pup tent. Elihud continued past the camp, the three men following close behind him.

Leda stopped. She wanted nothing more than to sit, to quit moving, to collapse on her sleeping bag. "Wait!" she said. Elihud halted. "Isn't this the camp?" she said. "Aren't we spending the night?"

Elihud shook his head. "No summit. No crater." He motioned down the trail with his hand.

David had talked about visiting the crater after they reached the summit. Since they had done neither, it appeared Elihud now wanted them to make up the mileage by hiking to a more distant camp. Leda couldn't believe it. They stood next to a perfectly good camp.

"We won't have as far to hike tomorrow," her father said. "We can be at the Mweka Gate by lunchtime."

Elihud and her father waited for her to start walking again, but Wyatt and Tom stepped past the porter and continued down the trail without comment.

"I'm going to the bathroom," Leda said. She turned and headed for the camp.

The cloud cover had gotten higher the lower they descended on the mountain. Even though they never saw the sun, the sky was growing darker; evening was close. Elihud, Tom and Wyatt had hiked ahead. Leda and her father were alone on the trail. It was well marked, so there was no fear of getting lost. Leda hoped they could make camp before dark. She didn't have her headlamp, having tucked it into her duffel at Barafu Camp. She doubted her father had his, as the goal each day was to carry the lightest load possible. They had never needed their headlamps on the trail before last night's summit ascent. The trail was fairly wide with steep sides cut out of the dirt. Low bushes similar to sagebrush lined the top of each bank, extending as far back as Leda could see. Despite their scraggly branches, the bushes were the most profuse display of plant life Leda had seen since their trek through the rain forest on the first day.

Leda's legs felt like pudding. She couldn't move faster than she already was. Each time she worked her way down another rocky ledge, placing her boots with ginger care, she was sure her leg muscles would cramp or give out. In the past twenty- four hours, the group had climbed to Barafu Camp, gotten close to the summit after very little sleep, and descended more than ten miles. A few miles back, Leda's mind had stopped worrying the shock of Gail's death like the constant turning of a jagged stone in the palm of her hand. Her whole self was fully dedicated to moving forward to the next camp, trusting she had trained well for this hike, forcing her body to obey the need to arrive before dark. They came to another rock ledge – she should expect them, she told herself, not dread each one, after all, they were going down the mountain.

Leda felt with her trekking poles for a firm spot to steady her as she scrambled down. She was close to the bottom when the rock under her foot wobbled. Any other time, she would have leapt to the trail. But she didn't have the energy or the will to keep her balance. She sank to the ground like her bones were made of mush and burst into tears.

Leda vaguely felt her father lift her by her elbow and guide her to the side of the trail. He helped her sit on the bank.

"Are you hurt?" he said.

Leda shook her head. "Just give me a minute." She sniffled and searched her pockets for a tissue, forgetting she had used them all up on the climb to Lava Tower. Wyatt had told her then to make a snot rocket. She cried harder, her head bowed over her hands still gripping her trekking poles. She missed Wyatt. She missed the easy camaraderie they shared. She didn't want to be bitter and angry. She didn't want Wyatt to think she was. She missed Gail. She missed her mother. She missed the old, easy days of hiking with her father.

"Use this," her father said. He held out his red kerchief.

Seeing her pop's signature red kerchief crumpled in his hand, Leda didn't think she would ever stop crying. She saw the trail now through a veil of tears, the blurred toes of her father's dusty boots and the wavery outline of her knuckles on the trekking poles. She didn't dare look up. She couldn't bear to see his expression go flat. Not now. She waited for his voice, soft and cool, as if he were talking to a stranger, but he stayed quiet, the kerchief steady in the open palm of his hand.

When she had calmed, Leda let go of one trekking pole and reached with tentative fingers for the kerchief. She blotted her cheeks; she wiped her nose with the back of her glove. Leda drew a deep breath in through her nose, and blew it out her mouth. She pushed up from the bank.

She offered the kerchief to her pop. "Thanks," she said.

He waved his hand. "Keep it," he said. "For now." A slight smile tipped the corners of his lips.

Leda's laugh felt watery. "I'll give it a good washing," she said. She put it in the pocket of her open fleece.

"There's no rush," he said.

Leda pressed her palm against the kerchief lump in her pocket. "I love you pop," she said. The tears felt like they might flow again, but this time Leda raised her eyes to her father's.

"I know," he said.

Chapter 50

The two stood in silence: their shadows long on the trail, taller than they were, merging at the bend of their necks. For the first time since London, Leda didn't feel out of sorts in her father's presence. She felt a fragile unfamiliar peace instead of anger that her father had hidden the truth about her mother. It was as if her tears had washed away all the tension between them. Leda didn't know if her father would ever answer all her questions about her mother, but for now, in this moment, she didn't care. Wyatt was right: her father was the one who had stuck around. She had clung to her childhood fantasy of her parent's tragic romance for too long. The little truth she now knew was raw and shocking and no less tragic. She didn't know if she would ever stop mourning the loss of her mother. But here was her pop, alive and standing next to her on this foreign trail.

She and her pop had shared a dream of reaching the highest summit of Mt. Kilimanjaro, and they had come close. But there wouldn't be a picture of the two of them at the summit for the top of her dresser. Leda reached for her father's hand where it rested on his trekking pole. The two stood with their hands clasped. For now, it was enough that they were together.

Leda's tears dried on her cheeks. She gave her father's hand a quick squeeze.

She wished she felt a sudden burst of energy, but she didn't. Her father's stance was relaxed, his feet wide. It seemed as if he was ready to wait for however long it took.

"I'm so tired," Leda said. "I just want this day to be over." She looked towards the direction of camp.

"I think camp is just over that hill," her father said.

"When hasn't it been?" Leda sighed. She adjusted the straps of her poles on her wrists. "Let's go."

"You ready?"

"Not really," she said. "But there's no other way to get there." She started walking, the trail wide enough for her pop to travel next to her, at least until they came upon more rocks to navigate.

It was past dusk, but not yet night when the two crested the final hill and entered the forested area of the sprawling Mweka Camp. The thicket of trees created a darker gloom. They hiked past a large building. Leda could see flush toilets inside. She vowed to come back later. A little further down the trail, Elihud approached. He led them to their camp, which to Leda, seemed to take forever to reach. Three pup tents had been set up in the small openings between the bushes and trees. The area felt confined after the panoramic vistas of the last four nights. Dinner was waiting for them in the dining tent. Leda and her father ate alone. Wyatt and Tom were already in their pup tents. Leda assumed they were asleep. She heard no noise when she walked past the tents. All she wanted to do when she finished dinner was sleep.

Leda climbed into the tent she shared with her father. Her sleeping bag felt like heaven, her thin mat like a cloud and she fell into a deep sleep, not opening her eyes until the next morning's wake- up call just after sunrise.

She crawled from the tent feeling buoyant and eager to talk with Wyatt. His stuff was already piled in front of his pup tent, as was Tom's in front of his tent, the single duffel and sleeping bag a stark reminder of Gail's absence. Leda assumed they were in the dining tent. She hurried to the rough camp toilet, walking all the way through the camp to the flush ones would take too long, and she didn't want to waste any time. This could be the last chance she had for a moment alone with Wyatt. But neither he nor Tom was in the dining tent. Her father sat at the table by himself, eating a last camp breakfast of oatmeal, eggs, watermelon and white bread.

"Where are Wyatt and Tom?" Leda said. She settled into a chair across from her pop. She reached for a serving spoon, and scooped up some eggs.

"They left," he said.

"Already?" Leda's hand hovered in mid-air. A small piece of egg dropped from the spoon onto the checkered tablecloth.

"They wanted to get to the Mweka Gate and see Chase and Jen," her father said. "Can't blame them."

"No, I guess not." Leda felt deflated. She dumped the eggs onto her plate. She didn't feel hungry anymore. But remembering yesterday, she filled her plate with watermelon and white bread and ate it all. The hot chocolate she had poured in celebration of making it this far tasted too sweet. She filled an empty cup with hot water. Watching the steam rise from the cup, she wondered if she would see Wyatt again.

This morning, Leda was glad they had hiked further the day before. She was anxious to get going, to reach the Mweka Gate and catch up with Wyatt. Since Elihud had gone ahead with Wyatt and Tom, an unfamiliar porter who spoke no English led Leda and her father. The three slipped and slid down the muddy rainforest trail. Leda didn't want to walk slowly, but the tread of her boots soon filled with mud and she lost traction. Each step became like skating on ice. The porter fell, landing on his butt with a thud. He stood up quickly and brushed off the mud. After that, Leda tried to scrape the mud out of her soles with her trekking poles. She was careful on the deep steps, shored up slim logs now covered with moss. She was sure Wyatt and Tom couldn't leave the Mweka Gate without the whole group. They had all arrived in the same Land Rover.

Leda rejoiced when they navigated the last step and reached a level dirt road cut through the rain forest. Deep gullies riddled the road like open wounds Leda and her father followed the porter as he jumped from one side of the road to the other, avoiding the worst of the crevices; sometimes he led them into an open rut and they had to scramble out of it at the end, their boots sinking into the soft soil. It made for a tortuous route, and Leda felt her anxiety rising. Where was the Mweka Gate? Where was Wyatt?

Small, thin children mysteriously appeared on the road, skipping along the sides, begging for chocolate. The children swarmed around Leda and her father, their hands held palms up, repeating "chocolate?" over and over again in sing song English. The hikers were still passing through the national forest, and Leda couldn't see any houses in the trees. If houses were there, they were illegal homesteaders. The porter shooed the children away like they were flies, shouting at them in Swahili.

Leda hoped the appearance of the children meant the gate was just around the next corner. But the three kept walking, leaping over fissures, descending into others only to surface back onto the ruined road. Leda was beginning to doubt the Mweka Gate existed when the three emerged from the rain forest.

Now, vendors buzzed around Leda and her father waving kerchiefs for sale that looked like the Tanzanian flag, t-shirts imprinted with Mt. Kilimanjaro, carved wooden animals and cheap African jewelry. Several vendors offered to wash mud caked boots. The cacophony of voices and the press of unwashed bodies overwhelmed after the windblown silence of the mountain. Leda pushed her way through the crowd, following the porter, standing as tall as she could, hoping to catch a glimpse of Wyatt in the sea of people. The porter took Leda and her father to a small wooden gazebo with a concrete floor. David waited for them there. He didn't smile. He looked as tired as Leda felt.

"Congratulations," he said. "You made it."

He held out two official certificates, one for Leda, and the other for her father. Leda took the certificate without looking at it. Her father handed David a wad of money and shook the guide's hand. Setting her trekking poles and the certificate on a bench, Leda reached into her money belt, pulling out the money she had brought for tips. She thanked David, but looked past him, still scanning the crowds at the gate for Wyatt.

"You are looking for someone?" David said.

"The rest of our group," Leda said. "Where are they?"

David shifted on his feet; he closed his eyes. When he opened them, his gaze was focused on something behind her. Leda was tempted to turn and look. Maybe he saw Wyatt. But his words stopped her. "They have gone," he said. "There are arrangements to make." David's voice sounded scratchy. His focus returned to Leda, and for a brief moment, Leda felt a shared grief with the guide, his eyes reflecting her own sadness. She touched David's arm. She thought about the guide waiting alone with Gail's body, and she wondered if Gail's death would make it hard for him to get work. She thought about Erik's footprints receding in the snow. She would never have to climb this mountain again, but climbing it was David's livelihood.

Another group burst into the gazebo, spirits high with their goal accomplished: the summit reached. Leda's hand dropped. She watched as hikers from the other group posed for pictures with their certificates; she listened to their applause. She didn't know what to say to David. She reached for her trekking poles, pressed them into David's hands. "*Asante sana*, thank you very much," she said. She hoped he understood that he should continue as a guide. David nodded.

Leda sat on the wooden bench, squeezed into the narrow space left by the celebrating hikers, her shoulder pressed against her father's. She stared at her certificate.

This is to certify that

Leda Stanton

Has successfully climbed Mt. Kilimanjaro the Highest in

Africa to Uhuru Peak 5895m

David had filled in Leda's name, the date and her age. The certificate was signed by David, the Chief Park Warden of Kilimanjaro National Park, and the Director General of the Tanzania National Parks. There was no asterisk, no notation that she hadn't really made it to the top, that she had simply come close. But Leda didn't care.

Wyatt was gone. Leda leaned against her father's shoulder and sobbed, the certificate slipping from her fingers.

Chapter 51

Leda looked around her bedroom. Faded paint rectangles spotted the wall where her awards used to hang. A fresh coat of paint would remove them. It had been too long since her room was painted. But that wasn't her worry now. Her awards were stashed in a box at the back of her empty closet. The dresser was bare of photographs. She had wiped the top with a crumpled newspaper. Dust swirled in a random pattern across the painted surface. She could refinish it when she moved into her new place wherever that might be. Or maybe she would just leave it behind. Two medium-sized boxes held the rest of her possessions, and were stacked by the dresser. Her whole life packed into three cardboard boxes. It could depress her, and it had at first when she sealed the final box with tape. But she was determined now to look at it as a blessing. Less to move when she got back from her trip: if she returned.

Her suitcase was open on the wrinkled comforter of her bed; it was hard packing when she didn't know how long she would be gone. If San Diego worked out, she might just have her father ship her boxes to her. Leda added a pair of jeans to the suitcase, and then leaned over her nearby desk to check her laptop.

The desk was clear except for the laptop. Leda opened the familiar browser with web cams showing the San Diego surf. It looked like some large swells today. The waves rose and fell, spraying flecks of white foam, in a constant rhythm she found inviting. Maybe she would go for a swim when she got there or even try surfing. What had Wyatt said about the ocean? He had quoted Thoreau who called the ocean "our last untamed wilderness." She was excited to experience it with Wyatt.

She opened her cell phone. Re-read the text from Wyatt. Smiled.

She hadn't been sure what David was giving her when he handed her the crumpled piece of granola bar wrapper. Was he reminding her not to litter on the trail? She remembered the monkey snatching her half-eaten bar at the beginning of the trip, but she didn't remember dropping any trash along the way, but maybe she had. She wadded the wrapper in her hand and stood to throw it away. But David stopped her; he took the wrapper and smoothed it out. He showed her the scribbled phone number scratched on the inside of the foil. Even then, it had taken Leda more than two weeks to contact Wyatt. She would hold the foil and look at the number, then go back to packing up her room. It wasn't until she took her awards down that she gave into the urge to text him.

The taxi would be there to take her to the airport soon. Leda pushed away from the desk and finished packing. She zipped the suitcase closed, and then slid her laptop into her backpack.

Her father rapped on her door, pushing it open. "All set?" he said. Her father hadn't been thrilled with her plans to move, but after his initial protests – "think of all the money you're saving" "I thought you liked living here" "you'll be lonely" – he accepted her decision. Every so often, he would come into her room while she was packing, look around and leave with his lips pressed tight. He hadn't told her more about her mother even though Leda kept asking. His silence wouldn't stop her questions; she still planned to continue her search for answers. When she got frustrated with her father's stubbornness, she would remember Gail forgiving Tom, she would think of Gail urging Wyatt to forgive him as well. She would remember how much she loved her pop. She just couldn't live in the same house anymore.

Leda surveyed the room. "I think so." She grabbed the handle of her suitcase.

"I wanted to give you this," her father said. He held out her mother's locket. It looked like it had been recently polished and it gleamed in his hand. "I got it fixed."

Leda stood with her hand still on her suitcase handle. She remembered yanking the delicate chain from her neck, hurling it into the corner of the pup tent. She hadn't thought of the locket since.

"Here." Her father stepped into the room, the thin gold chain dribbling from between his fingers.

Leda let go of the suitcase and took the locket.

"Don't you want to put it on?" her father said.

Leda slipped the locket into her jeans pocket. "No," she said. "Not right now."

Leda picked up her backpack, grabbed hold of the suitcase again. Her father looked around the room, his gaze touching the bare spots on the wall. His khaki pants were wrinkled, his loose t-shirt had a small tear at the neckline. His eyes were the same cool hazel, his hair somewhat disheveled like always yet he seemed older somehow, beaten.

Leda touched her throat. "I'm wearing a necklace," she said.

"Right, yes, of course." Her father took a step back towards the doorway. "Can I give you a ride?"

"A taxi's coming."

"Leda." Her father paused. His eyes strayed to the suitcase and back to Leda. "I hope you're making the right decision. Flying down there to see him."

Leda moved towards her father. She pressed her lips to his cheek, and then stepped away. "I know pop," she said. "It might be a complete failure. But I have to try."

The doorbell chimed.

"Let me get that." Her father hauled the suitcase to the front door where the taxi driver received it without comment. The two watched the driver load the suitcase in his trunk, and climb into the front. "I'll miss you," her father said. He put his arm around her, his fingers squeezing her shoulder. Leda wrapped her arms around his waist, rested her head on his chest. She felt his hand move to her back.

The taxi driver beeped his horn. Leda checked her smart phone. Her flight left in an hour.

"Don't be late," her father said.

Leda sprinted to the taxi.

Chapter 52

David surveyed the crowd of hikers at the Marangu Gate. Most appeared full of energy, bouncing on the toes of their clean hiking boots, talking in loud happy voices. The porters stood in a separate group, worn jackets loose on their shoulders. He hoped he was ready for this, his first trip back up the mountain in more than a month. Grace hadn't said a word this morning as she handed him his jacket and the trekking poles. She wasn't a woman of few words. She had plenty to say the past month. First she talked about the *wazungu* and how crazy they were to climb the mountain no matter what. Then she told David he couldn't be blamed. God couldn't be blamed either. These things just happened. No one could know what the mountain would do. Towards the end of the month she made comments about lazy husbands who sat around drinking *mbege*.

David's group was larger this time, eleven, all Europeans. They were a mixed group of men and women - old, young, big, small. He hoped to God all would summit. He hoped he could lead them past the narrow trail in the snowfield.

David turned his face up towards the gray sky. Groups usually started earlier on this route, hoping to get through the jungle before the afternoon brought thick showers. A short burst of laughter drew his attention. A young man without a coat – one of David's group – kicked a bit of foil like a soccer ball. He appeared to be in good shape, bits of his long hair flying about his head, the rapid movements didn't even make him catch his breath but David wondered.

They all knew the risk.

The doctor said no one could have known Gail would die. The American was born with a heart that didn't work right. It skipped beats. She could have lived her whole life not knowing anything about it - as long as she never climbed to the top of Mt. Kilimanjaro.

David hoped he remembered the doctor's words and Grace's words when this new group got close to the summit, that David could not be blamed. Some people brought things to the mountain that couldn't be seen. All he could do was his best.

The ranger waved to David. It was time for him to gather his group, time for them to sign the register and begin their ascent.

The End

I'd like to thank my family and friends for their support and input during the writing of this novel, their journals, recollections and critique were instrumental in the formation of this story. I'd also like to thank my writing partners – this novel wouldn't be the same without them. Although this book is a work of fiction, I drew upon my own experience of climbing Mt. Kilimanjaro in July 2010, as well as the experience of Cindy who organized our trip and shepherded our group up the mountain and our lead guide Peter Nathan who advised me via email from Tanzania. I also referred extensively to "Kilimanjaro: A Complete Trekker's Guide" by Alexander Stewart. My blog, **www.janicecoy.blogspot.com,** details my training and my climb. For more information about me, please visit **www.janicecoy.com**. Thank you for coming along this journey with me.

Made in the USA
San Bernardino, CA
12 July 2018